WHEN THE SON REFUSED TO SHINE

By

Vincent Banks

TABLE OF CONTENTS

PROLOGUE: JUDGES 16:31 v

PART I: HAZEL 1

Chapter 1: JUDGES 13:2 2

Chapter 2: JUDGES 13:3-23 7

Chapter 3: JUDGES 13:3-23 22

Chapter 4: JUDGES 13: 24-25 32

PART II: SAMSON 46

Chapter 5: JUDGES 13: 24-25 47

Chapter 6: JUDGES 14:1-4 71

Chapter 7: JUDGES 14:1-4 79

Chapter 8: JUDGES 14:7-10 87

Chapter 9: JUDGES 14:10-17 91

Chapter 10: JUDGES 14:18-19 100

Chapter 11: JUDGES 14:19-20, 15:1-2 106

Chapter 12: JUDGES 15:3-5 110

Chapter 13: JUDGES 15:6-7 113

Chapter 14: JUDGES 15:7-8 116

Chapter 15: JUDGES 15:7-8 122

Chapter 16: JUDGES 15:9-10 126

Chapter 17: JUDGES 15:11-13 129

Chapter 18: JUDGES 15:14-19 134

Chapter 19: JUDGES 15:20 142

Chapter 20: JUDGES 15:20 145

Chapter 21: JUDGES 16:31 152

Chapter 22: JUDGES 16:1-3 157

Chapter 23: JUDGES 16:4... 164

Chapter 24: JUDGES 16:4.. 168

PART III: DELILAH 172

Chapter 25: JUDGES 16:4.. 173

Chapter 26: JUDGES 16:5.. 178

Chapter 27: JUDGES 16:4.. 184

Chapter 28: JUDGES 16:5.. 191

Chapter 29: JUDGES 16:6.. 194

Chapter 30: JUDGES 16:6-7 197

Chapter 31: JUDGES 16:8-10 202

Chapter 32: JUDGES 16:11-13 209

Chapter 33: JUDGES 16:13-15 213

Chapter 34: JUDGES 16:15-17 217

Chapter 35: JUDGES 16:16.. 219

Chapter 36: JUDGES 16:16.. 222

Chapter 37: JUDGES 16:18-21 224

Chapter 38: JUDGES 16:21.. 231

Chapter 39: JUDGES 16:21.. 233

Chapter 40: JUDGES 16:21.. 236

Chapter 41: JUDGES 16:18, 16:23.. 239

Chapter 42: JUDGES 16:22-23 241

Chapter 43: JUDGES 16:23-30 245

Chapter 44: JUDGES 16:23-30 249

PART IV: HAZEL 252

EPILOGUE: JUDGES 16:31 253

> *"Good evening. We interrupt our regularly scheduled programming*
> *with breaking news: thousands have reportedly been killed tonight at*
> *a party hosted at the governor's mansion.*
> *Reports from the capital confirm that an explosion, felt for miles,*
> *occurred at approximately 9:52 PM. One moment, folks... we're*
> *receiving an update."*

The reporter presses his finger against the interruptible foldback while he receives a transmission.

The seasoned reporter squints and gazes at the ground, his weary expression betraying the weight of the grim details he's about to share.

His once-square shoulders slump, folding like a flimsy tent. With purpose, he draws a deep, steady breath as he prepares himself to deliver the solemn news.

> *"The 75,000-square-foot governor's mansion, a historic Philistine*
> *landmark, has been reduced to rubble. Sources report no known*
> *survivors or witnesses.*
> *Police are scrambling for answers. We do not yet have an exact death*
> *toll. What we do know at this point is that this event boasts an*
> *extensive guest list. In addition to the governor, attendees included*
> *prominent Philistines such as the mayor, politicians, and business*
> *owners.*
> *Wait! We are receiving additional reports..."*

The reporter, once again, presses his finger to his ear as he listens...

> *"This just in... Rendor, son of the police chief, has provided an*
> *eyewitness account that points to a possible suspect...Rendor states that*

Samson urged him to leave the building mere minutes before it crumbled.

Countless mysteries linger, but stay tuned, ladies and gentlemen, as we keep you updated with breaking news as this heart-wrenching tragedy unfolds.

A tragedy of this magnitude will undoubtedly have profound repercussions on the Philistine government. "

PART I: HAZEL

50 years before the explosion

Chapter 1

JUDGES 13:2

The pamphlet trembles in Hazel's hand as she paces the cool, tiled bathroom floor, her fingers twisting nervously through her curly, shoulder-length hair. Nervous energy keeps her walking in a tight circle on the cool surface for five minutes, but waiting for potentially life-altering news makes five minutes feel like an eternity.

Hazel sinks down on the side of the Jacuzzi tub. Her heel tapping on the floor echoes as she watches each second tick by on the clock. Unable to sit still, she rises again, making another lap around the bathroom, her gaze fixed on the blue tiles she counts with each step. Suppressed emotions bubble up as she catches a glimpse of herself in the bathroom mirror. *It's been five years; why do I keep doing this to myself?* Hazel's nostrils flare as a deep breath surges through her chest cavity. She exhales, fighting to maintain control of her breathing, her efforts futile. Her hopes, fragile and desperate, are tied to the result of that little pink stick.

Gripping the porcelain sink, Hazel closes her eyes, counting the final seconds. The timer beeps. Her eyelids fly open, searching, hoping—then she crumples to the floor. "What's wrong with me?" she mutters with crippling disappointment.

It takes all the strength she can muster to ascend from the depths of her newfound abyss - both emotionally and physically - but she does. Slowly, she rises, staring at her defeated reflection. Tears blur her vision as agony sharpens into rage. She strikes out blindly, and with one fell swoop, the evidence of her failure is knocked off the countertop and put into the trash can. She fills the sink with cold water, plunging her head beneath the surface until her lungs burn, forcing her up for air—a jolt her system desperately needs. As she dries her face, she reminds herself that time is the only thing that can wash away the pain of such a setback, something she learned through the wisdom of experience.

In the quiet waiting room of Dr. Galen's downtown Zorah office, Manoah flips through a magazine. The faint chatter of nurses and soft overhead music provide the only sounds.

Hazel's emerald eyes briefly flicker to the muted television on the wall. An immediate unease draws her gaze away, a reaction mirrored by Manoah as he follows her line of sight. Thick, black plumes of smoke billow from a burning tenement in a district near their home in Zorah. Manoah's jaw tightens, and the urge to shut off the television is written across his face.

The last thing their already agitated community needs is the appalling spectacle of Philistine political corruption cloaked as senseless gang violence. The Philistines always seek innovative ways to exploit their resources and perpetuate an ongoing cycle of distress. A tumultuous history of injustice and power struggles simmers beneath the surface, and the wounds of the past, thought to be healed, are prying open once more.

Manoah navigates an endless stream of cases as a civil lawyer, each a desperate plea for justice. However, even within the framework of their laws, specific provisions are manipulated to their detriment. The gnawing question remains: how much longer will this blood feud persist? How many more times will they be made to pay for the sins of generations long gone?

His gaze shifts to Hazel, her auburn hair framing sun-kissed skin—a beauty dulled by life's hardships. Her hands are in constant motion, her fingers fidgeting, and her leg trembles almost frantically. Manoah sets down his magazine and places a reassuring hand on her trembling thigh, grounding her in the moment.

"Sorry, butterflies," she admits.

"I know," Manoah says warmly. *Should I tell her now?* he wonders. *No, she's far too vulnerable right now.*

This appointment is their last hope. They've tried everything: acupuncture, fertility diets, ovulation tracking, vitamins, and even hiring a personal chef and trainer.

They even considered eccentric alternatives, which included Hazel performing handstands. Nothing is too crazy to be tried at least once.

"You folks can come in now," the nurse says, beckoning them with a wave. Manoah grabs Hazel's trembling hand and squeezes. "It's going to be okay," he whispers.

On the way to the examination room, the nurse hands Hazel a cup. "This is for your urine sample, Hazel," instructs the nurse. "You can leave it behind the small door when you are done. I'll have it tested."

After the urine sample is gathered, the nurse takes Hazel's blood pressure, checks her temperature, draws her blood, and then weighs her. "Any changes since your last visit?" The nurse uses her index finger to push her gold-framed glasses back up to the bridge of her nose.

"No," Hazel mutters.

"Ok, then. The doctor will see you shortly."

The couple settles into the room. Manoah stands behind Hazel and affectionately places his hand on her shoulder while she sits in the armchair. She touches his hand, caressing his knuckles until a knock at the door shatters the tender moment.

Dr. Scott Galen, a renowned infertility specialist, is celebrated worldwide for his success rates. The doctor enters wearing a plastered-on smile, but the truth can't be hidden away; it always breaks free. The truth is evident before a word is spoken in the good doctor's eyes.

"I thought this round of treatments would take, but the test results were negative. I'm sorry." Dr. Galen shoves his hands into his lab coat pockets and takes a step back. "I'm going to step out for a moment to give you folks some time to collect your thoughts."

Ten minutes elapse before Dr. Galen re-enters the room to find the couple engaged in a heart-wrenching embrace. The doctor clears his throat. Hazel moves to the examination table while Manoah leans against the furthest wall.

"I need to be very honest with you." Dr. Galen removes the stethoscope from his neck and places it on the counter. "I don't know if there is anything else we can do. Have you thought about adoption or possibly a surrogate?"

Manoah studies his wife's face. She tries to force a smile, but her lips are reluctant participants. "We have discussed it," Manoah replies, "but we don't think it's for us. We want a baby of our own."

"You have one year left of fertility, maybe two. Please, think about it."

"We'll keep trying," Manoah says, nodding with reassurance at Hazel as he gently strokes his wife's back. "Thank you, Dr. Galen. We will see you again." The two gather their things and head toward the parking garage. Manoah's stomach flips. "I have something I need to tell you," he yells.

Hazel notices the sadness on his face. "What's wrong?"

"I realize that this might not be the best time, given the news we just received…" his voice trails off.

"You're scaring me, Manoah. What is it?"

Hazel searches his face for clues. *I can't take any more bad news today.* A rogue car horn from the traffic below interrupts her thoughts and seems to urge Manoah on.

"I … I made partner today." An apprehensive grin appears on Manoah's face. Hazel squeezes his hands with all her strength.

"Oh! I'm happy and mad at the same time. I can't believe you are *just* telling me!" She wraps her arms around him. "Moe, this is wonderful." Cuffing his face with her hands, she softly kisses his lips. "You are an amazing man. I don't understand why it took them so long to realize it."

"Me neither, but I'll tell you more about it later. I have to get back to the office." Before leaving her, Manoah clutches Hazel's hands. "About the fertility treatments… I know you're frustrated. I am, too. But no matter how much we want a baby, sometimes things don't happen when or how we think they should. What I do know is that when the time is right, it *will* happen. We have to keep praying."

"That's easy for you to say," Hazel mutters. "You already have the boys."

"That isn't fair," he sighs. "I'm in this as much as you. It's stressful for me, too."

Hazel winces at the sting of her words, regretting the mention of his past relationship and the lingering pain of the boys' absence. She laces her fingers through his. "I'm sorry."

Manoah squeezes her hand. "It's fine," He rubs the frown lines forming between her eyebrows with his thumb. "I told you—no Botox—so stop frowning."

Hazel nods and chuckles. Manoah wraps his arms around her, pulling her close. "Now that I'm a partner, no one will mind if I sneak home. We can put in extra effort on that baby project," he teases, planting a tender kiss on her neck, his eyes sparkling with mischief.

"Later, I promise," Hazel ardently whispers.

After they part ways, Hazel heads to her boutique, lost in her thoughts. *I'm so proud of him. He deserves that promotion. But I want to give him something that he can't get for himself.*

"Welcome to *Something Unique*. Can I help you find anything today?"

Hazel delivers her usual greeting, only glancing up afterward. "Recognizing the customer, Hazel brightens and hurries to the front. 'Oh, hello! I just got some fabulous new pieces in since your last visit."

The woman browses a circular rack of scarves, her movements slowed by the flowing maternity maxi dress draped over her rounded belly. "I haven't been able to go out as often lately," the customer says, slowly massaging her tummy.

Hazel tries to avert her gaze but finds herself staring. Realizing, she smiles warmly and says, "Oh my goodness, congratulations! You look absolutely radiant."

"Thank you! I'm finally past the morning sickness—and most of the weird cravings, thank goodness."

Hazel and the customer stroll through the maze of tables and racks in her store. "We have personalized baby items. Do you know if the baby is a boy or girl?"

"Not for another couple of weeks."

Hazel guides the woman to a display table showcasing sterling silver baby frames, delicate rattles, and cozy cashmere hat-and-bootie sets. The woman frowns as her eyes search the gallery. Hazel tries to save the sale. "Have you decided on any names?"

"If it's a boy, we've narrowed it down to Ian. But if it's a girl, Alexandria, or Tracy. We can't agree on a girl's name."

"Those are all beautiful names. Once you decide, we can personalize almost anything—including these pink and blue crib blankets, which we can embroider with the baby's name."

She turned and walked towards the door. "Unfortunately, I won't be able to return. My husband and I are building a home in the suburbs of Sorek."

"You can order from our website. We will personalize and ship it to you. Let me grab my business card. Please send me pictures of the baby!"

"I will, thank you." She waves on her way out.

Hazel watches the woman exit through the glass doors, her gaze lingering as she disappears. Turning back to the rows of baby items, Hazel wonders if she'll ever have a reason to indulge in her vast inventory.

"Tell me about your promotion," Hazel says softly as they settle into bed that evening, her tone warm and inviting. He rubs her arm, evoking a shiver of pleasure, drawing her head against his chest.

"It was the real estate case I mentioned," he begins, his words accompanied by pride. "The Philistine company was cooking the books, falsifying statements to lure in investors—which, of course, is illegal. And when they couldn't fulfill their obligations to the investors, especially those from our community, we stepped in. Our firm initiated the prosecution, but their lawyers argued that the owner was oblivious, laying the blame solely on the chief financial officer. After all, it was his signature on those altered statements."

"And you didn't find that convincing?" Hazel probes, a hint of skepticism in her voice.

A small sigh escapes Manoah. "No, I didn't. But proving the owner's complicity was tricky. We had to settle for holding the CFO accountable."

In the soft moonlight filtering through the wooden blinds, Manoah's face becomes a canvas of joy, illuminated for Hazel to see. He pulls her closer to tenderly kiss her forehead before sleep. As Manoah's eyes drift shut, Hazel remains awake, restless even in the night's embrace.

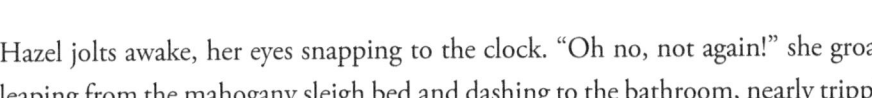

Hazel jolts awake, her eyes snapping to the clock. "Oh no, not again!" she groans, leaping from the mahogany sleigh bed and dashing to the bathroom, nearly tripping in haste. The cold travertine obliterates residual grogginess. She races around the bathroom, darts into the adjoining closet, searches for a dress, and hops down the stairs while pulling on black ballet flats.

With frantic fingers, she snatches her purse and keys from the kitchen counter and grabs a chef's prepared meal from the refrigerator. As she passes the hall mirror on her way to the garage, she realizes she hasn't put makeup on. *I'll have to do it in the car.*

Sunlight spills into the garage as Hazel hits the door's button. Her car is missing. She gasps. Her body is frozen until she remembers Manoah has taken it to the dealership today for a factory recall repair.

She walks back through the garage, passing the power tools and lawn equipment against the side wall, then exchanges keys in the kitchen. Today, her ride is Manoah's Fox Body Mustang. The car is all black, with red racing seats and a white Ford pony stitched at the top. Red calipers were visible through the spokes of its 20-inch black alloy wheels.

Back in the garage, she yanks the fleece-lined, waterproof cover off and throws her purse onto the front seat. The Mustang's five-liter V-8 remains silent when she turns the key. She flicks the lights and radio—nothing. With a frustrated sigh, Hazel pops the hood and retrieves the portable battery charger from the workbench.

"Excuse me, do you need a hand?" a voice calls out from the sidewalk.

Hazel startles, turning with the charger in hand to see a man standing at the edge of her driveway. "Uh, no, I think I've got it," she answers, heart racing.

For all she knew, he could be a stranger with bad intentions. Hazel swallows hard and forces a polite "No, thank you."

"You don't sound sure. I'd be happy to take a look." He walks up the driveway with his t-shirt and sweatpants waving in the light breeze. He doesn't look familiar, and his complexion lacks the telltale olive undertone of the Philistines. His voice is pleasant and friendly. A measure of Hazel's apprehension melts.

He must be new to the neighborhood or perhaps a guest—strangers were rare in their gated community. "Are you new to the area?" she asks, still trying to place him.

He stops short of entering the garage. "No, just passing through, he replies with an easy smile."

"I think the battery is dead. My husband showed me how to charge it." Hazel says, in a rush, setting up the charger.

"If you like, I can hang around for a while to make sure you get it started." His genuine smile makes his offer difficult to refuse. Hazel fumbles with the charger cables, her nervous hands betraying her attempt at casual small talk.

"That's really kind of you—thank you. It's just one of those mornings," she sighs. "How's your morning been?"

"So far, so good. It's a gorgeous day. Perfect for a jog."

"With all the rush, I haven't even had a chance to appreciate how beautiful it is outside," Hazel remarks, her words carrying a hint of surprise. She gestures towards a refrigerator tucked in the corner of the garage. "Can I offer you a bottle of water?" The situation she's in should leave her feeling uneasy – alone, stranded, engaged in conversation with a stranger in her garage – but an unexpected calm prevails.

"No, but thank you." He removes his cap and puts it back on his head, adjusting it as if trying to achieve a better fit.

Hazel climbs into the driver's seat to apply her makeup. In her peripheral view, the man is standing at the garage entrance, and she can see him admiring the car. She applies the finishing touches of her lip gloss and hops out of the vehicle to check the indicator light on the charger.

"That was fast," she whispers, disconnecting the cable and placing the charger on the shelf. Reaching through the driver's side window, Hazel turns the key. The Mustang engine growls: she loves that sound – the rumble, the power.

"Thanks for chatting. It made the time go by faster."

"No problem at all. Before I go, though, I have a message for you." His kind countenance turns pensive.

Hazel closes the hood and turns to face the dark-haired stranger, unease flickering in her eyes.

"Don't worry. It's good news," the man chuckles. "You're going to have a son."

Hazel searches his face, her thoughts racing. *Who is this man? How could he possibly know they've been trying for a child? And how could he be so sure it would be a son?*

"Is this some kind of cruel joke?" Hazel's voice trembles, sharp and cutting, as she glares at him. "Did someone put you up to this? Because I assure you, it's anything but funny!" A storm of frustration and confusion swirls in her eyes.

"No joke," he replies calmly. "I was sent to deliver this message. Your son will be a Nazirite. I know what you're thinking—don't you have to choose that for yourself? Normally, yes. But God has special plans for him."

Hazel's eyes widened at this news. Could it be? What kind of big plans?' she asks, her voice barely above a whisper."

"Your son's destiny lies in illuminating a path of hope and liberation for our people," the words carry a solemn weight, woven with the threads of a shared history. "For the Israelites, oppressed and struggling under the iron grip of the Philistine government, he is destined to be a beacon of light, a deliverer." As the words hang in the air, Hazel considers the magnitude of the task foretold, a task that carries the echoes of countless lives yearning for relief from their plight.

"Hmm, that's quite an immense plan," Hazel reflects inwardly, her thoughts tinged with skepticism and hope. She can't help but mull over the profound levels of suffering and grief their people have endured, weighed against the staggering might the Philistines wield. A shiver travels down her spine, a physical manifestation of the anxiety that grips her. The weight of the responsibility that would rest on someone's shoulders, especially on her child's, seems almost impossible. Hazel reflects on how answered prayers rarely come in the forms we expect.

The man holds up a hand before Hazel can speak again. "Now," he begins, ticking off on his fingers, "there are a few conditions. First, no alcohol."

"Does that include wine?" she scoffs, hoping he says no.

"Yes, it includes wine, wine coolers, cosmos, and any other form of alcohol. Secondly, you have to restrict the type of meat you eat."

"I rarely eat meat."

"Also, the fish you eat must have fins and scales."

"Don't all fish have fins and scales?"

"A catfish doesn't."

She frowns. *What if you don't fry it? Is that acceptable?*

He smiles and shakes his head, seemingly reading her mind. "That also includes lobster and shrimp."

Hazel drops her head and lets out a heavy sigh.

"The only red meat you can eat –"

"Wait," she interrupts. "There's *more?*"

"Yes. The only red meat you can eat must be from animals with a divided hoof that chews their cud."

"The meat I buy comes in a package; I don't know what kind of hooves the animals had!" Hazel raises her hands to her face and then drops them back down to her sides.

"Eat beef and goat, and you will be fine." He is about to go into greater detail about the final rule but decides against it when he sees her face. "You can eat chicken and turkey, too."

"Wow. Is that all?" Her voice is thick with sarcasm.

"Almost," he answers with a raised eyebrow. "Once your son is born, his hair must never be cut."

The look in the man's eyes is sincere. He checks his wristwatch. "I'm sorry. I must run. Remember what I said: no alcohol, no unclean food, and you mustn't cut his hair." He waves and dashes across the grass onto the sidewalk. "Take care."

"Wait!" She reaches through the window to turn off the car to catch up with him, but when she looks up again, he is gone. She rushes down to the end of the driveway, but he is nowhere in sight.

Her heartbeat reverberates in her ears while she walks back toward the car. Thoughts whizz around her head like a swarm of agitated bees. Hazel is still trying to figure out what to do next. She wants to ask the man if someone has put him up to this, but the more she thinks about it, the more she doesn't need to question the authenticity. The encounter was as real as it was odd.

When Hazel arrives at the boutique, her excitement makes working impossible. As much as she hates bothering Manoah while he is at the firm, she *has* to talk to him.

"Hello?" Manoah answers on the third ring.

"Hey."

"Is everything okay? It's not like you to call before noon."

"Umm, yeah. I guess."

"What do you mean?"

"While I charged the Mustang this morning, a guy jogged up to see if I needed help."

"What guy?"

"I don't know. I've never seen him before, but he seemed nice."

"Wait. What were you wearing?" Manoah interrupts, trying to keep his voice from sounding cold.

"What does that have to do with what I'm saying, Moe? You always worry about the wrong things."

"I know you. You were probably wearing that clingy dress that I like and stilettos. He saw you, and…" Manoah's tone morphs, punctuated by a slowed mocking cadence, "he just had to come over to see if the poor damsel in distress needed some help."

Ignoring him, she continues. "He said he was sent here to tell us we will have a baby—a son—and our baby will be important. I mean important to God. He said that we need to abstain from alcohol and eat restricted and specific types of meats."

"Aren't all kids important to God? If it's God's will, we will have a child when the time is right." Manoah doesn't like the sound of any of this. Some strange man approaches his wife and starts spouting this peculiar prediction. It's too much for him to believe.

"We weren't even talking about kids," Hazel says. "We were chatting about the weather and his jog. Then he said he was sent to tell me we will have a baby."

"Hold on…sent by whom?" Manoah asks, feeling a tightness in his chest.

"I don't know. He didn't say. He said our son would belong to God. So, I guess God sent him? Moe, what if he was an angel sent by God? Whoever he was, I believe him."

"Wait, hold on. Yeah…okay…great." The facetiousness returns to his voice. "I just received a message from an angel. He said I will have pizza and chips for dinner and watch sports."

Hazel doesn't respond right away. Instead, she allows an awkward silence to linger on the phone. She finally speaks up after what had to have been close to a ten count. "Moe, I am serious. I'm not talking about a new pair of shoes. I'm talking about a son."

"I'm serious, too. I don't think he was an angel. What if you were dreaming? Sometimes you dream and wake up mad at me because of something I did in your dream."

"Are you listening to me? I wasn't dreaming!"

"I think maybe you mentioned you wanted a child, and he responded in a way that made you feel better. I'm not saying there's anything wrong with him reassuring you, but I don't think a man jogging through the neighborhood is one of God's angels, either. God will have to send him back so I can meet him for myself before I believe anything he says."

"You're a killjoy."

"We will keep trying," Manoah says, now sensitive. "I'll talk to you later, babe. I have to finish up some work."

Despite her husband's skepticism about the identity of the man she encountered, Hazel's conviction remains steadfast. With a heart full of hope, she offers up prayers, her deepest wish being that the enigmatic figure reappears, allowing her husband to converse with him.

With a satisfied sigh, Hazel adjusts the last magnets on the shelf. Rays of morning sun pierce through the boutique's window, carrying the aura of a good day. Her eyes rove over the display: a collection of colorful souvenirs with different themes for teachers, nurses, police officers, firefighters, high schools, and colleges that she knows are perfect for her clientele.

As long as the professionals and entrepreneurs in her community found even a shred of encouragement through them against the Philistine oppression, then she would continue to distribute them. God knew they needed all the joy they could get.

The items are created by a new vendor in the area, Cloud 9 Magnets. She takes great pride in offering her customers one-of-a-kind pieces – from baby gifts to jewelry to home décor – that can't be found elsewhere. The items from Cloud 9 Magnets are a perfect addition to Hazel's boutique.

Hazel's growling stomach breaks her concentration. "Alexis," Hazel calls out to her clerk, who slings her purse over her shoulder and locks her office. "I didn't have a chance to eat my breakfast. I'm starving. I will have an early lunch at the deli on the corner. If anyone calls, I'll be back in an hour."

Five minutes later, a sign in the deli window stops her: Closed – Under Construction. Hazel's stomach roars in protest. She looks around to see if any of the people on the sidewalk heard it, but they seem unbothered by the noise. She has to eat – now.

As if on cue, a delicious aroma of spices fills her nostrils and draws her toward a café she has never noticed before. The wooden sign above the door reads *Vernell and Veronica's Café*. The place looks quaint and unique, but even better, it is open.

The chime on the door announces her arrival in the cozy restaurant. The patio is adorned with tomato vines that weave up a homemade trellis. A gentleman reads the paper in a comfy booth against the back wall while sipping his tea. Hazel starts to order pastrami and turkey on rye when she realizes the cafe doesn't process their meat. She reads the menu on the chalkboard in disbelief. The freshness and quality of each thoughtfully considered ingredient are astonishing.

"On second thought, make that a veggie wrap with grilled, organic eggplant and aged balsamic."

Hazel pays, thinking again about what the man said about forbidden foods. She decides then and there to eat healthily, following his instructions and ensuring his message comes true. *What do I have to lose?* Not only that, but she will also recruit Manoah to help her throw out all processed food in the house. No longer will they eat food loaded with antibiotics and hormones or covered in chemical pesticides and fertilizers. No more boxed food with a long list of unrecognizable ingredients. They may even start their organic vegetable garden in the backyard.

She selects a small table near the window while she waits for her food, casually watching the people walk by. Someone catches her eye. Suddenly, her back straightens, and her eyes widen.

Wait. Is that the man from the neighborhood?

The passerby resembles him. He is wearing dark-washed jeans with a red T-shirt and has just entered the gift shop on the corner. She digs in her purse for her cell phone.

"Hey babe, what's up?" Manoah answers.

"Moe, the jogger from the neighborhood, is at the gift shop across the street from the boutique. Can you take an early lunch?"

Manoah's law firm is two blocks west of her boutique. They each know this opportunity might never present itself again. "Walking out now," he says.

"Hurry..."

She watches the gift shop while she waits for Manoah and her wrap. The man exits the gift shop, and she watches him enter the florist next door. She quickly checks on her order just as it is coming up. "Grilled veggie wrap!" the woman behind the counter calls.

Hazel grabs her food and hastens out the door. Jaywalking across the street, she hurries to the other side to wait for her husband and to keep an eye on the door of the florist shop.

Manoah arrives disheveled. "Where is he?"

"He's in the florist." Manoah pushes the florist's shop door open. They walk into the store, but the man isn't there. "Where did he go? I didn't see him come out," Hazel says. She steps outside and scans the block in both directions but sees no sign of him.

Manoah places his hand on the small of her back. "It's okay. I'm sure we'll see him another day. Let's get some food, I'm starving."

Her face wrinkles with confusion. *How could I have lost him?* She follows her husband across the street, glancing back to check the sidewalk as they turn the corner. She needs Moe to believe her and the jogger to confirm God's message.

"Pasta?" Manoah asks. Hazel holds up her to-go bag in response. "Pasta for me, then. Will you join me?" Manoah formally requests. As Manoah opens the door, the jogger walks out.

"Hello," he says, surprised to see them as they are to see him. "I was looking for you. Your assistant told me you came here to eat. Manoah, I presume? Nice to meet you," he offers his hand to a shocked Manoah. Hazel hadn't mentioned Manoah's name earlier.

"Are you the man who told my wife we will have a baby?"

The man moves from the doorway onto the sidewalk so they aren't blocking the deli's entrance.

"I am."

"She told me you said we'll have a son."

"Yes, I did."

"Who sent you? What do we need to do once he's born? Are there special schools he should attend? What kind of career will he have?" His rapid-fire questions are slathered in sarcasm.

"As I told your wife, make sure you eat only permitted foods and don't drink alcohol. Your son is already promised to you; all you have to do is follow God's laws."

Hazel smiles. Manoah rubs his forehead as he considers the whole notion. He isn't convinced the man is an angel. On the other hand, what does he have to lose by believing him? He doesn't want to upset his wife, but he doesn't want to give her false hope.

"We were just about to eat. Please, join us." Manoah opens the door to the restaurant and gestures for the jogger to enter. "Let us buy you lunch for delivering us this wonderful news."

"No, thank you. Perhaps you could buy someone else's lunch."

"Wait, we don't even know your name," Hazel says.

Tires screech, and everyone turns to face the sudden commotion. A taxi has halted within inches of hitting a bike messenger, who has swerved and fallen off his bicycle, scattering manila envelopes in the intersection. The angry courier gathers the packages off the asphalt, muttering obscenities. Concerned bystanders help the messenger pull his bicycle to the sidewalk. He adjusts his yellow and black helmet, curses the cabbie, throws his hand in the air, and peddles away disgusted. Stunned, the taxi driver sits there, shaken by the near miss.

"Thank you for…" Manoah's voice trails off. As he turns back, he notices the jogger has disappeared. "Did you see where he went?" he asks Hazel, squinting as he looks down the street. It is close to lunchtime, so the street and sidewalk are packed with people.

"He did the same thing to me when he stopped by the house. I turned away for a quick second, and he was gone. Just like that, he'd vanished."

A bell chimes as the couple enter the diner. The scent of freshly cut meat and baked bread wafts through the air. Manoah orders his pasta as Hazel studies the clusters of seated people. Some lean in and speak in hushed tones, while others are boisterous. Apart from their distinct mannerisms, it's evident that they're all enjoying themselves.

With their orders in hand and fingers intertwined, the couple heads for the city's downtown water fountain district to finally eat. Before they sit down, Hazel notices a woman standing next to a dumpster.

"What is she doing with that child?" It's unclear if the woman is attempting to toss the child into the dumpster or holding him while he rummages inside. Regardless of intentions, Manoah doesn't see it as their place to inquire. But when he no longer feels Hazel's soft fingers, he stops.

"Ma'am, do you need help?" Hazel shouts, and the woman and child ignore her.

"Looks like chicken," the boy says, raising a bag of food into the air, his face gleaming with joy. The boy turns back to continue rummaging through the trash.

Hazel walks into the alley to get closer. Manoah knows his wife won't leave until she finds out what is happening, so he follows reluctantly before asking loudly, "Ma'am, are you and the child okay?"

"We're fine," says the woman, waving him away.

"Looks like you could use some help," Manoah returns, noticing their dirty, tattered clothes.

"We just wanted to make sure you were all right," Hazel adds. She looks at the boy's filthy clothes and notices he is now watching from inside the dumpster. "Are you hungry, baby?" she asks gently.

"Yes, ma'am. We're looking for something to eat." His smile is innocent, and her heart breaks for him, watching him approach the front of the dumpster.

"Boy!" his mother snaps at him. With her head still hung, she peers at the strangers through her lashes and between greasy strands of unwashed hair. "We're just looking for a bit of food. We aren't hurting anybody."

A lump rises in Manoah's throat. How many of their people roamed the streets like this, scavenging for food, while Philistines reveled in luxury with embezzled funds?

He blinks away the red haze forming behind his vision. "If you're hungry, please take this." Manoah extends his hand and presents his brown paper bag to the woman. Hazel offers her meal as well. For an eternity, the woman stands motionless and stares at the bags without meeting their gaze.

"Thank you," the woman whispers nearly inaudibly. The child's eyes light up as he jumps out of the dumpster and reaches for the bags. After an awkward moment, the hardened look on the woman's face softens. "I do appreciate this," she says. The anguish on her face is apparent when she eventually lifts her head. "I've prayed all morning for God to send us food, and today, you showed up. I don't know what else to say, but thank you. You both are truly a blessing."

"There's not a shred of doubt left in my mind that the man we met was a divine messenger," Manoah's voice carries a sense of awe as he sits at the edge of their bed, extending his hand toward Hazel for her inspection as they readied for bed. "I tried to keep my composure, but when he vanished, I'll admit, I was shaken. I didn't know what to make of it. He seemed to know we were destined to find that boy and his mother. It was as if God intended us to witness that miracle."

Hazel's smile widens as she recalls the faces of the young boy and his mother. "Their expressions were unforgettable."

Manoah's response carries a sense of humility. "I'm just grateful we could be of assistance."

Hazel's voice softens, and her eyes shimmer with belief. "And that same angel promised us a son. I believe it wholeheartedly." Her fingers trace a soothing path down his back as he lies beside her. Their eyes meet, his hand cupping her cheek before he presses a loving kiss to her forehead.

"I apologize for doubting you earlier. I was concerned. A stranger suddenly appears, tells you what you long to hear, and then vanishes," Manoah admits. As Hazel makes her way towards the bathroom, he watches her, his expression a mix of surprise and curiosity.

"Are you heading to sleep?" he asks, adjusting himself to lean against the headboard.

"Yes, why?" Hazel replies from behind the bathroom door, her voice muffled.

"You're wearing my shirt," Manoah's eyes widen in astonishment and amusement.

Hazel emerges from behind the door, clad in one of his button-down shirts. "I know," she whispers as she moves toward the bed, her movements a graceful glide.

Manoah's surprise lingers, but a hint of playful teasing emerges. "Are you trying to seduce me?"

Hazel hushes him, placing a finger over his lips as she settles into bed. "Enough talking, and could you please turn off the light?"

The morning air is chilled on this day, but the sun is out. Leaves on the trees lining the street are beginning to turn ruby red. Hazel strolls from the boutique to the parking garage. While digging around her purse, her keys fell to the ground. She bends to pick them up and suddenly feels hot and dizzy. She loses her balance. Hazel leans on her car to cool off and let the dizziness pass. It doesn't help. She unlocks the car, still dazed, and slides inside, closing the door.

Hazel lowers the car windows, soothingly inviting the breeze to brush against her cheeks. Lost in her thoughts, she reflects on her meals from both breakfast and lunch, a subtle unease settling in her stomach. She mentally scrolls through the contents of her plate, searching for any culprits that might be causing this sudden discomfort. Yet, her meals had been ordinary, nothing out of the ordinary. Frowning slightly, she dismisses the idea of anything amiss.

"It must be something I ate," she moans aloud, her words laced with resignation as if unwilling to allow herself to entertain any other possibility. The possibility that hovers in the back of her mind, the one she's been trying to suppress, is almost too overwhelming to confront.

Chapter 3

JUDGES 13:3-23

Hazel finally finds one, rips open the box and pulls the test from its package.

This time, the instructional pamphlet lies forgotten on the counter. She paces the cool floor of the tiled bathroom, twisting her curly, shoulder-length hair around her fingers—five minutes – an eternity.

She sinks down on the side of the Jacuzzi tub. This time, she does not tap her heel on the floor, and no sound echoes as she watches each second tick by on the clock. Jumping up from the tub, she makes another lap around the bathroom, counting the blue tiles. Hazel catches a glimpse of herself in the bathroom mirror. *What if it's negative again? No. God promised us a son...* "This has to be it," she reassures herself aloud.

After taking a deep breath, she stands in front of the porcelain sink and closes her eyes to pray. *God, you know I trust you. I believe you sent that angel to us and will bless us with a son. Let me have the strength to accept your timing. In your glorious name, Amen.*

Slowly, she opens her eyes and peeks. It is positive. Her heart began to race. In disbelief, she yanks out another test and quickly takes it. While she sits on the edge of the bathtub to absorb the results, she calls Manoah. His phone goes to voicemail, so she decides to wait until he comes home to tell him in person, although she doesn't know how to wait that long. She is bursting with excitement.

Hazel walks to the mirror in her bedroom, raises her shirt, and pushes her stomach out as far as she can, imagining what it would look like, swollen with new life. A delighted giggle escapes her lips as she pictures it. *How can I tell Manoah?*

Not wanting him to find them, she pushes the tests into the kitchen garbage under some trash. She then scribbled a note on the whiteboard on the refrigerator, letting him know she had run to the store. Driving to her shop, she heads straight for the baby aisle. *Yes! That's it.* Before she makes it that far, she spots a red and blue baby bib with "#1 Dad" stitched above a baseball glove, bat, and ball. *This is perfect.* She grins, grabbing it with a small gift bag and tissue paper.

Manoah pulls into the driveway at the same time Hazel returns home. "How was your day?" she asks, stretching to the tips of her toes to kiss him as he meets her at her car.

"You know…same thing, different day. How about you?"

"Hmmm. I have something for you," Hazel says, holding the small bag behind her back.

"What's today? Did I forget our anniversary?"

"No, silly. I got you a little something."

His lips curl to one side. "What is it? Wait! What do you want?"

"Open it," Hazel smiles, pushing the bag toward him. It takes every ounce of composure Hazel can muster to keep from jumping for joy while she watches Moe open the gift.

He sifts through the tissue paper and pulls out the bib. His brows furrow, then shoot up. "Wait—really?" A broad smile spreads across his face as he realizes its meaning. "Are you sure?"

"I'm sure." Hazel sings the words as she dances around the kitchen.

"There is so much to think about. Where do we begin?"

Hazel continues her happy dance, then suddenly pauses at the counter. "Names! That's a good place to start. I have always liked Theodore, Troy, and…" She bounces around the kitchen island, almost making Manoah dizzy.

"Babe," Manoah interrupts, laughing at Hazel's antics, "*slow down.*"

"I know, I know. I'm just so excited!" She hugs him again and dances up the stairs, singing as she goes along.

The excitement didn't fade as the weeks turned into months. Hazel reads everything she can get her hands on about babies. The mother-to-be website she follows tells her what to expect week-to-week, what she will feel, and what is going on in her body. At thirteen weeks, she checks it to see if her belly is the right size. Hazel has given up many of her favorite indulgences: morning coffee, creamy cheeses, and flavorful fish dishes. When her belly button itches, she checks the website for the best anti-stretching creams. As delighted as she was to be carrying a baby, she had not realized what a chore pregnancy would be.

When Manoah isn't taking pictures of her expanding belly or inundating her with baby information he finds online, he is readying the baby's room. After work, he comes home and puts furniture together. It is all he talks about.

Late this particular morning, Hazel starts having cramps. She first assumes that her breakfast doesn't agree with her, but the cramps become more substantial and more regular. Finally, it seems, the day has come. "I think we should go to the hospital. The contractions are stronger," she tells him.

"You ready?" Manoah asks minutes later. "I spoke with the nurse at Dr. Galen's office, and she paged him. He said he would meet us at the hospital."

Seated at the edge of the bed, Hazel's fingers clench the fabric beneath her, her leg quivering with anticipation and anxiety. The rhythm of her contractions continues to surge, now arriving every seven minutes, their intensity gnawing at her resolve. With determination etched onto her features, she forces words through gritted teeth.

"I don't know if I have the strength for this," she confides, the edges of her voice frayed with a blend of pain and vulnerability. The sensation gripping her feels like a relentless blaze, tearing through her being with an unyielding force. Manoah sits beside her, opening his arms and motioning for his wife to lay her head on his chest. "Come here."

Hazel slides her body closer and wraps her arms around his waist. "I'm scared, Moe."

He strokes her back gently. "You are not in this alone. I was here when you became pregnant; I will be there when our son arrives. I am here for the rest of our lives."

Hazel raises her head, looking into her husband's eyes. He leans down and kisses her forehead. A contraction tightens in the pit of her stomach, causing a sudden, sharp intake of breath. She breathes through it slowly as she waits for the pain to pass.

Manoah stands and reaches out for her hand. "You'll do great, babe."

"Ok. Here we go," she says, surrendering.

Manoah picks up the hospital bag next to the door on the way to the garage. Hazel snatches her purse off the counter.

"Manoah."

He fumbles about the kitchen, patting himself down. He checks every pocket, scans the counter, and then the key hooks on the wall.

"Manoah!"

"I can't find the keys," he mumbles, checking his pockets for the fifth time.

"Manoah!" she screams.

Manoah jumps and spins around. Hazel stands in the doorway to the garage with the keys in one hand and gripping the door jamb with the other.

"Is it another contraction?"

"My…" Hazel's voice falters as her hands grip the doorframe. A sharp jolt tears through her stomach and lower back, stealing her breath. Manoah gently pries the keys from her clenched fingers. Hazel takes a deep breath, the pain temporarily subsiding.

Manoah follows her eyes to her legs.

"…water broke."

Water is everywhere. He hurries her to the car, supporting her as they walk. Hazel holds her breath through another contraction. It hurts more than breathing through it, but she forgets all her breathing techniques every time a contraction rolls in.

Somehow, she manages to fasten her seatbelt while trying to take longer, steady breaths.

Manoah tosses her bag into the trunk, slides behind the wheel, and drives off with a controlled urgency.

Staring out of the window in tremendous pain, Hazel gazes at the bright blue sky and rubs her tummy. She'd waited for this day for years, and now that it was finally here, she should have been ecstatic, but she wasn't. Nervousness is the only emotion she has. *Is it the labor I'm afraid of, or is it the thought of taking care of a fragile baby?*

Up ahead, two uniformed officers signal them to stop.

"What's going on?" Hazel forces out through another contraction.

Manoah's features darken. "Philistines." He mutters under his breath.

"Not now." Tears sting her eyes—part anger and part pain.

They pull over, but Manoah keeps the engine running as the men approach. Years of being with him informed her that from the stiff tenseness of his shoulders, anything could happen from here. She lays a trembling hand of caution on his solid muscles.

"Officers, my wife is in labor as I speak. Is there a problem?" She knows by his tone and worries that he will provoke the officers.

The one with a *too*-groomed brown mustache peeps into the car and releases a chuckle void of humor, "You don't say."

The other officer gives a crooked smile. "Papers, sir." He taps his stubby knuckles on the hood. "And for the sake of wifey, they better be up to date."

It feels like an eternity passes afterward. A rush of fear and hatred overtakes Hazel in the break between contractions. *How could they?* In a flash, the faces of relatives and friends she'd lost to their kind all those years past filled her mind. How long would this last? Was this the end for her? What about her child?

Manoah fishes out the papers. Even through her haze, she can tell the legal wheels in his head are turning, seeking a fast and clean way out of the situation. The officers take their sweet time perusing the impeccable licenses. Another stab of pain stretches within her, and a strangled half-scream escapes her lips.

"Everything is up to date," her husband hisses. "What more do you want?"

"Quiet down, Israelite," the officer snaps, his disdain as clear as the sneer curling his lips.

Hazel's heart sinks even further.

"Honey." Manoah turns in his seat to grasp her hand. The look in his eyes is raw desperation. He holds her gaze, wordlessly transmitting all his love and strength. What she gives him in return is a pitiful attempt at a smile.

In a flash, something shifts within her, and the heaviness of her child descends like never before. It's a miracle she doesn't pass out from the abrupt pain. Breath is knocked out of her and then resumes in short, strained chops.

"Give me my papers." Manoah's voice is barely above a whisper, so chilling in its quality that both men stop their gimmicks to look at him.

With something between a smirk and a leer plastered on his face. The officer with the mustache asked, "Are you the first woman to ever be pregnant?"

A strange tremble overtakes her body. Before she can process the shift in her, she feels an odd warmth trickle down her legs.

"Moe!"

He glances back, and his eyes widen.

Everything after that was a blur. Her husband tears the papers from the officer's grip with astonishing speed and force and hits the gas. The shouts that trail them are more than angry — but she barely registers them.

Hazel clutches her maxi dress in a death grip. If He had promised this child to them so specifically, wouldn't He have also been faithful in protecting him from harm? Tears sting her eyes.

Lord, please... my baby...

Upon their arrival at the hospital, a nurse rushes to their car with a wheelchair.

Hazel's thoughts race with fear. Manoah strides alongside her, clutching her bag, his face reflecting his anxiety. The nurse, dressed in red and white heart-patterned scrubs, guides them to their room. Urgently, she calls for the doctor, who appears promptly, issuing rapid medical directives. As another wave of contractions courses through Hazel, she offers up a silent gratitude for the wheelchair that supports her.

In a room bathed in light, they lift Hazel onto the bed, moving swiftly to assess her and the baby's vital signs. The anxiety stemming from the blood on the car seat lingers.

"Everything appears to be in order," the OB-GYN announces. "No complications detected."

A shiver of thankfulness sweeps over her. Thank you, Lord. The ominous threat hadn't taken away this precious life. Hazel would willingly face the harshest pain rather than endure the loss of this newfound joy.

With the doctor's consent, the necessary preparations for the next steps are set into motion.

"Welcome to your delivery and recovery room," the nurse explains warmly. "The bed is designed to separate when it's time for you to deliver the baby. Here's your gown. Once you've changed, I'll proceed to draw some blood and connect both you and the baby to monitors, which will track your contractions and vitals. If either of you have any questions, don't hesitate to push the button on your bed. Either I or the other nurse on duty will be here to assist you."

With contractions occurring roughly every four minutes, Manoah assists Hazel in going to the restroom to change clothes. Meanwhile, the nurse readjusts the bed's cover and pillows. While Hazel changes, Manoah places the bag on a nearby chair and takes out a video camera. Once Hazel returns, the camera focuses on her belly.

"Son, we'll meet you very soon." Manoah addresses her belly, his earlier pallor replaced by a newfound steadiness, though his voice still carries a hint of tremor from recent events. She understands why.

"Moe, could you put on some music?" Hazel requests as she eases herself onto the hospital bed. Manoah plays music from his phone, and Hazel rests her head on the pillow.

One of the nurses comes in smiling. "I will insert your IV and review what you need to know. Please don't hesitate to stop me if I'm moving too fast."

Hazel adjusts her arm and closes her eyes, trying to slow her heartbeat and wait out another contraction. The nurse's voice babbles in the background.

Another nurse, petite and dressed in blue with short, dark hair, enters the room. She places a device on Hazel's stomach to monitor the contractions and the baby's heart rate. Then she takes her blood pressure, wrapping the cuff around Hazel's arm. "Mommy, you need to relax. You are in good hands." The short-haired nurse squeezes Hazel's hand, smiling gently at her. Hazel can't help but squeeze back, maybe a bit too hard, as a contraction causes her to double over.

"I know," Hazel mutters and takes a deep breath. "I'm just so nervous." To ease her fears, both nurses reassure Hazel and give her as much information as possible about what they are doing. She is trying to listen to everything they tell her, but she is in so much pain that it is difficult to concentrate. She glances over at her husband, who is still videotaping from the corner of the room; she waves to the baby, who will, one day, see this video. That helps lighten her mood.

"Can she eat now?" Manoah asks.

"No, not until after the baby is born. But I will bring her water and a cup of ice to suck on. Dr. Galen will check your progress in just a minute." Both nurses leave the room.

The TV playing above Manoah and Hazel's heads is muted. The machine monitors the mother and baby's heartbeat and beeps in the background. Manoah begins to pace the floor with the phone in one hand and the camera in the other. "How is your pain?"

"Getting worse. I'm trying to breathe through the contractions as they taught us in Lamaze." Hazel pauses as another contraction begins. She turns on her side and pulls her legs to her chest. Shutting her eyes, she breathes through her mouth in short puffs. Manoah rubs her back until it passes.

Dr. Galen appears in the doorway moments later and asks Hazel to lie back so that he can check her dilation. The exam was uncomfortable but quick. "All set, mommy; you are eight centimeters and 80% effaced. We should be able to start pushing soon. In the meantime, call the nurses and use your breathing techniques if you feel the urge to push."

Manoah hugs his wife and strokes her hair. "What happens now?" Manoah asks the petite nurse as she walks back into the room.

"My shift is ending, but I will update your oncoming nurse. She will check on you in about an hour to see how many centimeters you are dilated. Feel free to get up and walk around if you like it – it will help your labor progress."

Another muscular contraction comes on. Hazel squeezes her eyes tight and clenches her husband's hand, her eyes watering from the pain. Manoah rubs her arm while kissing her on the forehead to calm her. "Something's wrong. I feel weird. It felt like something inside me just ripped!" The nurse pauses. Hazel's face is pale, and her eyes are panicked. The nurse looks at the monitor, and without saying a word, the nurse rushes out, and Dr. Galen rushes in.

By now, Hazel has realized that she is bleeding again. She pleads with Manoah and Dr. Galen to save him – to save her son. Dr. Galen suspects a placental abruption that Hazel's placenta has torn away from her uterus. The baby is showing signs of distress, and they need to conduct an emergency cesarean. Time seems to slow around Hazel; people are rushing around and shouting. She hears someone say, "We've got to get him out." She can't speak. She looks right into her husband's eyes. *Pray... pray for him... pray for our son. He has to live.*

Because it is emergency surgery, Hazel is whisked out of the labor room with Manoah running alongside her bed until they get to the Operating Room doors, but he is not allowed inside. She can hear him calling her name even after she can't see him anymore.

In the OR, everyone is moving and jabbering, instruments clanging, plastic tape unraveling. The surgeon pokes her with the scalpel to start the incision, asking, "Can you feel this?"

Not wanting to waste any time, Hazel shrieks, "Just do it! Get him out! Save him!" Moments later, the sedation that the anesthesiologist pushed through her IV starts to take effect. Hazel attempts to fight it, wanting to be awake when her son enters the world, but she drifts off.

Hazel groggily opens her eyes to find Manoah's face hovering over her. It feels like home. The flood of memories quickly drowns a fleeting rush of warmth and confusion: the searing pain, the blood, and the frenzied blur of rushing bodies. Her motherly instincts kick in. "My baby!" Her throat burns. She can't breathe. "Where is he? Please…" she manages to croak. Tears spill onto her cheeks as she searches Manoah's face for answers. "He has to be alive. God gave him to me… he *has* to be."

"He's alive!" Manoah's joyous exclamation fills the room. His face lights up as he gazes at his wife; his touch instantly eases the weight in her heart. With his words, Hazel sobs uncontrollably, letting go of the tension that had been building within her. Manoah gently cradles her, swaying until her tears are exhausted. Wrapped in his protective embrace, he whispers reassuring words into her hair, waiting for the storm of emotions to subside.

"Because you'd lost so much blood," Manoah explains, "they were worried his brain had been deprived of oxygen. They rushed him straight to the NICU. He needed to be cooled down to slow the progression of any possible brain damage," Moe says.

"How is he now?"

"I haven't been to see him yet. I couldn't leave until I knew you would be all right."

"*What?* He's been alone all this time?! My poor baby! Please take me to him. I want to see him now!"

Chapter 4

JUDGES 13: 24-25

"What is his name?" the doctor asks.

Manoah beams through tears, his voice steady despite the overwhelming emotions. "Samson," he declares, the name carrying the weight of God's promise fulfilled.

"Your turn," Hazel mumbles, rolling over onto her side.

Manoah's eyes flutter open, the faint glow of 3:00 am casting soft light over the room. Samson's cries pierce the stillness, drawing Manoah's tired gaze toward the bassinet. Though the routine is familiar, the years between now and his older boys make it feel like starting anew. Manoah pushed himself to sit, startled that he hadn't noticed the baby's fussing earlier. He shifts his gaze toward his wife, who is already asleep. With an inward sigh, he maneuvers himself out of bed, each leg moving one laborious step at a time. "No amount of reading could have truly prepared me for this," he muses, acknowledging the challenges of caring for a baby despite having done it before, even after a considerable lapse of time.

Hazel's side of the bed conveniently stations Samson's bassinet. Manoah stumbles across the room, his steps somewhat unsteady, to insert a pacifier into his son's mouth to provide comfort until Samson's milk is ready. When they decide that Hazel will breastfeed, she pumps milk to allow Manoah to share in the feeding duties. He retrieves a bottle from the refrigerator, placing it into the bottle warmer with a soft clink. As the milk warms, Manoah eases himself into a chair. His hands rubbed his eyes, followed by a weary yawn. Eventually, his head rests on the table's surface, a brief moment of respite.

The beep of the bottle warmer startles him awake. Samson might have rejected the pacifier, given the renewed crying. Manoah can't help but wonder how parents of multiple children successfully juggle these responsibilities, his experience reminding him that this isn't always an easy feat.

He picks Samson up the blanket in the bedroom and climbs back into bed. He inserts the nipple of the bottle into the baby's mouth and watches him drink for a moment before dozing off a second time. He awakes with a jerk. The last time he fell asleep during a feeding, the bottle had dropped to the floor, leaving Samson crying. To his amazement, this time, Samson grasps the bottle with both hands, suckling the milk. *Lil man, you're strong. Holding your bottle at three months.* Manoah grins. Manoah watches Samson as he drinks. Black, curly locks frame the child's sweet face. After finishing the bottle, Manoah burps and places him back into his bassinet.

The following day, Hazel awakens alone in the bedroom. She hears the television downstairs and Manoah talking. The bassinet is empty. *Samson must have woken up early.* She walks over to the window to let in the morning sun. Bright yellow streaks appear on her walls, and she takes a deep, joyful breath. After a quick shower, she goes downstairs to join her family. She enters the kitchen and notices Manoah giving Samson a bottle with a scoop of cereal.

"Look at this," Manoah says, his eyes gleaming with pride. He places Samson gently on the kitchen table and slowly removes his hands. To their amazement, Samson sits unassisted, cooing and smiling.

"Let me check the book," she whispers, her voice barely audible as if afraid to disrupt the moment. "At three months, he's supposed to lift his head and grasp objects, not sit up," Hazel marvels, her fingers flipping through the pages. "And definitely not hold his bottle. He shouldn't be strong enough to sit up until he is at least *six months old.*"

"What does it say about him holding his bottle? Last night, he held it by himself."

"I don't think that is for another few months either," she says, intently flipping through pages.

Manoah places the bottle in Samson's hands, guides it to his mouth, and then lets it go. Samson grips his bottle with both of his hands and continues to drink.

"Oh, my goodness, you're right!" Hazel runs over to Samson just as he throws the bottle across the floor. "Well, maybe he can't hold it," she questions.

"Naw, that was his pitching arm. Did you see how far it flew? That's my boy; he's got talent!"

The following year marks a significant learning period for the new parents. Even though Manoah has prior experience, it has been a while since he's worn the shoes of a new parent. They gradually establish a structured routine, navigating a learning curve with a blend of trial and teamwork. There are nights when Hazel responds to their son's needs while Manoah occasionally steps in. This balanced approach ensures that they both get a chance to rest.

Samson's development trajectory far outpaces other children his age. Walking is no challenge for him. As soon as he can pull himself up, he attempts to put one foot in front of the other. With the cheers of his adoring parents, Samson starts walking in 6 months – a feat that takes most kids over a year. His vocabulary expands, and he soaks up everything they teach him.

The next few years sped by, filled with "Mommy-and-Me" classes, playing with the neighbor's toddlers—amongst whom a bubbly curly-haired boy named Asher reigned supreme—and birthday parties. Although work remains demanding, Manoah and Hazel find ways to spend time with their growing son. Hazel takes him to work at the boutique during the week, and Manoah works four days a week whenever possible.

"Moe, are you ready? It's almost time to go," Hazel calls from the bottom of the stairs.

"I'll be down in a minute," he replies from their bathroom.

"Sam, you, too. Come on down here. Your breakfast is getting cold."

Samson runs down the stairs.

"What did I tell you about running? One of these days, you might fall down those stairs. Come here. Let me fix your shirt."

"How can I hurry without running?" Samson asks his mother. "Asher and I are going to run for the *Olympics!*"

Hazel chuckles. *Wouldn't that be something?* Throughout the summer, Samson and Asher alternated sleepovers in their houses, cultivating a warm friendship between Asher's parents, Deborah and Zain, Manoah, and herself. Four years ago, they had lost their daughter in the crossfire of a Philistine gang shootout. Their resilience and unswerving trust in God through all the pain was inspiring.

Samson's shirt is tucked in the front but not in the back. Hazel smiles at the five-year-old's attempt. She looks down at him momentarily but doesn't answer his question. "Did you brush your hair?" She knows the answer before he says anything – it was brushed on one side and frizzy on the other.

"Yes, ma'am." Samson beams with pride at his accomplishment.

Hazel kisses him on the cheek and runs her fingers through the other side of his hair. "Where's your backpack?"

"Huh?"

Hazel gives him the side-eye look that all mothers have perfected. The boy leaps from the table and returns to his room, re-emerging moments later with his backpack.

Manoah walks into the kitchen as Samson sits down to eat his breakfast. Samson's first day of kindergarten is today, and his parents are both elated. It seems like only yesterday they brought him home from the hospital, and now it's his first day of school.

"Come on, eat up so we can go," Hazel instructs Samson, pouring her husband a cup of coffee.

After breakfast, the three pile into her station wagon and drive to Samson's K-12 private school. As they pass Philistine traffic officers, Hazel's entire body reflexively stiffens.

"Mommy! Daddy!" Samson squeals from the back seat, bouncing as much as his seatbelt will allow, pulling Hazel's mind from that old terror.

Once more, Hazel's heart swells with gratitude. Her delight is difficult to conceal, evident in the amused glances between her and Manoah. "Another one of your riddles, Sam?" she playfully inquires, an unspoken acknowledgment that riddles are simply part and parcel of their time together.

"How'd you know?" His laughter is pure joy. Riddles gathered from a kids' TV show have been his passion for months. "What is as big as you are but doesn't weigh anything?"

"Umm…Moe, you want to do the honors?"

"I…" Manoah chuckles, turning the steering wheel. "I don't know. Tell us, Sam."

"Your shadow, silly!"

A rush of motherly pleasure shoots through her chest. "That's brilliant, honey. You're brilliant."

After a while, they notice a small crowd up ahead. Manoah squints. "What in the…"

Before her mind can process the battered bodies lying on the sidewalk—a testament to yet another act of Philistine gang violence—Hazel swivels in her seat to grasp Samson's hand, heart pounding.

"Put your head down, baby."

His brown eyes are round saucers. "Why, mommy?"

"Just trust me, honey." To her husband, she says, "Speed up!"

Only when the scene falls far behind them does she exhale. Manoah's mouth is a grim line. Her eyes prickle. *How long, Lord?*

The school rises in the distance. It is renowned for its curriculum and outstanding academic and athletic programs. Manoah doesn't believe this school is as important as his wife's, but from an early age, their son has excelled in everything he has tried, so she insists on attending it.

Hazel gives her son the once-over when they arrive, ensuring his blue and yellow plaid shirt is tucked into his khakis. She turns down one side of his collar and runs her fingers through his hair again.

"Mommy, I can do it," Samson protests, puffing his chest as though to prove his growing independence.

Hazel smiles softly, brushing a stray curl from his forehead. She knows this day marks a turning point, yet she can't resist the urge to ensure everything is just right. "I know you're a big kid. I want to make sure it's exactly right." She kisses him on the cheek.

"I can't wait to hear about all the fun stuff you do today," Manoah says, giving his son a big hug. "You ready?"

"Yes," he smiles.

"Sammy!"

They turn to find Asher standing at the school doors beside his mother, waving with such vigor that he hasn't toppled over. Samson's features brighten like a bulb. Hazel laughs. "See you later, honey."

He grins up at her and then dashes toward his friend.

Manoah and Hazel follow him into the massive school and crowd in with other parents. Deborah leans in and whispers, "It's happening, Haze. Our boys are leaving the nest."

Hazel sighs, a mixture of pride and longing fluttering in her chest. "Tell me about it."

They go down the brick hallway to the kindergarten and first-grade wing. They find Samson's name on one of the lists tacked outside each classroom.

"Good morning. My name is Ms. Moran, and I will be your teacher."

Samson notices the adult is shorter than his parents, has thick red hair, and bold, black-framed glasses. "Hello," Samson says, but his attention is not on his teacher. His eyes dart around the room, trying to take it all in.

"Please, find a desk," his teacher instructs, patting him on his shoulder.

Manoah and Hazel introduce themselves as Samson strolls around the room, looking for a seat. He finds one beside a boy he recognizes from the park near his house.

"Are you going to be okay?" Hazel interrupts the boys' chatter.

"I will be fine, Mommy." Samson's face flushes, peeking at his friend's face to see if he thought his mother was being overprotective.

"I will pick you up right after school." She kisses him on his forehead.

"Have a good day, son," Manoah says, ruffling his hair. Samson waves goodbye.

Manoah takes Hazel's hand and pulls her close. "It's okay to cry."

She sniffles and laughs. "I can't believe how big our baby is."

Manoah stares at the phone on his office desk. The message he received from Samson's school crackled and gurgled like it had been placed underwater. Samson has just started first grade, so the teacher's voice doesn't yet sound familiar. He noticed Hazel had also called but hadn't left a voicemail. He takes a slow, steadying breath and reaches for the phone to call Hazel.

"Manoah…"

He doesn't like the calm rasp in her tone. "Honey?"

"Oh, Manoah. Thank heaven."

Manoah straightens in his leather chair. "Babe, what is it?"

Hazel fishes for her keys along the bottom of her purse. She finds the key, angles her shoulder, and slips the purse over her arm. "Moe… It's Sam." The voice on the other end rumbles in a familiar baritone, and Hazel feels her shoulders drop as she lets out a tiny breath. The steadiness of her husband's timbre somehow reaches through the phone and comforts her. Manoah had that ability. His steadfast and practical approach was the perfect counterbalance to her propensity to go off the rails before hearing all the facts.

"Is he at school?"

"Yes," she answers, entering their home and dropping the keys back into her purse as she runs up the stairs to Samson's room.

"Well? What happened?" Manoah's voice dripped with urgency, prompting her to burst into Sam's bedroom. Frantically sifting through his haphazardly scattered clothing - the very same clothes she had repeatedly requested he tidy up - she couldn't help but think back to the conversation she had with Samson after she discovered the reason why his first-grade teacher, Ms. Dron, had approached her with a pointed question.

"Moe, all I know is she sounded frenzied." Hazel digs around the closet floor in Samson's room. "I can't find anything in here."

"What? Honey, what did you say?" Manoah inquires. In her mind's eye, Hazel sees Manoah seated in his office chair, back straight as a board, his countenance impassive. She imagines his neck elongated like a cobra, coiled and poised to strike at the slightest hint of provocation.

Suddenly, a lone knapsack in the corner of the closet catches Hazel's eye. She snags the sack and stands. "Got it!" The smell makes her wince. "Ugh, boys!"

"Hazel, what is going on? What happened at school?" Silence. "Hazel? What is it?" he repeats, anxious for answers.

Quickly descending the stairs, she mentally berates herself for failing to clarify her earlier warning to Samson about what he should avoid. She had assumed he would understand, but clearly, her message lacked specificity. "Can you meet me at the school?" she asks, picking up her conversation with Manoah, exasperation still evident in her voice.

"On my way now. Love you." The phone clicks off abruptly.

Stuffing Samson's knapsack into the car, Hazel lets the garage door stand agape as she reverses out of the driveway. Within moments, she reaches Samson's private school. Moe maneuvers into an adjacent space, just about to stretch her legs from the parking spot. Her steps stall, and she shoots him an arched-brow look. "You're aware that parking like that bends all the traffic rules?" she teases, her eyes dancing with humor and affection.

Moe switches off the engine and bounds up beside her. "Funny." He takes her by the hand and marches, with her in tow, to the school office. Hazel smiles warmly. Two minutes later, the pair stand with Samson's first-grade teacher, Ms. Dron, in the school's recreation room. The slim woman glances at Manoah and Hazel as she turns her attention back to their child.

Hazel follows the teacher's line of sight, her gaze landing on her son at a miniature table, engrossed in crafting what seems like a castle from a folded brown construction paper. A closer look uncovers the impressive artistry within that modest medium. Encircling the paper fortress are stacks of building blocks, forming towering walls that reach a foot high. A surge of admiration rushes through her as she discerns that her son is animatedly directing the other children, guiding them to position the blocks and the ideal mix of colors. She can't help but think, *probably weaving riddles into the instructions.*

Moving with Manoah alongside the scene, she wonders what the to-do had been about. *Did I overreact to Ms. Dron's plea that we come to Samson's first-grade class as soon as possible?* She catches her husband's eye, noticing his expression. She is just as surprised but full of the same pride she feels. He squeezed her hand with his firm grip, and they shared a silent, joyous moment, exchanging a look of relief.

They follow Ms. Dron to the assistant principal's office. Mr. Samuels, the associate principal, stands, extending his hand to greet them, and Ms. Dron carefully clears her throat. Manoah and Hazel both notice the brief nod the teacher gives him and the great look of concern she wears; the parents are confused as to what is happening and why they are here.

"Hello."

Hazel sits Sam's small knapsack on a nearby chair and starts to offer her hand when Manoah presses to stand between her and Mr. Samuels.

"Good afternoon, Mr. Samuels. We received a phone call from our son's teacher, Ms. Dron."

"Yes, I asked Ms. Dron to follow up with you."

Hazel moves beside her husband. "Follow up, as in two calls, that our son was not getting along with his classmates?"

"I phoned once today," Ms. Dron remarks.

"Yes," Manoah replies, "and the tone was very urgent." His lawyer's mind swiftly sorts facts from the general information he and Hazel received from Samson's school over the past month. This most recent voice message sounded vitally important.

Hazel spins to face the smartly dressed woman. "What about Samson?"

"How about we get right to the point?" Manoah interjects. "You've previously contacted us about Sam not integrating with the other kids."

"Which is not true," Hazel chimes in.

"Not only is it not true, but we also watched our son in the recreation room. If Sam is anything, he appears to be a natural-born leader."

"And he was building with the other children," adds Hazel.

"Quite industriously," Manoah agrees, glancing at her. An unconquerable pride at seeing his son engaged with something he enjoys is evident in his eyes. "And not a care in the world about him."

Ms. Dron clears her throat louder. "It isn't Samson's getting along with the others in the class that is a concern..."

Manoah turns to the teacher. "No? Then what is it?" Ms. Dron hangs her head.

Hazel touches Manoah's suit sleeve and sets her purse by the backpack she brought with Sam's favorite racing car. He glances at the sadness in her eyes and shakes his head, "No."

"Manoah, you know why we're here."

"It isn't that Samson is not a good pupil. On the contrary, he's very bright," the teacher offers.

As Manoah observes the teacher twining her thumb and finger through a single strand of hair missing from her tightly pinned updo, he glances over at Hazel, who nods at him slightly. "Here we go again," he thinks.

"Manoah—" begins Mr. Samuels.

"Are you seriously suggesting we alter our son's hair?"

The assistant principal rounds a desk overflowing with stacks of applications whose parents hope to send their children there for next year's fall class. Manoah makes them out instantly, aware that it hasn't been long since he and Hazel have done the same.

"We told you, it's a matter of our culture. There is no disregard for this institution's guidelines," Manoah gestures, using air quotes to show his disdain.

"We've tried to get Samson to understand," Ms. Dron starts.

"What? There is nothing to understand here," Manoah interrupts, rising from his chair to stand before the teacher. "Our child's hair is our family's concern, no one else's."

Hazel turns to face the schoolteacher. "This isn't why you brought us down here, right?" Ms. Dron nods solemnly.

Manoah looks back and forth between the two of them. "Am I missing something here?" When no one answers, he glares at the school representatives and then at his wife. "Hazel, *what* is going on here?"

Before she responds, she turns to the teacher, asking, "How serious was it?"

Manoah pauses. He glances from Hazel to the others who seem to fit together – the worry, the grave expressions. "Our son's been in a fight?"

"No, Manoah," Mr. Samuels clears his throat, his gaze darting between the concerned parents. "He's being bullied," he finally states, the words hanging in the air like thunderclaps. Hazel feels her breath hitch, her mind racing to piece together what could have led to this moment.

Later that day, nestled in the warmth of their kitchen, Manoah glares at Hazel. "You *knew?*"

Hazel eyes him softly. "I didn't until I remembered Sam stopped playing with the car you gave him for his birthday."

Manoah nods. "Yeah, he's never been around the house without it."

"Then, just last month, during one of our usual mornings, as we were all getting ready, I saw him quietly stashing his toy car into his backpack before he darted past us. And then, suddenly, the sight of that little car vanished," she recounts, her tone tinged with sadness. The unspoken implication hangs in the air – he ceased taking the toy to school to end the torment he faced over his hair.

Manoah shakes his head, a trace of gray touching his left temple. "He didn't say anything about this. I mean, with how excited he got having Asher in his class, I couldn't have guessed."

"You remember how school was when you were growing up," Hazel remarks. Meanwhile, the inviting scent of chamomile dances through the air, wrapping the space in an embrace of tranquility. "I'm getting us some tea," she says.

Manoah grumbles, "I don't want any."

"I'm making it because we will talk about this."

"About what?"

"Sam needs to go to another school."

"No, absolutely not." Manoah's voice holds a resolute tone as he cuts in. He's confident she wouldn't purposefully make things more challenging for them. "Hazel, let's consider this carefully. If we give in to your suggestion and move Samson to another school, we might create a web of complications we'll have to untangle later," he reasons.

She mimics the final trio of words before he notices the sharp pang in her usually bubbly soprano. "If you think we are going to allow our son to go through any more attacks at that, that, that…" Her hands ball into fists. "That 'school'. Do you realize what that assistant principal said?"

He nodded. "I do, Hazel."

"It wasn't what he said; it was how he said it." Hazel stands in front of him. "*We feel your son is drawing too much attention away from the rest of the classroom*," she mimics.

"That isn't exactly what the assistant principal said," Manoah remarks.

Hazel rushes by him, retrieving a piece of paper in haste. "Seriously? Show me," she exclaims, raising the plain white sheet she had pulled from their printer file holder. He's well aware that their lives are complex – he just ascended to partnership, and Hazel recently launched her new store. Their future endeavors weigh heavily on his mind, prompting him to opt for a path of minimal disruption.

"Let's not complicate things further," he muses. "It's true, he's bound to attract attention if targeted. And you're right; why didn't they involve the other students? There's more to this."

"Maybe the teacher scared them off?"

"Then they should have been in the school's office, with their parents, like us."

Suddenly, Moe feels her pin him with a pointed stare, "You're blasé about this."

Manoah's game face breaks into a thousand-watt smile. "I'm just taking in this moment."

He watches his spouse casually fold her arms. "How so, Moe?"

"In our 11 years together, I have seen you champion many causes. Even when you saw me short-winded after testing out that toy motorcycle, I'd wanted to give Samson."

Hazel smiles a little. "We were just starting. Neither of us had a great deal of money then. We'd been trying to have a child for so long; I didn't want you to feel like you had to buy us things." Manoah eyes her still slim figure as she sidles closer. "We both knew I'd join in and try to get him the world."

Manoah laughs. She bats her lashes and grins at him boldly. "Amen to that; it's one of the umpteen reasons I'm in love with you."

Hazel playfully frowns. "Only *umpteen*?"

"Okay, a lot more," he admits. Hazel quietly stands. "A whole lot more," he adds.

Her smile widens again momentarily before it snaps back into a frown. "What will we do about our son having trouble in school?" She waved the paper in her hands back and forth. "This letter says…"

"Hazel, he isn't in trouble. He has long hair that makes people notice his appearance."

"If we don't find him another school where he can realize his true potential, what will become of him?" She glances at Manoah. "You know I'm right."

Manoah smiles. "Which institute of higher learning did you have in mind?"

A slow grin spreads across Hazel's face as she speaks. "I-have been thinking about one school. *Excelsior* has a 95% Israelite population. Deborah herself testified to its quality, even though she and Zain cannot afford the tuition right now for Asher. What more could we ask for?"

"Mm-hm," he pulls his wife into his broad arms. Whatever you think is best, honey.

PART II: SAMSON

38 years before the explosion

Chapter 5

JUDGES 13: 24-25

The gates to Excelsior Preparatory School towers over Samson.

He reaches into his pocket, holding the bear's claw he'd found while walking up the cobbled driveway. Other students file in between the gates, but he isn't ready to meet all of them. It was the first day of the 7th grade. Frankly, he'd rather play with the bear whose claw he had found than make new friends.

Maybe there will be something he can put himself into after the reading, rhyming, and arithmetic. Or perhaps a flood will wipe out everyone and everything, allowing him to go home.

Home.

If that doesn't work, maybe homeschooling will be an option.

He sighs. *Better get here soon, Ash.*

As it is, the halls of Excelsior are a far cry from kindergarten, but then again, Middle School did carry its vibe. He pushes a long lock of dark hair from his face as he climbs the steps, nervous that he will probably hate going to school.

But nothing ventured....

The recess bell clangs, and Samson beelines for the school gym, along with every other student, for the Town Hall—the patter and stomps of private school students from 6th to 8th grade pile onto the polished linoleum. The halls of Excelsior are buffed to perfection. The students jockey to sit on the wooden benches lining the gymnasium.

By the time he reaches the bleacher stairs, Samson is swarmed by students filing onto the bleachers and claiming their seats. He circles back to the farthest stairs – also the highest – where only one other student sits - a girl. He climbs swiftly, hearing scoffs and catching stares from students, and observes lingering looks from a cluster of girls, some even older than he was whispering, as he makes his way to the top stair.

The mic on the podium at the other side of the high school gym screeches from a gruff tap. Samson and the rest of the student body grimace, except for that lone girl sitting on the same bleacher three feet away. She is now facing Samson, resting on her elbows, wearing a blazer like his and a sly smile. As a second ping rings from the microphone, he jerks his head so she won't catch him staring.

"Hello… Testing. Welcome! Some of you may recognize me. My name is Clive Reynolds. I'm the Assistant Headmaster of Excelsior Preparatory School. Thank you all for being here. This is our first Town Hall of the academic year. For those who are transfers from another institution or part of our foreign exchange program…"

Samson turns his body to face her directly, his brows raised in question as he watches her reach inside her blazer and pull out a silvery flask. She uncaps it and silently toasts to everyone in the gym. He stares, noticing that the din from the mic drowns out any sound anyone might hear but him. "What the—" She grins, dragging a swig from the container, offering him a wink.

Headmaster Reynolds has started his announcements, but Samson finds it challenging to pay attention. Is she doing what he thinks she is?

"We will hold abbreviated school hours because of the recent brush fires. I appreciate your patience as your studies start slowly, including this Orientation Week."

Samson's throat tightens as he discreetly scans his surroundings. Relief washes over him – no teacher has caught on to his actions. Thank God for that. His gaze then returns to her, drawn to her like a magnet. His eyes fixate on the distinctive sheen of her charcoal hair. His mind races, unraveling the enigma before him. What kind of riddle does she embody?

"...*to* and *from* the grounds will be security-checked, as will all backpacks, outer jackets, and cell phones to ensure the safety of all students following the attack on our beloved city after the election of our new Mayor. We ask all students to comply with these new measures as we adjust to greater monitoring until there is a certainty of no further Philistine threats..."

Her pearly grin is intact, and she raises the container to him and winks again before another swift drag.

After a satisfied exhalation lost in the blast of the headmaster's mic, the girl points a perfectly manicured finger at Samson. Then, her crimson lips part, and she winks again; Samson blinks, presses his gaping mouth shut, and looks away.

"...for the second year in a row, the school is offering additional electives during the season, and they include water polo, etiquette for social media, and shop class. These and more electives will be added as we enter the year. Interested students must check the bulletins posted outside the Commons' Office after lunchtime on Friday."

Samson's ears perk at the mention of shop class. He wonders if there are actual cars or motorcycles students work on.

"You must scan your school badge at one of the kiosks to enter any electives. If space is available, you each may audition for the class you are interested in. You will receive word from your elective teacher if you are accepted into your class of choice.

"As we navigate the civil unrest caused by factions from outer-lying regions, such as Canaan, and the ongoing outbreaks of fires that you are all aware of, Town Meetings will now take place every first day of the week, and class electives will occur every mid-week and Friday. We will continue with this adjusted schedule until the situation is either neutralized or contained. Once that happens, we will resume a full class and elective schedule."

A rumble floats among the students.

"To those who have questions about the dress code, see either me or our librarian, Ms. Gemma Amerton, who is also one of the finest historians in our beloved city."

The girl straightens, never taking her gaze off Samson. "Right, like that's going to happen." She twists her dark hair into a ponytail and drags a long sip from her flask.

Mr. Reynolds grabs the mic, closing the assembly. "Everyone new to our Excelsior community, *welcome*."

Samson merges with the rest of the crowd, making their way back down the stairs. The girl in the blue stockings is now right behind him. "If this is your first year of middle school, let me be the harbinger of bad tidings and tell you it's all downhill from here." She follows Samson's gaze to her hand holding the metal flask. "And *what* are you looking at?"

"That," Samson mumbles.

"This? It's just orange juice," she explains, a casual shrug punctuating her words. Her gaze lingers on him with a glimmer of amusement, her tone holding playful caution. "You might want to be careful. Not everyone around here has the same spirit of exploration that I do. And you, well, you seem like quite the adventurer, a lone wolf with your striking hair. Is that what you're aiming for? Standing out?" Just as he's about to respond, a newcomer joins her side. Swiftly, she stashes away the flask, waving a quick farewell before departing with her companion. The scene unfolds like a snapshot, leaving him to mull over her words.

Crazy place. Asher has no idea.

Samson watches her from across the gym, shaking his head. *What just happened?*

At home, the first thing he does is look at himself in the bathroom mirror. He shrugs out of his school uniform, undoing his striped necktie and unbuttoning the top of his long-sleeved white shirt. He is a little over average in height. His face was angular, his shoulders broad. The build he has, he guesses, is what some would call *stocky*.

The girl had mentioned Samson's locs, which are so dark that they appear navy in the daylight. They are slightly longer than how most other guys wear their hair at school. Samson heard people commenting as they took him in, and their reactions were mostly the same - not shock or dismay, but rather marvel at the sight of his long, curly hair. On the other hand, Asher teased him relentlessly but with jokes that always left them doubled over with laughter.

During the Town Hall meeting, the girl had posed a question that lingered in Samson's mind: was he accustomed to standing out? As he pondered, the puzzle grew more complex. He struggled to grasp her underlying meaning. Admittedly, some on the school grounds and common areas cast curious glances his way, but it didn't bother him – he saw no reason why it should. Girls often seem drawn to him, which he's content with. Yet, at times, a lingering uncertainty nags at him, leaving him to question the intricacies of it all.

"Sam, are you home?"

"Yeah, Ma," he calls from the stairs.

"Have you been home long?" Hazel asks from the foyer.

"Nah."

"I haven't had anything since breakfast. From the looks of the cabinets and the fridges inside, you and your father devoured anything that wasn't nailed down or frozen. Are you hungry?"

"I could eat. I'll take whatever you've got."

"That's spot-on. We've run out of food entirely," she says, exasperated. "The wildlife rummaging through town for scraps probably keeps everyone hunkered down indoors. Plus, those forest fires are wreaking havoc, disrupting people's ability to get to work. Your dad hasn't made it to his office for a week. Are you finding difficulties getting to class?"

"School was fine," Samson replies. He realizes that he isn't catching everything his mom is saying. "What did you say?"

"I asked if you wanted Falafel or organic truffle pizza; both are in the freezer. Your father's been wanting us to be vegan these days."

"I don't care."

"What do you mean *you don't care*? I had nothing but limes and truffles for three weeks straight before you arrived. You were reared on truffles," she lightheartedly replies.

Suddenly, Sam races down and glares at his mother. "I said, I don't care!"

Hazel responds quietly. "What did you just say?"

"You heard me." His mother's eyes flash hot, and he immediately regrets muttering the words.

"Sam, is something bothering you? How are things at school?"

"I said I was fine," Sam mumbles, rolling his eyes.

"Then you may go to your room until dinner."

Sam's eyes pop wide. "What? I don't get a say about what's for dinner now?"

Hazel places her hands on her hips. "What has gotten into you? I don't appreciate your tone."

"Come on, Ma, don't have a coronary. It was just a question."

"Go to your room," Hazel orders. "And remember, your choices always will have consequences."

Samson stifles a flippant response and heads straight to his room.

Hazel sidles up to Manoah. "Honey, is there anything bothering Sam at school? Did he mention anything to you last night?"

Manoah shrugs. "Like what?"

"Boys," she says in disgust.

Manoah cocks a brow, confused. "Pardon?"

"He seems to be troubled, is all."

Manoah pulls her onto his lap. "Don't worry, you're pretty head about it. He's probably just lonely now that Asher's in a different school. He needs to make new friends."

Hazel chews on her lip. If Deborah and Zain had not experienced financial struggles, both boys would have been at Excelsior and had a much easier time together. At least the weekly sleepovers and regular excursions have helped. She sends a silent prayer for the family just as Samson skips down the stairs.

"I'm going to be late for class. Gotta go."

Manoah frowns. "Greet your mom like you've been taught before you leave."

Samson pauses for a moment. "Sorry, Ma." The apology is as much for the talking back as for ignoring his mother all morning. Samson walks over to his mom and hugs her tightly.

"Have a blessed day at school, Sam," Hazel whispers. The boy races out the door.

Moe observes their exchange. "Maybe something is going on with our son?"

"Pssst!" Samson's voice is thick with agitation. "Get moving, Ash!"

The towering forms of the arching Philistine building equipment create an otherworldly backdrop against which the figure of Asher materializes. The heavy machinery looms like colossal sentinels, their mechanical arms and steel structures casting elongated shadows that seem to stretch toward the horizon. Amid this mechanical grandeur, Asher's presence starkly contrasts the industrial setting.

His voice emerges as a playful melody, a brief respite breaking through the air. "Dude, you need to take a chill pill," he remarks.

How the guy manages humor in such a dangerous situation is beyond Samson. For the umpteenth time, he casts a frazzled look over his shoulders, trying to calm his pounding heart. That initial exhilaration disappeared. The many times they've done this doesn't make it any less rattling.

Samson's desire for vengeance started with a single comment he'd overheard from a kid at school about how Philistine authorities planned to tear down their tenement building and raise a casino. To this day, the memory still sends rage coursing through his veins. Forged documents claimed the property belonged to the Philistines. Then, without notice, parents and neighbors were forcefully evicted.

Fueled by a surge of anger, a daring idea took shape—the seeds of a sabotage mission that aimed to scatter their demolition equipment in subtle yet pivotal ways. The purpose was simple: carve out precious moments and extend a lifeline to the innocent Israelites under the shadow of oppression. The concept, sparked by Samson, was initially talked about. But now, they stood here, doing something to make a difference.

His motives ran deeper in this clandestine pursuit beyond assisting those in need. The intensity in Asher's eyes reflected a burning desire to dismantle the very system that claimed his sister's life, to tear down the oppressive regime piece by piece until justice was served and vengeance delivered.

So far, their efforts cutting bulldozer wires and pouring water down gas tanks have paid off. A month after the deadline, the demolition still hasn't begun. Ma will lose it if she finds that this sleepover at Asher's house is the fifth of such escapades.

Samson presses his lips together. Tonight, he is lookout. They have already slashed some tires, but still, Asher refuses to leave, insisting on the 'icing on the cake'—whatever that means. "Are you almost done, though?" Samson's whisper cuts through the dusk.

"Um...just a sec..." Asher's muffled voice returns.

Somewhere to the right, a shuffle sounds. Samson's throat tightens. If they are caught...it is too terrible to contemplate.

"*Ash!*"

"OK, OK, done." He emerges from the shadows, grinning. "See? Nothing to do—" In that very instant, he bumps into a stack of tin paint containers. Samson squeezes his eyes shut, breath held as the ugly crash reverberates.

"Hey, who's there?" A rough voice demands, followed immediately by quick, heavy footsteps.

"Run!" Samson grounds out, even as both boys take off, using the escape route they'd gone over, just in case.

They don't stop until two streets from Asher's house. They collapse against an alley wall, panting.

Asher releases a winded chuckle, "I bet your fancy new classmates can't match this."

"Crazy," Samson manages past his heart racing as they reach the house's back porch. "You're so crazy."

Asher elbows him, "I learned from the best."

Samson surveys the track field where most of his 7th-grade class is splayed across eight running lanes. The track is part of the curriculum for any student who wants to advance to the next grade year. Samson craves something different, though; something he can put his heart and soul into that won't have him looking like a dweeb. He completes the heats that the P.E. instructor insists upon, and while he doesn't entirely end in last place across the finish line, he hasn't exactly given it his all, either. The teacher isn't thrilled by his disinterest either. Sam finds himself sitting outside the Assistant Headmaster's office later that day.

Mr. Reynolds seems cool enough with his wire-rimmed specs and buzz-cut hairstyle. He also genuinely appears concerned with why Samson isn't more active in his studies or extracurricular opportunities. "Because that's what they are: chances to improve your mental faculties and overall well-being," he explains.

"I know, Mr. Reynolds," Samson nods curtly.

"But?" replies the Assistant Headmaster, coaxing Samson to keep going.

It isn't just the exercise and the academia Samson isn't gung-ho for. He feels there is something more out in the world for him. None of the things in school make him want to put himself out there. "I just thought there might be something more I hadn't tried."

The Assistant Headmaster eyes Samson, his nearly bald head contrasting with Samson's long, flowing curls that reach past his school blazer jacket collar and shoulders. "Tell you what. You try to find something in the electives, and I'll hold off mentioning anything about your academic and extracurricular performances to your family."

Sam shoots straight up in his chair. "My parents?!"

"Excelsior's rigorous curriculum is designed to push our students to peak academic performance," says Mr. Reynolds. "Our student body is in the top 10th percentile of collegiate-preparatory education that places its students in the most competitive universities and colleges. When our students exhibit a less than B-level performance in any area, the school's policy is to notify the families and suggest a tactic to propel our pupils into A-grade performance."

"But my parents are... Mr. Reynolds, you can't. They won't understand."

"Then finding something to improve your grades should be at the top of your mind so that the school has only stellar reports about your performance."

Samson is quiet, but he nods slowly. "Yes, Sir."

"Good. We will meet again at the end of the semester."

Samson begins to stand.

"Samson."

"Sir?"

"You'll do fine."

Accepting the Assistant Headmaster's hand with a firm shake, Samson exits the office and navigates the school's corridors during his recess period. His mind is a maelstrom of thoughts and emotions. Amidst the chaos, a familiar longing resurfaces, a dream that has ignited his spirit countless times before — motorcycles.

As he walks through the halls, the pull of being a diligent student tugs at him, urging him to immerse himself in his school life. Yet, in the next heartbeat, a yearning to be on the motorcycle track consumes him— to stand among the elite racers and indulge in the thrill of competition, to weave his way through the wind and leave everyone trailing in his wake.

But even as these dreams stir within him, there's a persistent thorn—the matter of his long hair.

Mr. Reynolds had also asked him if he was doing fine with the other kids in his classes. Then he'd taken a long glance at his hair. Samson wracks his brain to recall what the girl at the recent Town Hall assembly had said. *Not everyone might see my long hair as adventurous.* Samson hasn't made any friends. There isn't anyone he wants to get to know. Though, there are plenty of girls in his class (and the higher grades, too) that he has noticed sizing him up.

Lost in his thoughts, it takes him a second to orient to his surroundings. He is outside a dark and dank room, but when he peeks inside, he sees tons of equipment: tools, torches, and even machinery parts. He is smack in the middle of an auto shop. His eyes widen.

"Is anybody here? Hello!" Samson is greeted with an almost palpable quiet. He doesn't find a light switch, but he notices he can see well enough after he looks around a bit more, his eyes adjusting to the dim light. He weaves between deconstructed engines and car and motorcycle fenders wholly stripped of paint and others in serious need of soldering.

As the door bursts open, two-spirited 5th graders charge into the room, prompting Samson to slip behind the shelter of a commercial-class engine, a formidable barrier that conceals him from view. Eavesdropping on their hushed conversation, Samson can't help but be intrigued by their ignorance of the school's hidden treasure—an auto shop concealed in the heart of the building.

With the door swinging shut behind them, the young intruders departed with the same haste they entered, leaving Samson alone in the room's quiet. Now, his gaze sweeps across the space, revealing a shop station adorned with a motorcycle chassis and an assortment of cycle parts strewn around like the scattered pieces of an intricate jigsaw puzzle.

The room is saturated with a soft, diffused light filtering through the skylight, casting an ethereal pallor that bathes the scene in a captivating glow. The bell, its metallic chime ringing in the air, signals the onset of recess. This call goes unnoticed by Samson, whose attention is captivated by the arrangement of possibilities before him.

A wide grin spreads across his face, an irrepressible expression of exhilaration and discovery. In this hidden haven of machinery and tools, he senses an opportunity to immerse himself in the world of motorcycles—the passion that ignites his heart. With each breath he takes, the air seems charged with the promise of hands-on exploration, of turning fragmented components into roaring engines, of bringing life to the dormant forms before him. As the echo of the bell's chime gradually fades,

Samson stands among the tools of his dreams, and the realization dawns upon him: this is his shop class, a realm where he can begin to weave his aspirations into reality.

Samson picks up a pocket wrench from the workstation, admiring having access to such tools. He begins to clean motorcycle parts with a dingy piece of tarp he had found while walking around the school grounds. When he stops to glance at the wall clock, it surprises him to see how quickly time passed. Returning to his studies, Samson can't believe the class isn't more popular with his peers.

Samson's not officially enrolled in the class, so his school badge doesn't grant him access to the Shop room. Nevertheless, he's discovered that his school ID can cleverly manipulate the door lock, allowing him entry with minimal effort. That day, when two boys curiously stumble into the shop, Samson realizes they likely encountered the same challenge and devises the same solution.

And that doesn't go over too well when he bumps into the shop teacher.

This newfound obsession is so enthralling to Samson that he doesn't hear the teacher enter the room. He is tinkering with a large motorcycle section when someone clears their throat.

Mr. Krevorkian's voice snares Samson's attention. The teacher stands with arms crossed and a single eyebrow quizzically arched. "Good afternoon," Samson stammers, taken aback by the unexpected encounter. But instead of formulating a response, his mouth hangs open like a drawbridge stuck mid-motion. Mr. Krevorkian's gaze questions something unspoken.

"Have you been tinkering with the dilapidated auto parts in the Shop Class?" The teacher probes, his tone suspicious. Samson's heart pounds a little faster. Before he can utter a word, his instincts drive him to exit the shop. Yet, his hurried escape takes an unforeseen turn as he unintentionally collides with the same girl he'd encountered during the school meeting at Town Hall.

Caught off guard by the collision, Samson stumbles into an unexpected encounter. To his chagrin, Mr. Krevorkian appears in close pursuit, as if his steps are synchronized with Samson's every move, making it clear that the teacher isn't letting this situation go unnoticed.

"Class is only on Mondays, Wednesdays, and Fridays," she spins to hasten with him. "I'm one of the few students enrolled. Most of the electives are upperclassmen playgrounds,"

She smooths her hairband and shakes it to make herself less recognizable as their uniform shoes clack across the floor.

"Hey, you two!" shouts Mr. Krevorkian. "Get back here."

"This way," the girl says, leading him around a corner. They find themselves in the school gymnasium where students are doing calisthenics. Sam feels her push him toward the lockers, hissing, "Get in here."

"What?" He's not sure that he's heard her correctly.

Samson's gaze remains fixed as the girl deftly kicks at a small lever near the closest locker, coaxing a concealed crevice to spring open. With a graceful pull, the locker shifts, revealing a concealed space. Inside is a sprawling storage room, haphazardly crammed with gym equipment.

As his eyes adjust to the dimmer lighting of this newfound chamber, a quartet of distinct figures comes into view. One wears a hoodie, and the other is blonde, with their hair a cascade of golden strands framing their face. A tall figure stretches their legs atop a foam cushion, while a more reserved presence sits with a contemplative air.

Samson's sharp eyes catch the glint of something between their fingers – a device that, from his vantage point, he can only deduce to be an e-cigarette. The air carries a subtle haze, hinting at the vaporous evidence of their shared indulgence.

With raised eyebrows, Samson took in the situation before him. The dots were starting to connect. He remembered Asher's tales from one of their trips, describing his well-to-do peers as a secretly adventurous and sketchy bunch. Samson had brushed it off at the time, but now he could almost hear Ash saying, "I told you so."

"You barely made it," a blond kid remarks to the girl as she takes a vape from an older student, ready to puff.

"I know. Had to deal with a rebellious student," she replies, rolling her eyes towards Samson.

"Hey, I didn't ask for assistance," Samson retorts.

"True, but it seemed like you could use some," the tallest kid adds between drags while the other kids in hoodies snicker.

"So, what's your name?" Samson asks, curious.

The girl glances up through the vape smoke and responds, "No names. And this isn't charity. I'll know who to ask."

"Was the help some sort of blackmail?" Samson inquires.

"It's about fitting in," the kid in a hoodie chimes in.

"Or not," the girl adds.

"And how you don't," the tall kid smirks, taking another puff.

"Yeah, and what's with the long hair? Are you planning to grow a matching goatee?" the blond kid jokes. Laughter fills the air, though Samson doesn't join.

"Thanks for your help," Samson manages, keeping his sarcasm in check.

"No problem," the tall kid snickers back. Samson turns to leave.

"Where are you headed?" the reserved group member asks. "There is still time left before recess resumes," they add.

Samson notices their curious glances directed at his hair. "I just need to go."

"Oh, here comes Lonely Guy again," the girl sighs.

He glances at the group – all well-dressed and from privileged backgrounds – huddled in a storage room, vaping and engaging in unknown activities. "What's wrong with that?" he challenges. Laughter erupts among the other kids.

"That's some impressive hair," the blond kid remarks, popping bubble gum.

Hazel turns from the brick oven in the kitchen and runs smack dab into Samson. Setting down the muffin tray she's just removed from the oven; she eyes Samson puckishly. "What are you doing at home at this hour?"

"Same as you."

"We are not back to you getting all irritated."

"Ma, I want to ask you something," he sighs.

"All right," she nudges.

He watches her as she sets down a delicate porcelain platter and then reaches for the muffin tray, gathering the courage to ask his mother the one question that has lingered for so long.

"Ma, why do I have long hair, and why have you and Dad never let me cut it?"

Hazel falls silent, fully aware that this moment might arrive someday. He's always had a unique quality that sets him apart from the other kids. She reflects on the miraculous events that brought him into her life, which she explains to him now.

"So, you're saying I stand out because of a prophecy about my hair?"

Hazel searches for a way to put it less dramatically but realizes that straightforwardness is best. "Yes, Sam, that's the truth." Samson doesn't respond with laughter, which she half-wishes he would; it would make this weighty conversation feel lighter. "It's a calling I received from the Lord, conveyed through one of His angels." She notices his expression – wariness, thoughtfulness, and curiosity.

"Why are you making up stories? That's not why I shouldn't cut off all this hair!"

Hazel leaves the cherry raisin muffins in the baking tray. "Where is all this coming from?"

"What's all the to-do about?" Manoah interjects. Samson and Hazel turn to Manoah, who is standing in the doorway.

Hazel looks at Manoah pointedly. "Please, talk with your son!"

Despite his abrupt exit from the teacher's presence, Samson's determination to explore the world of Shop class remained unshaken. Mr. Krevorkian eventually relented and allowed him to sign up for Shop. Within those workshop walls, he's embraced by the welcoming embrace of cars' hoods, a ritual that extends from junior high through high school.

Amid the potent bouquet of grease and the satisfying weight of tools in his grip, Samson finds an unwavering sense of freedom. In this haven of engines and machinery, he's uncovering an identity that profoundly resonates. The intricate dance of steel entwines him with an unbreakable fascination day after day. The prospect of unveiling their secrets, of teasing out more speed from their mechanical hearts, holds an enchanting allure. The prospect of racing these mechanical masterpieces is singing to him like an irresistible siren.

So, he's becoming immersed in this realm, finding comfort and exhilaration amidst the tools, the fragrant symphony, and the whisper of velocity. However, among the nuts and bolts, a more profound metamorphosis is stirring, awaiting its chance to unfurl and define him in ways he's only just beginning to fathom.

Samson's and Asher's visit to the War Museum had been an absolute blast. As far as solo excursions go, this has to be the best one yet. Now, riddles and jokes fill the taxi as they head home. Samson's ribs hurt from laughter, and Asher's grin is megawatt bright.

"We have got to do that again," he says, slapping his friend on the back.

"You bet," Ash says with a satisfied sigh as he slumps into the seat, his body relaxed. "You know, when—"

But their burly driver hisses a curse into the air. Just beyond the confines of the vehicle, the streets unfold in a scene of unexpected chaos, the air crackling with tension. Before them, a sad and disarrayed crowd lingers, and a wide array of emotions dance across their faces.

Samson scoots forward, "What's going on?"

"Bloody Philistines," the man spits. "Looks like a forced evacuation."

Samson's heart plummets to the pit of his stomach. It's a sensation as poignant as that distant memory from years ago. After months of resisting the ruthless government, that tenement was ultimately surrendered and razed to make way for the accursed casino. Each time the Philistines seize another Israelite tenement building, helplessness coils around him and constricts. Presently, Philistine officers stand guard, their presence a stark embodiment of authority, forcibly evicting both people and possessions from their rightful places.

A strained hush descends over them as their car crawls by. The driver dials a number and begins speaking under his breath.

"We can only do so much," Asher finally says, voice like sandpaper. "God sees, and God knows." The lump in Samson's throat doesn't allow words to pass. "Let them wait until I join the Force."

The next hour sees them caught in the ensuing traffic jam. Just as they round the corner onto the freeway, a loud siren pierces the afternoon. "What now?" The driver snaps, straining to see through the rear-view mirror. Samson swivels back.

"A convoy, " he whistles. "Check out those rides!" He counts at least two power bikes, eight sleek black Highlanders, one armored truck, and an ambulance fast approaching the other lane.

"Must be a VIP." Asher's mutters. "Philistia's written all over them."

"A thieving one, no doubt." The driver chuckles without humor. "Just sell one of those engines, and I can retire today with that dough."

Sighing, Samson slumps against the car seat. "It bites, though, that we can't do much to stop them."

"That's exactly what they think, which is great for us." Asher's feet tap on the car floor as they always do when the wheels in his head start turning. "They won't see this next one coming, I tell you. We'll ta—"

The car abruptly stops, throwing both guys forward. Amidst their struggle for balance and the driver's unrestrained cussing, the convoy cuts into their lane, bullying vehicles out of their way.

"Crazy people," the man spits but still steers the taxi to park on the side.

Even then, another car from the convoy brushes too close. "Hey!" The driver yells. "I'm out of your way, man. Stay in your bloody lane!"

The words are barely out of his mouth when another sleek black car skids by them. The breeze from them rattled the taxi.

"What is the matter with these people?" Asher yells. "What point are they trying to prove?"

Successive collisions follow, driving the taxi farther off the road's edge. The driver's cry is hoarse; his fingers battle to retain control of the steering wheel. Samson's grip tightens on the door handle. An ear-piercing screech of tires and a thick cloud of acrid smoke erupt into the air from the violent clash of rubber against the road. The moment crystallizes in heart-pounding chaos.

"Ash!" Samson's cry reverberates, his heart a wild drumbeat.

In an instant, the armored truck hurtles closer. Their driver's hand slips from the steering wheel, a fleeting realization that the battle is lost. Samson's eyes connect with his best friend's, a desperate terror exchange. The car smashes into the bridge.

A shrill, ear-piercing whistle pierces his senses, a cacophony filling his head as the impact's vibrations consume him. Just as the relentless jarring within his body begins to wane, another force strikes the car, a vicious onslaught from behind.

Then, all fades into darkness.

Samson groans, struggling to open his eyelids. Even that slight movement sends pain searing through his entire body. He swallows a cry and lays still. Consciousness slowly returns. A steady beeping rises to the surface, along with the heavy scent of antiseptic.

A hospital?

How did he get here? His mind is a terrible blank. Searching the recesses of it amplifies a vicious headache. It drags him to the edge of that nothingness.

Darkness envelops him.

When he stirs again, something warm brushes against his fingers. He remains still, the memory of pain still too fresh. He will need to build momentum before attempting anything drastic. Instead, he focuses on moving those fingers against that warm, comforting object.

A gasp fills the space. "Sam?"

He knows that voice.

More shuffling. "Oh, thank God! Manny! Nurse!"

Mom. Her voice, and those of the others filling the room, are like sledgehammers to his head. Those dark hands begin pulling him to the cliff again. He fights it, trying to see, to blink. *What is going on here? Why...?*

In a staggering flash, the memories of the excursion, the echoing laughter, the traffic jam, the overwhelming hopelessness, the ominous Philistine convoy, the angry cussing, and the desperate struggle all descend upon him.

The first crash.

Then, the second.

His eyes fly open, and lights pierce through. Ignoring the torturous pain, he struggles against the bed and the restraining hands.

"Ash." He groaned. "Where's..." he trails off, resisting the urge to retch.

Mom's jasmine scent embraces him. "Oh, honey." At the same time, an unfamiliar voice, a nurse, says, "Please, try to calm down, sir." But the sadness, the sorrow in his mom's voice, is too deep, too complete.

"Where's Asher?" His scream threatens to split his head open, but he doesn't care. He struggles harder. "Where's Ash? Where is he?"

More hands restrain him. "Let me go! I need to find Ash..."

Broken sobs reach his ears. "I'm so sorry, baby."

"No!" she can't mean that... "*No!*"

"Help calm him, please,"

"*Asher! Asher!*" he starts to bellow with the heady rush of adrenaline. The force of his struggle shoves people across the room: the bed strains and creaks under his unrestrained strength.

Something cold snakes into him, spreads fast, and settles. He thrashes even harder and yells louder.

"Administer more doses!" a panicked voice cries. "He's too strong, and his blood pressure is rising astronomically!"

More engulfing coolness. Those dark hands return with greater force, grab him, and pull him to the cliff's edge. "No, please..." his limbs feel like water, too rubbery. He knows he is losing the fight. But what about Ash? He needs to find him. "*Asher...*"

They push him over the cliff.

And darkness, painful and empty, engulfs him.

"Sam?" His mother pokes her head through the door.

He sits motionless on the couch, his gaze fixed on the birch tree leaves in the yard. The hot summer wind hits him like a punch to the gut. When Hazel walks into the room, he doesn't attempt to conceal his raw left knuckles, bruised from repeatedly striking the wall.

"Sam?" She settles beside him, careful not to brush against the heavy cast around his right arm and leg. Her soft palm brushes his shoulder. "You don't have to go now if you're not up to it."

All over again, that dagger claws deeper into his heart. Who knew that pain has levels and segments that defy explanation until experienced? He had missed the funeral; he had been too broken and unconscious to say goodbye. The thought makes him want to vomit.

Samson blinks and shrugs away her hand. "I'll come."

Getting his broken body into the van is a struggle, with his pain-filled, crutch-assisted wobble. On the way to the gravesite, they pass Philistine officers on patrol. It takes every single ounce of willpower in him not to wrench the door open, come down, and unleash himself on any one of them his hand first finds. Hatred, he has discovered, has an imposing, acrid taste.

His parents guide him to the grave and then retreat to the car, giving him just enough space. The way his parents treat him as though he's fragile stirs up frustration and regret. How they have endured his tumultuous behavior since the crash is a mystery to him.

Samson stands alone, trembling.

So, this is it: Asher *Jonas, beloved son, friend, and defender of the right.*

Dreams, hopes, and life were all snatched away in a split second. The driver survived, albeit as broken as he. Samson lifts his eyes to the heavens. "Why didn't you let me die instead of him?" The memory of his parents, Zain and Deborah, drained and pain-wracked by his hospital bedside, yet trying to look brave for his sake, cut him to the quick. How would they deal with the loss of yet another child at Philistine hands?

Oh, Ash.

The ugly, crippling reality that he would never see him again, never hear his voice, whether in a joke, riddle, or blatant calling out, dawns on him. For the first time since the unthinkable news came, Samson lets his defenses collapse and lets the broken sobs wrack through him.

He lets the pain sink in and birth a ravenous fire for vengeance.

"Ma!" Samson calls from down the hall. "*Ma!*"

There are days Hazel wants to ban the words Ma, Mom, Mother, and Mama from her son's vocabulary. It had been a frustrating day at the boutique, and she was willing to bet money her son had called her name fifty times since she'd come home. In the year that had passed since Asher's death, the despair and fury had only just begun to loosen its grasp on him. Nevertheless, there are occasions when she catches a glimpse of profound grief etched onto his face, moments when muffled sobs persistently emanate from behind his closed bedroom door.

"Ma, I need your help."

"You want me to come into the bathroom?" she asked, tapping the closed door.

"Yes, please. I met this girl, and I need to make a good impression. I want to buy her something nice or take her somewhere special. What do you think she'll like?" He is facing the mirror, rubbing his upper lip with his finger.

"Is that dirt on your face?"

"No, it's a mustache. The ladies are starting to notice."

"No girls until you're at least eighteen," she jests.

After his hand and leg had healed, there were nights he'd return home well past his curfew, evidence of scuffles clear—his knuckles bruised, eyes occasionally blackened. She can't shake the suspicion that the news reports detailing vandalism on the Philistine property over the months may be linked to Samson. In recent times, such incidents dwindled, renewing hope within her.

Gratitude to God fills Hazel with the possibility of healing for her son and Asher's parents. For her boy, if a relationship could hasten the process, she will allow it—so long as it is Godly with a good Israelite girl.

"Come on, Mom, you know I've been dating for forever. Plus, that's only in another two years." With her velvet pixie cut and dry humor, Carmen is too different from the girls he's been with; the challenge she spikes is impossible to resist.

"Against my will. You and your father conspired to slip those girls under my nose."

"There is this one girl. She's different from the others. Her body, Ma, it's bad—in a good way."

"*Samson!*" she gasps.

He laughs. Teasing mom about girls never growing old, knowing he can always get a rise out of her. "No, for real. I need your help. You're a girl—what do you like?"

Hazel watches her son rub his peach fuzz and talk about a girl he's met. He is growing up so fast—whether she likes it or not—and she isn't sure she likes it. A handsome young man: she knew it was only a matter of time before the girls started to notice.

Samson stands out amongst other boys because of his shoulder-length, jet-black hair, which seems to want to grow into locs all on its own. His skin is a sun-kissed caramel, his features striking. He resembles his father closely. She remembers how taken she was by Manoah the moment she first saw him. The sole difference between Manoah today and when they met in college is the gray sprinkles throughout his hair. She appreciates the distinguished salt-and-pepper look in men.

From the time Samson was a young boy, the girls in the neighborhood constantly came by to ask if he was home and allowed to play. She chuckles, recalling his eighth birthday when Manoah had bought him an electric motorcycle. Samson cruised up and down their street wearing sunglasses, and she just knew the girls would love her son.

"Samson," she answers, snapping out of her daydream, "you don't impress someone by buying gifts. How you treat them is what they remember—like writing sweet notes or a poem. Plus, don't forget you were born to serve a purpose. You never know when God is going to call you. You need to stay focused on school and stay out of trouble. We can worry about girls later."

He sighs. "I remember. I was a miracle, born to do important things, blah, blah. You tell me all the time, Ma."

She pats him on the cheek. "I want you to remember you're special."

"I will. Not to change the subject, but I need a faster bike—" Before he finishes his statement, his mother's face is already wrinkling with concern. "Don't freak out. I've been going to the racetrack. I need a faster bike so I can start racing professionally."

"Samson, I just became okay with your riding, let alone—" The telephone interrupts their conversation. "We'll finish this in a minute," Hazel says. The call is from her husband, letting her know he will be home late. She turns toward the bathroom to finish her conversation with Samson, but before she reaches the door, Samson has already bounced past her and is in the hallway on his phone, arranging to meet a friend. *Teenagers.* Hazel shakes her head. *Between the girls and that motorcycle, I don't know which will be the death of me.*

Chapter 6

JUDGES 14:1-4

"Thanks, bye." Samson falls backward on his bed, staring up at the ceiling.

He let out a sigh. "Race motorcycles are *so* expensive." He can almost hear Asher's snarky comment if he had been there physically: *Quit whining and rob a bank!* A fierce ache tears through his chest at the thought of his friend. But through the haze of pain, he finds his lips loosen into slightly bittersweet smiles.

Sitting up, he flips open a magazine to research how to build a motorcycle that could win races. What he finds doesn't make him feel much better, but he keeps seeing the message: *buy a used race bike.* His frown morphs into a devious smile as he reviews the tasks needed to make a motorcycle race-ready. "I can do this myself."

Reflecting on the past year, Samson is struck by the magnitude of his efforts to amass the necessary funds for his dream motorcycle. This bike isn't just any ordinary ride; it's his canvas for crafting a racing masterpiece. He's dedicated himself to various odd jobs – mowing lawns, maintaining pools, washing vehicles, and even selling used parts online – all in pursuit of the financial jigsaw pieces he requires. As money flows in like a trickling stream, he receives the rewards of his persistence. With rising excitement, he meticulously crosses items off his wish list: shocks, case covers, rear sets, exhaust, fuel module, bodywork, clip-ons, braided brake lines, frame sliders, steering damper, 520 sprockets front and rear, 520 chain, spools, and grip tape. However, his awareness remains sharp – this checklist only marks the beginning. The most potent metamorphosis – the engine overhaul to increase horsepower – awaits him on the distant horizon. Nevertheless, the exhilaration of witnessing his vision materialize, of feeling the wind whip through his hair as he speeds down the open road, provides ample fuel for his anticipation.

Before the race season starts, Samson decides to race despite his agreement with his parents to wait until after graduation. His parents won't like it, but this is something he wants to do. Besides, the repercussions would be minor when it came to his parents. His dad loves to race, so Samson knows his father won't be upset if he finds out. And he can always wiggle his way out of trouble with his mother. After all, he is her baby.

He dreams of hearing his knee puck grinding across the track as he makes a pass for the lead. He watches professional races for hours and even sneaks in at night to ride his bicycle on the track. The slower pace will give him intimate knowledge of the track and prove an advantage.

Samson's bike is not even close to being race-ready, with more than half the parts he needs on his list. He doesn't have enough money. He isn't sure he can be competitive and win races. How will he lower his lap times without the added horsepower and tuned suspension?

The long-awaited day finally arrives. Samson strides onto the track and clinches a commendable 4th place in his debut race. Yet, his elation remains pent up, lacking an immediate outlet. Devoid of sponsorship, he lacks a team or even someone close to confide in. In the bustling hubbub of the paddock, the vibrant heart of the racing arena where riders, mechanics, and teams converge, discussions center around the spirited privateer hailing from Israel. Yet, amid the bustling crowd, Samson stands alone, immersed in a solitary celebration of his achievement.

Weeks later, Samson is at the track evaluating his new suspension settings when he notices a girl walking through the paddock. He watches her for a minute—her walk, her style, even the way the wind tosses her hair. *I need that in my life*, he thinks to himself. She walks by him, smiles, and nods. He inclines his head slightly.

"Hey, who was that?" Samson whispers to another racer who is also working on their bike.

"Not sure; I think she's an umbrella girl, or maybe she is dating one of the Lion Motorsport guys," the racer replies.

Samson tries to hold out as long as he can but gives into temptation and looks back. The mystery girl turns back for a second glimpse, and the two lock eyes momentarily.

She reluctantly walks toward the Lion Motorsport pavilion, where one of the racers calls her over. "Lilith, who is that guy you were talking to? With the long hair? Number 74?"

Her eyes roll as she takes a deep breath. "You called me to ask me a question you already know the answer to?" She pats him on the back like a puppy. Buddy has been crushing on Lilith since grade school. "You know you're like a brother to me, Buddy, and I can't date my brother."

"Repeatedly turning me down is one thing, but fraternizing with the enemy is almost worse," he says. "Almost."

She lingers to watch Samson walk away. His stride intrigues her; it is confident, almost cocky.

On her ride home, the good-looking, long-haired guy consumes her thoughts. She doesn't know who he is but knows she will find out.

In the middle of a brisk walk with his headphones on and blasting, Samson crashes into a girl approaching the corner. He drops his phone on the ground. "Sorry about that," he mumbles, reaching for his phone.

"It's okay. You're new, aren't you?"

Samson is so engrossed in preparing for the race that he doesn't realize the girl he'd bumped into was the beautiful one from weeks prior. He puffs up his chest and clears his throat before answering in a refined tone, "I'm not sure how new I am, but my name is Samson." He extends his hand.

"I'm Lilith," she says. He flinches when her hand touches his hand. *Philistine.* A sour taste fills his mouth and slides down his throat to his stomach. "I like your hair," the girl continues. "How long have you been growing it?" she asks, reaching out her hand but stopping short of his locs. "Can I touch it?"

"Sure. I have been growing it for a while." Samson tries to downplay his hair and change the subject. "Which team are you with?"

"I'm not really with any particular team, but Lion Motorsports contracted me for this race." She musters up her best imitation of a professional voice.

Against his better judgment, he smiles. "Well, I won't hold it against you."

"If I ask for your number, you won't get in trouble, will you?"

"I won't tell if you won't."

"Deal." Her eyes sparkle, and Samson catches his breath.

On the rooftop deck of a café in Timnah, Samson reaches across the table and scoops a spoonful of Lilith's soup. She rolls her eyes and tucks a long, graceful curl behind her ear. "If I had a dollar for every time you did this, Sam, I'd be able to afford a luxury trip somewhere by now."

Samson chuckles, allowing that familiar warmth to spread across his chest. His lips still tingled from their kiss earlier in the car. The memory of his fingers running through those silken tresses digs deep. These feelings she whips up in him never grow old.

But he is conflicted because she is a Philistine, and their treatment of Israelites makes him feel like she belongs to the people who killed his best friend. Her fierce banter about politics or sports can make his blood boil at one moment. However, in the next moment, she can make his heart race just by running her slender fingers through his locks.

The woman was like ambrosia.

Their chemistry has been instant and undeniable; she is unlike any girl he's met. Samson knows he could spend the rest of his life with Lilith. It is only a matter of months before he acknowledges what he has to do.

The past few months have brought them closer together than he'd expected. Aside from racing, discovering she adores cycling and canoeing like he does draws him in. Lilith is not only athletic, but he finds it easy to talk to her about any subject. Nothing tiresome exists among the long hours they spend discussing life.

When he told her about Asher, she wept.

With each passing day in her company, the war within him lessens. How can he hold a murder she had nothing to do with against her?

A cool breeze, fresh with the promise of spring, fills the air. "I've been thinking," Samson starts. Her gaze met his. "Let's get married."

"Are you serious?"

"Of course I am. Don't you feel the same about me?"

"You know I do. I love you. I'm just…are you…?" Lilith pauses. "I would love to…but…"

"But what?"

"My Dad is traditional. You have to ask for his approval first. Can you handle that?"

"Of course. Your dad loves me." Samson's chest inflates with self-assurance.

"You've only seen him a couple of times," she teases.

"I'm serious. That's no problem. I can tell he likes me. I know these things."

"Can we afford to get married? Where are we going to live? Are we going to have a big wedding or a small one? How many kids do you want? There is so much we haven't discussed."

"We can discuss that. I know I want to spend my life with you. I can't imagine being with anyone else." Samson asserts.

"Why don't you invite your parents to the championship race, and I'll bring mine. That way, everyone can meet each other." Lilith suggests.

"Yeah, about that—I haven't told my parents I'm racing. They told me I couldn't race until I graduated. I don't think it would be a good idea."

"You need to tell them before they find out."

"It's only three weeks until graduation. Plus, I don't think they'll find out."

"If you say so, we should arrange a meeting in Timnah next weekend."

Samson nods his head and changes the subject. "Now, may I get a kiss?"

Later that evening, Samson talks to his parents about his marriage plans.

"You know I've been with Lilith for quite some time now, and I can confidently say I've fallen in love. I'm certain about this, and I want to marry her," he asserts, his words brimming with confidence.

Hazel almost choked on her food, startled by Samson's confession. "You think you're in love? Sam, that's not funny."

"I don't know how to explain it, but I know: she's the one."

His mother stands up, gathers the plates off the table, and enters the kitchen. Samson sits beside his father, speaking loud enough for his mother to hear. He explains to them how—from the moment he saw her—he knew Lilith was the one. She makes him laugh, gets his jokes, and perfectly balances his life. He makes sure his mother hears him say she is friendly, sweet, and caring, just like his mother.

He tells them she is intelligent, and after graduation, she is attending a web design program at college. "Lilith is creative and artistic. She created a website for her father's modeling agency, and some of his customers want her to design their websites now. She's amazing."

Manoah listens to his son but doesn't take him seriously. He has learned that over the years, Samson's excitement for things doesn't always last too long.

"Nice, sweet, and educated. Don't pay the bills," his mother yells from the kitchen.

"Pop, she's *fine* though," Samson whispers so his mother can't hear him. Samson traces an hourglass shape in the air with his hands. They both laugh and high-five.

At that moment, Hazel returns to the room.

"What are we high-fiving about?" she asks, displeased.

"Ma, Lilith is gorgeous, funny, everything I want in a woman. I want you to meet her this coming weekend. She lives in Timnah. We could go there so you can meet her and her parents."

"Timnah? Sam, you can't tell me there are no Israelite girls to date. There are plenty of beautiful and intelligent Israelite girls." She adds, "Why did you choose a Philistine? I'd rather you race motorcycles."

Samson's eyes widen. He asks, "How do you know she's Philistine?"

"You're right," she replies, "I assumed. Is she a Philistine?"

He pauses and gulps. "Yes."

Hazel rolls her eyes and crosses her arms across her chest.

Samson elbows his father. "When you see her, you will agree." His father laughs. His mother does not.

"This is what happens when kids don't learn their family history," she says, her eyes locking onto Samson's with intensity—her voice trembles. "Forty years, Sam," Hazel steadies her tone, though the underlying emotion remains. "For four decades, they've relentlessly strived to undermine our people's rights, imposed burdensome taxes, and inflicted suffering upon our community." Her voice falters, her gaze becoming watery and heavy. "Remember—"

"Don't, Mom," he halts her, unable to stop the coldness that spreads within him. That familiar rage wraps its arms around him, whispering sweet vengeance in his ears. "With the last breath in me, I will destroy the people that took him from us," he leans in. "But Lilith isn't one of them."

"Sam, you are a Nazirite and promised to God," Manoah says.

"If God wanted me to marry an Israelite girl, he'd make them prettier. Have you seen the girls around here?" Samson raises his hand to high-five his dad again.

Manoah knows better. Hazel would give him a look that meant he'd be sleeping on the couch. "Samson, listen to your mother," Manoah orders.

She fixes her son with a stern gaze, a spark of anger igniting in her eyes. "You're still in high school. Are you truly prepared for marriage? Should we shoulder the responsibility not just for ourselves but for our wives, too? You haven't even experienced living on your own yet," she asserts.

"Mom, I am. We're working on plans. We'll find a place, and I'll get a job. We'll have it all figured out." Samson smiles at his mother. "Don't worry, Ma, you'll always be my number one girl." Samson knows his mother always gives in because no matter how old he is, he is always her baby.

Hazel sucks the air in through her teeth. "I refuse to agree. You are too young. She's not an Israelite. I will meet her, but that is all."

Chapter 7
JUDGES 14:1-4

The air horns snap Samson from his trance.

The track map image in his head disintegrates until nothing is left to see. As he stands next to his 160-horsepower, V-twin metal stallion, a light breeze brings a whiff of race fuel into his face. The sweet smell gives him goosebumps and infuses him with an intense sizzle. Most of the Philistine crowd cheers, and a sickening lurch pulls his stomach.

Just like in those early days after Asher's death, racing takes the edge away and stops him from imploding from that sickening rush of rage.

Lilith is the only good thing about them.

Other racers' tents bustle with golf carts, motorized scooters, and people wearing team colors running back and forth. A parade of decorated 18-wheelers position in a single-file line, blocking the racers from the rest of the crowd.

"Attention, attention. The track is going hot in 30 minutes," a race official announces over the loudspeakers.

In an instant, Samson's adrenaline kicks in. He claps his hands together. "Let's go," he barks and walks over to where his gear is lined up. Samson's "race team" consists of an air compressor, duct tape, zip ties, ten gallons of fuel, a generator, tire warmers, and a cooler full of water. The full-body leather race suit, gauntlet gloves, shin-high racing boots, and helmet—all in black—give him a menacing façade that fits his riding style. Without sponsorship, he is a true privateer – a privateer with a real chance of winning the championship.

The closed-circuit monitor in his paddock area comes to life with the announcers introducing the race.

Welcome to the Vineyard. What began as simple country roads have evolved through the years to become the most demanding track in all motorsports. Once a year, this circuit welcomes the best two-wheeled riders whose desire is to follow in the tracks of racing superstars. They must place past victories and defeats behind them to focus on the challenging Vineyard track ahead because this is their last chance at glory!

Known for its fast straights and hard-braking corners, the Vineyard tests man and machine, bravery and horsepower, skill and strategy. Every decision must be calculated, and every move must be near-perfect because this course is unforgiving.

Roaring engines mix cheers and idle crowd conversations – all an ear-piercing cacophony.

Fifteen riders arrived in Timnah for greatness, shouts the announcer, but only one will be mentioned alongside the legends who have won here before! Welcome to the Milk and Honey Grand Prix!

A second announcer emerges and grabs the microphone. "I'm Ethan Frances, and I'm here today to announce the final round of this road-racing championship. I have Chuck Hermes in the booth with me. He has won many races at this very track."

"Thanks for having me, Ethan," Chuck says, making his presence known. "We are at the great Vineyard Circuit in Timnah, one of the most beautiful tracks in the country. Today is a gorgeous, sunny day, and the temperature is a pleasant 78 degrees—perfect weather for a race!" Chuck pauses for the audience to voice their appreciation. "We have hundreds of eager fans, dressed in the colors and numbers of their favorite riders, who have lined the stands and nearby hills to witness the sights and sounds of today's race. Thousands of them rode their own motorcycles to the track today to be a part of the final race festivities."

"For those unfamiliar with The Milk and Honey Grand Prix, it started as an incubator to develop young talent, but it has grown into much more," Ethan adds. "It is now one of the top racing series in the world. Young riders compete to win a championship, some not old enough to drive and none old enough to drink. They pop milk instead of champagne, Chuck."

Ethan laughs at his joke, and Chuck nods in agreement, the two men working in perfect harmony.

"They sure do," Chuck acknowledges. "But despite their age, these guys are fierce competitors and have come here with one thing in mind: winning. The championship has come down to this final race. Two men are at the top of their class: Corbin and Samson. Due to their age, both have been competing in Milk and Honey for the last time. Who will end up victorious?"

"Chuck, I spoke with Corbin of Lion Motorsports this afternoon. Although people are betting on him to win again this year, he has a lot to worry about. You have a target on your back when you are the reigning champion. It looks like the newcomer, Samson, has Corbin in his crosshairs. Corbin runs his race clean and fast."

Chuck counters Ethan's endorsement of Corbin.

"Speaking of Samson, I can't say enough about this kid. First, he is racing on a V-twin motorcycle while the other riders are on in-line machines. This is a testament to his racing skills. Besides his pure racing ability, his hair and all-black gear make picking him out on the track easy. He is a privateer who has turned this racing series upside down. He is only two points behind the leader and has a real chance at winning this thing."

"Samson is on fire, and that is going to make for an interesting race," Ethan chimes in.

"Samson has given this sport a new face on the top step of the podium that, in the past, has been dominated by Lion Motorsports. I think he will give them a run for their money, and I, for one, can't wait."

Attention, attention. The track is going hot in 10 minutes.

The announcement spills out from the intercom. Racers fire up their motorcycles and head toward their starting positions. Samson tops off his fuel tank and starts his engine.

"Wait, where is my tech sticker?" Samson starts searching all around his bike, confused about its disappearance. Without the tech sticker, he can't race. All rider equipment and machines must undergo a technical inspection before each race. As he looks closer at where his sticker used to be, he notices a small corner of the sticker is still there.

"Somebody stole my sticker."

Samson tries not to panic. He puts on his racing suit, helmet, and gloves, kicks the motorcycle stand, and rides to the inspection area. "I'm trying to start the next race; can you please give me another tech sticker?"

"Give you a sticker? That is not how this works," says the crotchety man, standing up from his chair.

"Look," Samson argues, "I went through tech already, but someone stole my sticker."

Utterly unmoved by Samson's plea, he replies. "To make this race, you better remove your lower fairing."

Before Samson can debate, the inspection technician gets his clipboard. Out of options, Samson hops up and grabs a rear stand for his bike while the inspector examines his helmet, tire, etc. Samson rushes to remove his lower fairing. His stomach is in knots. He had worked so hard to qualify fourth on the grid; was all his hard work about to go to waste?

"You're good to go."

Samson returns to his bike and heads to pit lane, but he is too late. All the racers have already lined up and on their warm-up lap. His penalty for missing the warmup lap is to start at the back of the pack. Before the penalty, Corbin was positioned directly in front of Samson on the racing grid. Now, Samson's chances of winning are slim.

A track marshal taps him on the shoulder while on pit lane, watching the racers line up in their grid positions. "Sorry, kid, you missed the lineup. Now you have to start the race in last place." The marshal starts to walk away but suddenly turns back around. "Oh, by the way, number 13 wanted me to ask if you found your tech sticker. I saw it on your bike, so I assume you did. Good luck."

He took my sticker.

Samson glares in Corbin's direction. At the front of the grid, Corbin seems relaxed on his bright red motorcycle, joking with his crew. The gold wheels accentuate the lion on each side of his bike and helmet. His race suit is adorned with multiple sponsors: oil and gas, telecom, and soft drink companies. It is more than evident that the Lion Motorsports operation has deep pockets.

I need to ride my own race and focus. Samson closes his eyes. *Focus. Just focus.*

Samson takes his grid position on the back row. Racers rev their engines all around him, waiting for the start light to turn green. Samson initially hoped to finish in the top five, but now he will be lucky even to finish the race. "Lord help me," he mutters under his breath.

Flipping down his visor and clicking his bike into gear, Samson takes a deep breath. The umbrella girls clear the track. Air horns and the crowd both scream with anticipation. He leans over the front tire to keep it from rising at the start, then eyeballs the flag marshal. The flag drops. Samson lets off the clutch and races full throttle to the first corner. It isn't his best start, but he feels good heading toward turn one. He brakes, sticks out his knee, and he tips into it. Then, turn two, three, and four. He assumes Corbin must have gotten off to a blazing start because he can't see the cheater in the sea of bikes surrounding him.

Samson's initial plan was to save his tires for the end of the race, though being forced to start at the back of the pack changed that tactic. His front tire points skyward as he blasts down the straightaway. From that vantage point, he can see the vertical leaderboard — Corbin has a hefty lead. Samson charges forward, claiming victims one by one. Three riders in one corner. Two more in another corner.

"Looks like we have a bit of a mystery with Samson's positioning," Chuck Hermes remarks, his tone reflecting a mix of curiosity and concern. "He was supposed to start in the front row, but now he's back in the pack. Tough break for the privateer – and in the championship race, no less! He's definitely got his work cut out if he hopes to make any headway in this competition."

"Indeed, Chuck," Ethan chimes in. "It's a daunting task to fight your way up from the back in a race of this caliber. But remember, he's no stranger to adversity. This could be a real advantage for Corbin and the other front-runners, allowing them to capitalize on the situation and secure a strong lead."

"It could be several things, Chuck," Ethan retorts, "Maybe his tire choice. He could have a harder tire that's starting to soften now that we're in the heat of the race. That could be what's helping him with his corner speed. That Ducati is a bit heavy, so burning off half a tank of fuel can't hurt. This is the kind of race Samson loves. His style is to come from behind. I don't know many racers who like to come from behind, but Samson makes it look easy."

Samson continues to make up ground. After fourteen laps, he is in second place, catching up to Corbin like a lion stalking his prey.

"Six laps to go," Chuck announces. "Samson is now only one second behind the leader, Corbin."

"It's heating up," Ethan agrees.

"What a fight we have here, Ethan."

Corbin can hear the distinctive sound of Samson's V-twin engine coming up behind him. He looks over his shoulder, yelling, "You aren't going to win today, pretty boy!"

"It looks as if Corbin missed his braking point," Ethan says. "He overshot the corner. Samson is right behind him now!"

"One lap to go, Ethan," Chuck adds.

Yes! That's what I needed; Samson rejoiced silently.

The crowd stands to their feet. Samson is on Corbin's back wheel. Samson moves to the inside on the small straightaway between corners and shows Corbin his front wheel, hoping he will take the bait. Then Samson slides back behind Corbin to take advantage of the draft from the subsequent corner for a split second. Corbin protects the inside racing line, just as Samson anticipated. Samson storms around him on the outside to take the lead.

"Folks, I think we just witnessed the most unbelievable pass I have ever seen," Ethan announces. "I don't even know how he pulled it off. Where did that speed come from?"

The crowd is stunned. Corbin is rattled. With two corners left, it is down to the wire. Corbin hammers on the throttle. With his knee almost kissing the ground, Samson straightens his lean angle to rocket down toward the finish line.

In the middle of the final corner, Corbin refuses to let Samson win without a fight. He yanks on the throttle and shifts his weight a little farther off the side of the bike to help propel him around the corner, but his abrupt adjustment mid-corner disrupts the grip of the rear tire. It begins to slide out from under him. He shifts his weight back and lets off the throttle, thinking he can save himself and the bike from a thrashing, but within milliseconds, he feels the bike buck as it regains grip—stopping, sliding, and tilting against the lean of the turn all at the same time.

Suddenly, Corbin is ejected and thrown over the high side of the tremulous bike. His momentum launches him head-over-heels into the air, the bike spinning off in the opposite direction. The racer hits the ground head-first and rolls another fifteen feet, coming to rest alongside the track. The bike lies in pieces across from him.

Unaware of the mayhem behind him, Samson pins the throttle and tries to tuck it down under the windscreen. He clicks into fifth gear. He glances over his shoulder, seeing he is alone; Samson pulls a long wheelie across the finish line in celebration.

"And Samson wins The Milk and Honey Championship! I can't believe it, folks. Samson wins! Samson wins!"

Ethan interrupts. "Chuck, Corbin is down."

"Corbin is down and not moving. The medics are out." Chuck's voice becomes somber. "The ambulance has been called. Corbin is still not moving."

Small groups of Samson's fans celebrate. They are ecstatic. They couldn't believe the newcomer, the Israelite, had won. Samson rides a victory lap filled with wheelies and burnouts. Most of his competitors ride by to shake his hand. He stops at every bleacher to show his fans love. The ambulance drives away as Samson approaches the end of his circuit. He glances at Corbin's mangled bike and then coasts to the pit area; he doesn't want this moment to end.

"Samson, they're waiting on you!" yells a track official.

Samson parks his bike in the #1 spot, removes his helmet, and strides to take his place on the podium, veins pumping with adrenaline. While standing at the top, he sets his helmet down, picks up the celebratory glass quart of milk, and raises a toast.

For you, Asher.

"This year's Milk and Honey Champion is Samson!"

The crowd erupts. Samson closes his eyes and tries to soak it all in. The warm sun on his face, the cheers from the crowd, his hands thrust high in the air, clasping the Cup and the $100,000 in cash. A champion in his first season *and* enough money to lessen Israel's grief, at least for a while—what could be better? This will be a day he will never forget.

However, the celebration is cut short as a wave of whispers washes across the circuit.

"Ethan, we have some heavy news to report. Corbin, last year's champion from Lion Motorsport, has sustained serious injuries and has already been taken to the ER. We pray for his speedy recovery…"

"**G**ood shot," Hazel compliments, scanning the horizon. "I'm impressed."

"Don't be," Manoah says, frowning as he reaches into his bag for a different club. "I should have hit the ball twice as far."

"I'm still impressed," Hazel says under her breath, at once referring to her husband's shot and what they'd been discussing beforehand—the massive donation anonymously made toward Israelite orphanage upkeep and job creation. Her heart swells in gratitude. She moves to answer her cell phone.

"Hey, Ma," Samson says.

"Hey, what's the plan, Stan?" Silence on the other end of the phone. "What's the deal, pickle?" she continues. Samson can't hold in his laughter any longer, and Hazel giggles helplessly. "Isn't that what the kids say these days?"

"Not any kids I know. What are you two doing?"

"We're at the driving range, waiting to hear from you."

"Okay, I'm almost there." Ten minutes later, Samson arrives at the driving range and greets his parents with hugs and kisses. He pulls his right arm from behind his back and hands his mother a sizeable yellow gift bag overflowing with white tissue paper. "I was thinking today about how much you have done for me over the years and how you've always been there. I wanted to tell you I love you and show you my appreciation."

"Wow! Aren't you in a generous mood," Hazel says, taking the gift. She hugs him and then carefully extracts the tissue from the bag without tearing it. It is a large jar of honey. "This must be love," she teases. In unison, they laugh at her sarcasm.

"It's gourmet honey. You can bake with it or use it in your tea." Samson looks at Manoah, dressed in a tangerine-colored polo shirt and khaki pants, and pats his father's stomach. "Dad likes to eat."

"Thanks. I'm sure that honey will go a long way," Manoah says, taking his jab at the enormous jar. "But we do appreciate it. Just giving you a hard time."

"Where did you get it?" Hazel asks, holding the jar up to the sunlight. "How much did it cost?"

"I got it from a bee, and for you, it's free."

Hazel checks her watch. "What time is the dinner supposed to start?"

"I'm hungry," Manoah agrees.

"We can head that way now, Dad. Just follow me."

Samson's parents follow his truck to a street lined with Red Maple trees in east Timnah. He pulls up to the curb in front of Lilith's family's impressive two-story peach-bricked house.

Lilith's parents greet Samson and his family at the door. "We're so glad you could join us!" her mother gushes, urging her guests in with a welcoming wave. "Please, come in." They exchange pleasantries while making their way to the dining room. Samson smiles at his fiancée across the room. Lilith winks at him as she walks around the table to greet his parents with hugs. Samson yearns for the families to get along. He and Lilith are young, and the political unrest between the Philistines and the Israelites is not in their favor. All he knows for sure is that he loves Lilith.

They sit around the ebony-colored dinner table, with white china set on navy-blue placemats. Under the table, Samson rests his hand on Lilith's leg. She smiles up at him, exposing the dimple on her right cheek. Her eyes flicker with the same glow as the day they first met. As their parents are engrossed in conversation, Samson pretends to whisper something to his future bride and kisses her on the cheek. Her cheeks flush, and she nods along as though he had told her something interesting, all while trying to suppress the smile waiting behind her cheeks.

"When do you two kids plan on getting married, and where do you plan on living?" Hazel asks, breaking them from their trance.

"We were thinking about having the ceremony in two months," Lilith answers. "We looked at apartments around this area."

Hazel sighs. Samson spots his mother's disappointment and speaks up. "We don't see any reason to wait. We've been together a while, and we love each other. We will have graduated by the wedding. Why wait?" He pauses, but her face doesn't change. He continues to plead his case. "I know it seems sudden, but we are mature adults. We know what we are doing."

"Samson, how will you support your family?" Hazel asks. "What about a job?"

Manoah asks, "Are you still planning to go to college?"

Samson doesn't want to fuel the fire by telling his parents about his race winnings, so he answers their exact question. "We are both still going to pursue post-secondary degrees while we work and build a life together."

Hazel isn't impressed or convinced, but she knows he has to make his own decisions and mistakes.

Lilith's father speaks up. "We can have the wedding here, in Timnah. The modeling agency I own has a huge warehouse where we hold castings. We can perform the wedding at our church and the reception at the warehouse."

"Oh, that's true, Dad," Lilith agrees. "I forgot about the warehouse. We don't want a big church wedding anyway. Now that you mentioned the warehouse, we can set up an area behind it along the lake." She is close to bouncing out of her chair.

"Let's toast our new family," Lilith's Dad announces. "Lilith, bring in the champagne."

"Samson doesn't drink, Dad."

"I don't drink alcohol," Samson confirms, "but I will toast if you have juice or something else."

"I'm sorry, I didn't know that. Well, more for me," her father muses, raising his glass and smiling at his guests. Everyone at the table laughs except Hazel.

"To my future son-in-law and beautiful daughter, may you have a long, fulfilling life together. Cheers!"

Everyone raises their glass in unison. "Cheers!"

Samson and his mother exchange glances but don't say a word.

Chapter 9
JUDGES 14:10-17

"**N**ow, *this* is a party," Samson declares, walking toward the building.

Music escapes from the front door as two men walk out. The door remains ajar, so Samson slips in—late, as usual. As he strolls around the room, he realizes he doesn't know most people there. He recognizes some of Lilith's family, but many guests are her father's business clients. Her dad even invited models from the agency. Samson notices celebrities and wealthy businessmen whom he'd seen around town. He watches as most of the crowd mingle and talk, and they eat while others sip champagne and dance.

There was much to do during the wedding week – from the final tuxedo and dress fittings, bachelor's and bachelorette parties, to the rehearsal dinner. In addition, the bride's parents are throwing a party for Samson and Lilith at their home in Timnah.

"The more you take, the more you leave behind. What am I?" A tall guy asks. The small crowd of guys moan at the complexity of the tall guy's riddle.

"Samson!" one of the models from the nearby couch call. "Dude, that suit is sweet. Where did you get it?"

"You're put together every time I see you," another guy confers.

"Thanks. It's just a little something I picked up." Samson dismisses the compliment, smoothing over the sleeve of his designer suit. "What are you guys doing over here, having story time?"

"No, we are having mature intellectual banter. Think you can keep up?" a guy in glasses smirks.

"Any takers?" The tall guy looks around the room.

"Repeat the question," Samson requests.

"It was a riddle, not a question," he remarks, then repeats, "*The more you take, the more you leave behind. What am I?*"

"Footsteps," Samson replies with little effort.

"Beginners luck," someone yells as the growing crowd erupts in oohs and aahs. Samson chuckles; hundreds of the riddles he's dabbled in over the years flood his mind. *They have no idea.*

The tall guy proposes, "How about we put some money on it? A hundred dollars if you get it right, lose a hundred if you get it wrong."

"I will take those odds," Samson agrees. "I will even let you go first."

"I am not alive, but I grow; I don't have lungs, but I need air; I don't have a mouth, but water kills me. What am I?"

"Fire. That's a hundred dollars; what else you got?" Samson quips.

"I remember seeing you race," remarks another male model, trying to change the subject. "You were good. A little cocky," the man puts his fist over his mouth and fakes a cough, "but good. You're a one-hit-wonder. I bet you can't win next year."

Samson laughs a little. He knows most of these men are Lilith's friends, and he doesn't let them bother him. "You're right; next year, I'm moving to the premier class as the champion. But today, I need immediate gratification. "Now it's my turn," Samson challenges.

"Drinks, anyone?" A waiter approaches the crowd, crashing the conversation.

Some men head to the bar once they see the server only offering champagne. Samson scans the room. People dance as if they don't have a care in the world. His parents are huddled in a corner with Lilith's parents, laughing and joking. Another waiter with a tray pauses beside him, interrupting his thoughts.

"Seafood salad?" the waiter asks.

"No, thank you," Samson answers with a polite nod of the head.

"Now, what were you saying about your riddle, Samson?" The male model returns from the bar with two drinks in hand.

Samson glances at the bar where Lilith is talking with her girlfriends. They are hugging and congratulating her. Samson can't hear what they are saying but can see her smile.

He surveys the crowd around him and challenges, "Alright, how about this? I'll tell you a riddle." Samson's tone is relaxed, confident they cannot decipher his riddle. "If you can tell me the answer by the end of the wedding, I won't give you $100, but I will buy you all this same suit."

"Deal. I could use a new suit." Two models high-five one another. "Me, too—and those cufflinks."

After hearing Samson's challenge, thirty models decide to participate in the bet.

"But! You each have to buy me a new suit if no one answers it," Samson warns, upping the stakes of the bet.

"We have this in the bag, man," one of the models assures his friends.

"Okay, here is the riddle: out of the one who eats came something to eat; out of the strong came something sweet." Everyone looks at each other, puzzled.

Samson laughs inwardly, relishing in the source of this masterpiece: his record in crushing Lion Motorsport's Corban and blazing home with the sweetest victory so far: The Milk and Honey Grand Prix Cup and the stunning cash prize for his ailing people.

Out of the lion came the honey.

Smugness seeps through him, and he strolls off, optimistic they will never solve it.

Under the radiant sun, Timnah revels in celebrating the wedding day. Rows of pristine chairs, brimming with well-wishers, flank the aisle adorned with a monogrammed runner that stretches ahead. This path is embellished with fuchsia, mango, and lime flower petals that seem plucked from the heart of a tropical paradise.

As the guests follow this vibrant trail, their anticipation builds, leading them to a magnificent wedding arch. Crafted from elegant white wood, it stands proudly, adorned with hibiscus, lilies, and orchids in a kaleidoscope of hues. These natural blooms offer a tropical atmosphere, fulfilling the couple's vision for a day of vibrant celebration and timeless beauty.

Samson stands behind and watches their families and friends chat before the festivities start. He is elated to marry such a beautiful woman and that his family is there to share the moment. He is also excited to win thirty new suits, although he hasn't yet determined where he will put the new suits since his two closets are packed with clothes.

"Are you happy?" Hazel questions, approaching him from behind.

"Yeah, I'm happy." He grins and places his hand on his mother's shoulder. An old weight has dislodged from his chest. "Lilith is the one, Mom. I couldn't ask for a better woman."

"I'm glad you found someone who could make you feel like you do. I wish—"

"Is this how you felt about Dad when you got married?" Samson interrupts. He watches a shimmer dance in her eye. She glances away as though reminiscing. "Ma," he says, snapping his finger after a moment to break her trance.

"I was remembering our wedding," she says. "Your father was calm, but I was so nervous. My palms were sweaty, and I thought my knees would buckle while I stood there. But I kept reminding myself how much I loved him and how I knew he was the one." She smiles again. "Even though we've been through rough times, there was, and still is, no other person I would rather be with. Then you came, and you made what was already great amazing."

"Thank you, Mom."

"I hope you believe me when I say that you are a gift from God. I prayed for you, and God answered my prayers. I look at you now, all grown up, and my heart is full. I'm proud of the man you have become, Samson. I hope you and Lilith have the kind of love your father and I share."

Hazel's eyes pool with tears, and she blinks them back.

"Aww, don't do that," Samson chokes out, kissing his mother on the cheek.

"It's almost time!" announces the wedding planner, lighting candles along the end of the aisle and jolting the pair from their moment.

Lilith slips into her dress after the finishing touches are applied to her hair and makeup. "Does anyone know where the garter is? I can't go out there without something blue."

"Calm down, I have it," her younger sister reassures, rushing over with the garter.

Lilith's bridesmaids surround her and offer comforting words to keep her calm. Her stylist pins the veil in her hair and places a tangerine-colored Oriental lily on the side. When Lilith is dressed, she can't believe her eyes and can't think of another day when she feels so beautiful.

As they wait for the wedding to commence, the girls chat.

"Lilith, our boyfriends, and their friends are pestering us about this riddle. Do you know the answer to the riddle? If you do, will you please tell us the answer?" One of the bridesmaids pleads.

"It's my wedding day; I don't want to discuss that stupid riddle. Your men ask me for the answer whenever I am at the agency. They call me and ask me. They asked me if they would visit the house to see my dad. I wish this were done already so they would stop bothering me."

"Adrian is a struggling model. He can't afford to buy Samson a new suit," the maid of honor complains. "Samson is rich. He can buy those suits."

"Rich? You are exaggerating a bit," Lilith replies.

"All we are saying is this isn't fair, and you know it. We are all struggling to make ends meet. Porter and I just moved in together and have a baby. We can't afford a fancy new suit," another bridesmaid chimes in.

"I get it. You look out for your men, but I'm doing the same. Samson can't afford to buy the suits, either. Even if he could, it's a bet—fair and square. Your men shouldn't have taken the bet if they didn't think they could win."

The pestering was becoming more than she could bear. She feels bad for her friends, but what can she do? As much as Samson spent on clothes, ties, and his cufflink collection, buying thirty new suits would be a stretch. This was her man, and she had to seek his best interests.

Lilith steps into the reception area. In the heart of it all, the dance floor takes center stage, its spotlight illuminating the couple's monogram both on the floor and against the backdrop of the bridal party table.

Encircling the dance floor, a constellation of dining tables beckons. Each is adorned with a pristine white cloth as a canvas for a magnificent centerpiece. These centerpieces burst with life, boasting an array of fresh, fragrant flowers artfully arranged in tall, transparent vases. Crystal-clear water and glistening Swarovski crystals within the vases cast a mesmerizing shimmer in every direction.

What truly captivates Lilith, however, is the unique theme that graces each table. Each set tells its own story, with colored petals and additional crystals thoughtfully scattered across the tablescape. The effect is enchanting, a testament to the meticulous care that has gone into every detail.

Overwhelmed by the beauty surrounding her, Lilith finds herself speechless. She can't help but reflect on Samson's mother, whose unwavering support and blessings have guided the planning process. This moment is more than she could have ever imagined, a testament to the love and dedication that have shaped this day into a dream come true.

"Psst."

The voice behind Lilith startles her. She turns around to see Adrian, Porter, and four other models from her father's agency.

"We need to talk to you for a minute."

"If this is about that stupid riddle—"

"We've asked you as nicely as possible, but you don't seem to understand the seriousness of this situation. We can't afford to buy your man new suits. We will be the town's laughingstock if we don't make good on our debts. Our reputations will be in shambles. We need the answer to the riddle, and you will find out for us."

"I can't just—"

"If you don't get us the answer by the end of your wedding, we are going to ruin your father."

"My father?"

"Your father made a pass at me when I first started working there," Adrian states.

"Your father paid me for a sexual favor," another declares.

"Your father stashes child porn in his desk," Porter adds.

"None of that is true. How could you all say such things about him?" Lilith asks incredulously. "He is the reason you have work and do so well."

"Who said it was true? We'll just put it out there and see where the media takes it."

"The truth doesn't matter, sweetheart. There are thirty of us. Who do you think the media will believe?"

Porter seizes Lilith tightly by the arm, sending shooting pain through her wrist.

"You have an hour. And you better not tell your husband you gave us the answer, or that will be the end of your father's business."

The men walk away, leaving her speechless and trembling.

This is crazy. Are they willing to ruin lives over a stupid riddle? I've got to ask Samson for the answer. I can't let them humiliate my father. After the service, I will ask Samson the truth. He can pay off the debt, and then later, I'll get the money from Dad to pay him back. It won't be a big deal.

The ceremony is beautiful, but Lilith is so shaken by the threat that she can't remember her vows. After the nuptials, the bride, groom, and the wedding party head outside for photographs.

"Samson, why don't you tell me the answer to the riddle?" Lilith purrs while the photographer positions them.

"I'll tell you tomorrow," Samson mumbles.

"Come on, tell me now. You know they won't get it. How does it hurt for me to know? I'm your wife now; you're supposed to tell me everything. There should be no secrets between us."

Samson ignores her. Lilith rambles about his apparent lack of trust in her for the entire forty-five-minute photography session. His mood is beginning to sour.

"Look," he says through gritted teeth, "I said I would tell you tomorrow. Don't ask me again."

Lilith stares at him. He sees her chest rising and falling, faster and faster. She fights back tears.

"Don't cry." Samson reaches for her hand. "I'll tell you the answer," he sighs, "but not if you have raccoon eyes."

Lilith manages to crack a smile.

Samson figures there is no harm in telling her at this point. He leans in and whispers in her ear.

Once the pictures are taken, they enter the reception area. The crowd erupts into cheers when they are announced as husband and wife. The band plays soft music as they go to the dance floor for their first dance. Lilith feels the models' glares burn a hole in her as she dances with Samson. Everyone claps and cheers again as the newlyweds take their seats on the stage.

"Honey, I need to use the bathroom," Lilith whispers when the wedding party is served.

Samson smiles, teasingly kissing her knuckles, "You'd better come back."

E veryone stands and claps while the bandleader smiles and waves.

"Thank you, thank you," the bandleader remarks. "We will be back in ten."

The pause in the music makes Samson aware that most of the wedding party is off, mingling with guests. After a sip of water, he pushes back from the table to meet his new extended family.

"We have the answer," Porter whispers, touching Samson's shoulder.

Samson turns to face him as Adrian and other models walk over. "You do remember the riddle, right?" The huddle turns to look as the band starts up again, then all eyes return to Samson. "Out of the one who eats came something to eat; out of the strong came something sweet," repeats Samson in a slow cadence.

"It was tough to figure out, but I think we got it," Porter says, stroking his chin. "I mean, what's stronger than a lion and sweeter than honey?" he asks rhetorically, feeding Samson the words he had just shared with his new bride.

"I know, I know. Pick me, pick me," Adrian raises his hand, jumping up and down. "Money!" The beginning of another musical selection drowns out the loud laughter.

"Wow…you got it," Samson concedes in disbelief. He swallows hard. His jaw tightens. His face gets warmer.

"When are you going to pay up?" Porter inquires, licking his lips and rubbing his hands together.

Catching a glimpse of Lilith strolling through the celebration, thanking her guests, Samson storms off, knocking down one of the groomsmen with his shoulder. "As soon as I get back," he yells over his shoulder.

He couldn't *believe* she had told them. There's no way they had figured this out on their own. When Samson turns to make his way through the crowd, he can no longer hear the music or see the guests dancing. All he can see is Lilith. All he can hear are echoes of his pounding heart. He grabs Lilith's arm and sharply whispers in her ear, "We need to talk – *now*."

Lilith whips around. Samson's face and tone tell her all she needs to know. Before he could say another word, she came clean. "I'm sorry. They were harassing me, and they started to threaten me. I felt like I had no choice. I had to tell them *something*. Please, don't make a scene."

"Make a *scene*?" Samson's voice rises. "You're more worried about making a scene?"

"No, that's not what I meant." Lilith places her hand on his arm. "I'm so sorry." She is on the verge of tears. "You have to believe me. I didn't mean to—"

"Get off me," he snaps, pulling away. "If you felt threatened, why didn't you tell me? Instead, you asked me for the answer and gave it to them. I trusted you, Lilith! How could you do this to me?" The cost of the suits—obscenely expensive as they are—doesn't even matter. The ugly weight of her betrayal settles over him, nearly cutting off his air.

"I'm sorry, I...I—"

He lets out a bitter chuckle. Philistine blood, through and through. What did he expect? "You know what? I'm gone. I don't want to talk about this anymore. I can't even look at you right now." Samson storms out of the reception hall with Lilith right behind him in tears.

"Don't do this. Not today." Lilith's bridesmaids rush to her rescue.

Samson bursts through the double doors and charges down the brick stairs to his motorcycle—a black and chrome pro-street-style chopper—his first purchase with his winnings. The bike is embellished with ribbons, streamers, and a "Just Married" sign. He yanks off the decorations. After starting the engine, he sits there momentarily, chest heaving with each breath.

Lilith ruined everything. They had all fallen for a riddle that could never be solved. It was supposed to be easy money, but now I'm paying.

Tightness spreads across his shoulders and creeps down his arms as he grips the handlebars. Samson's ears burn with fury as he pops the transmission into gear and revs the engine. He leaves a ten-foot black streak on the concrete and a trail of white smoke in the air as he disappears into the night. All he has with him is his wallet and the hope that the wind on his face will wipe his cares away. Unfortunately, no matter how fast he rides, his thoughts keep racing back to the evening's events. Samson tunes out the roar of his engine, hearing only the incessant thoughts running through his mind.

There's no way they should have known that answer. I didn't tell anyone, not my parents, about the riddle or winning the Milk & Honey championship. They worry about me enough as it is.

I can't believe she told them. My parents were right; I should have married an Israelite. Maybe I did rush into this. Perhaps I don't know Lilith as well as I thought I did. I trusted her more than I'd ever trusted anyone, and she betrayed me.

As tears begin to well in his eyes, he wipes them with the back of his hand and speeds up, trying to outrun his anger, the scenery flashing in a blur. It takes a blinking fuel light and a pounding headache to pull him back to reality.

Samson looks for a familiar sight and realizes he'd passed through many small towns in the small coastal city of Ashkelon. A brightly lit gas sign stands ahead of him off the main road. It is a small gas station with two pumps. The area surrounding it is dark and overgrown with weeds. It reminds him of something he'd seen in a scary movie. Motorcycles and pickup trucks are parked around the building, and he can hear loud music from the gas pumps.

He fills his tank and heads inside to pay, noticing another sign that reads *Regular Old Gas Station*. It is funny and to the point. As he enters, he sees something he'd never seen before.

"A *bar* inside of a gas station? Only in Ashkelon," he laughs aloud, shaking his head. "I hope they serve food."

The small place is packed. At least fifty people are crowding in booths, standing against the wall, and sitting at the bar, where he eyes an open seat. The place looks like it hasn't been wiped down in years. He debates whether to search for somewhere else to eat, but his stomach rumble reminds him there might not be another place for miles. Reluctantly, he heads to the bar.

"I need to pay for my gas. Can I see a menu?" he asks, sitting down and nodding towards the bartender.

Staring at Samson, the bartender points at a sign above the bar:

MENU

Hamburgers – $5.00*

Hot Wings – $5.00*

Nachos – $5.00*

Price includes fries and a beer

"I'll have nachos and water." Some of the men at the bar hear his order and chuckle.

"Did you just walk into a bar at two in the morning and order *water*?" one mocked. Everyone around him laughs.

Glancing around the room, Samson notices some men staring out the window. He hopes these men will not be in any trouble tonight. After the fight with Lilith and trying to figure out how to pay for thirty suits, dealing with these clowns is the last thing he needs.

"Where are you going in that tux?" A man taunts Samson from a table across the room. "Who rides a motorcycle in a suit? Did you just come from a funeral?"

Samson laughs tiredly. "Look, guys, I'm having a rough night. I just came in to get something to eat. I'm not here to start any trouble."

"I think you came to the wrong place if you didn't want trouble," a messy-haired man cautions from a booth against the wall.

"Why don't you buy us a drink, rich boy?" says a husky man wearing a black leather biker vest. Samson notices that all the men are wearing the same black leather biker vests as this one. One of the men has the image of a wolf on his back.

"Rich…" Samson chuckles, thinking about his lost bet. "Look, I'm not buying you all drinks."

"I can tell by that bike of yours that you have money. And I'm not asking; I'm *telling* you to buy us all a round, Richie-Rich." The husky biker stands and saunters toward Samson. Another biker behind Samson rakes his fingers through Samson's locks. Samson jerks his head to face the biker.

"Come on, pretty boy. Where's my drink?"

Samson stands. "Trust me, if you touch me again, we are going to have a problem."

Menacing "oohs" and "ahhs" echo around the bar. The biker staggers away, mumbling. Samson turns away to face the bar, satisfied that he can now eat his food peacefully. As he takes a sip of water, he looks in the mirror above the bar, noticing the same biker standing behind him with a bottle in his hand, aiming for his head.

Samson quickly slides sideways. The biker misses and stumbles forward. Samson grabs him, smashes his head against the bar as hard as possible, and then tries to run for the door. But the bartender comes out from behind the counter and blocks his path. "You're not leaving just yet, are you?" protests the bartender, locking the door.

"I think you need to give us your wallet before you leave, rich boy," one of the bikers advises, smiling devilishly. Samson laughs.

"You think this is a joke?" questions the biker who'd lost a tooth after kissing the bar. The man punches Samson in the stomach and threatens, "Come off the wallet, pretty boy!"

As Samson struggles to catch his breath, another man knocks him into the bar. Samson catches himself on a folding chair that is against the wall. He hits his attacker over the head with the chair, sending the biker to the ground. As Samson yelled, "Have a seat!"

Samson starts hitting men with whatever he can reach. He feels as strong as a thousand men and as if nothing and no one could hurt him. He isn't afraid at all.

By the end of the fight, Samson is the only one standing on the tiled floor, bathed in blood.

Samson takes a moment to assess himself, ensuring none of the bloodstains belong to him.

"You gentlemen attempted to rob me, and now, well, just look at you!" he taunts, his words a subtle reminder of their failed endeavor. He contemplates leaving the scene but rifles through their pockets, not with overpowering strength, but with a shrewdness that belies his physical prowess. From their pockets, he liberates whatever meager sum of money he can find, leaving them in disarray and empty-handed.

"**L**et me get this straight," the short bald man behind the counter questions. "You want to buy *thirty* suits?"

"No, no. I want to open an account with enough money to buy thirty suits. The suits aren't for me."

The man calculates the amount, writes it on paper, and slides it to Samson. "We only take cash."

Samson reaches into his brown leather satchel and slowly counts out the money. "I'd like a receipt, please," Samson says, expressionless.

"Yes, sir." The clerk rushes to the back of the store with the money.

Samson's phone rings again; everyone, including Lilith, has called him countless times, but he isn't ready to talk to anyone—*especially* Lilith.

He is only in Timnah to pay off his debt and then intends to return to his family. His *real* family would never be disloyal to him. He thought it would be the same when he married—that he could trust Lilith—but he'd been wrong. And it hadn't taken her long at all to prove it.

"I have been worried sick about you," his mother says, fighting to hold back the tears. "We've called you. Where have you been?"

"Ma, calm down. I'm fine, I promise," he says, reassuring her with a hug.

Manoah hears the commotion and rushes downstairs to see his son. Samson doesn't want to alarm his parents, so he doesn't tell them about the debt or the bar fight;

he only needs more time apart from Lilith. "I just need time to think and clear my head."

"Okay, but if you need anything, your dad and I are here." Despite their concern, Samson's parents recognize that he will have to make his own decisions and deal with things in his way. Still, Hazel wonders if this would have happened if he had just listened to them.

Samson puts on a smile for his parents. "Love you guys. I'm going to bed now. I'm tired."

Everyone says goodnight, and Samson heads upstairs to his room. He silences his phone as it lights up, Lilith calling again. He sends her to voicemail and scrolls through the call log. Her father had called as well. As much as Samson likes him, he can't talk to him now.

Although Samson tells his parents he needs a few days, those days turn into weeks. He hangs around preparing for his next racing season and helps his parents with tasks. Hazel wants to repaint the living room and remove the wallpaper in the kitchen, so Samson and his father work on it together.

A month goes by, and Samson is still trying not to think about things and cool down, but he knows it is time to deal with the outside world again. He turns his phone on and finds his voicemail full. He doesn't listen to the messages; instead, he deletes them and decides it is time to see his wife in person.

Samson makes sure he looks good and smells even better before heading to Lilith's parents' house in his father's car. He hopes she will understand. Lilith had to know she was wrong.

He stops by a restaurant to grab her favorite meal, chicken enchiladas with sour cream sauce and picks up flowers. Arriving at her place, he holds his head high while approaching his in-law's house. Lilith's father answers the door after he knocks. "Samson, where have you been? We've been calling you for weeks!" he asks, surprised to see him on the doorstep. Shifting his eyes away, he continues, "Lilith doesn't want to see you right now."

"I know she's mad, but I must talk to her. I have some things for her."

"Why don't you tell me what you have to say, and I will pass the message along," her father says.

"Sir, can I talk to you, man to man?" Samson insists. He sits down and talks to Lilith's father, explaining his version of what happened the day of the wedding. He is shocked when her father understands and sympathizes.

"I didn't know. Lilith didn't tell me that part of the story." He pauses, his face solemn. "I wish we had known you were trying to clear your mind. Maybe it wouldn't have turned out like this."

"Like what?"

"I hate to tell you this, son, but when you didn't answer our calls, we gave up on you. We thought you weren't coming back. Weeks after the-wedding, she got the marriage annulled."

Samson doesn't respond. He is sure he has misunderstood him. Samson stares stoically as Lilith's father continues. "She's known him since elementary school. He was there for her through all of this, and they already had a bit of history. One day, they came to me and said they wanted to make it official, so they went down to the Justice of the Peace and had a quick ceremony."

Samson's heart sinks. The more he thinks about it, the angrier he becomes. He'd waited too long, and the first woman he'd ever loved ran off with someone else, and there was nothing he could do about it. "I guess I'll go." Samson hesitantly hands Lilith's father the food and the flowers. "Can you at least tell Lilith I wish her the best? And that I never meant to hurt her?"

"I sure will, Sam. You were like a son to me," he says warmly. "My youngest daughter is eighteen now. You sure you don't want to marry her so I can keep you in the family?" He attempts levity, but Samson's demeanor remains solemn.

Lilith's father, perceptive and sensitive to the situation, catches the shift in Samson's mood and offers a reassuring smile. "Take care, son. I'm sorry about all of this," he says, his genuine concern for Samson.

Samson waves and turns to leave. He collapses into the driver's seat, slamming his fist on the dashboard. The more he thinks about Lilith being with someone else, the more infuriated he becomes. "Who runs off with another man? These

Philistines marry for the gifts. It's just business to them. They've ruined my life!" He jams the key into the ignition, grappling with what he just learned. "They played me, but I'm going to send all of them a message."

Chapter 12

JUDGES 15:3-5

A new nightclub called *The Firefox Lounge* has opened in downtown Sorek. The Valley of Sorek is a city between Dan and Timnah. It is a haven for the rich and famous with its posh neighborhoods and ritzy nightlife, but it also has homes for average families and honest, down-to-earth residents who don't need to go clubbing on the weekends.

Samson knows it is the hottest spot in town. He parks across the street, angling his truck to catch a glimpse of the patrons on one of its busiest nights. He plans to dig up as much dirt as possible. To his surprise, not only are Timnah celebrities at the club but also well-known government officials are stepping out of limos and high-end cars.

Jackpot.

Samson is ecstatic; his plan is coming together. He will have to use his race winnings to hire help to pull it off, but to him, it is worth more than the cost. He jots down some notes and heads home. The next day, he places an ad in the local entertainment publication:

> *Casting Call: Attention alluring ladies aged 21 to 30! An extraordinary expedition into the realm of dating dynamics beckons. Picture this: The illustrious Ambassador Hotel sets the stage for auditions, commencing promptly at 10 am. A tantalizing opportunity awaits, crowned by a generous $300 compensation for those who partake. Dare to be part of this captivating saga!*

When he arrives at the hotel that morning, a thousand women are waiting to audition. Samson explains to the women they will be paired up and assigned to one man. "To receive payment, you must get a picture of them in a compromising situation. Use any means necessary: flirt with him, seduce him, do whatever you have to do."

"That's easy," one of the women blurts. The others laugh in agreement. Samson smiles, loving their enthusiasm.

He works through his selection process and chooses the women he thinks will be perfect to execute his plan. He then gives them precise instructions about his expectations.

Before the women begin their assignment, Samson sends one of them into the club on a fact-finding mission. He needs to know the club's layout and what goes on inside. – he knows that if he goes in, someone will recognize him.

The next day, the young woman reached out to him, unveiling a world of intrigue. She painted a vivid image of an exclusive, sophisticated nocturnal haven. In her words, it was a place where men held coveted memberships, obtained through substantial fees, while women were graciously granted complimentary entry.

As she described, the higher the membership tier, the more extraordinary the treatment bestowed upon the fortunate men who held it. There were strict requirements for women: beauty and impeccable attire were non-negotiable. Falling short of these standards meant being turned away at this elusive sanctuary's threshold.

Samson writes it all down; he will need to emphasize the standards the women need to meet. He now has everything in place and is ready to begin. He compiles a list of men and assigns a pair of women to each one. He gives them until the end of the week to go to the club and meet their mark. Some women come back within a day. Samson is in awe of the excellence of the photos; from inappropriate sexual situations to drug binges, his plan is exceeding his expectations.

One by one, Samson compiles his file. He has chosen the perfect venue. The repercussions of this information could financially cripple the entire Philistine community. Once he has all the evidence he needs, he contacts a local tabloid magazine to sell his photos. His price is $500,000. Once the magazine receives a sample, they willingly pay every penny.

Samson pays the girls off and still has hundreds of thousands in his pocket. But this isn't about the money; it's about making *them pay*. The cash was merely a bonus.

Chapter 13

JUDGES 15:6-7

"The ripple effect will be enormous," the news anchor cautions. "There are many industries touched by this scandal. There is no way to gauge the depth of the economic fallout."

Satisfied, Samson laid back on his bed before turning off the news. Word quickly reverberated all over town. The media, online, and social networks are abuzz. Everyone wants to know about the public officials involved. There are distraught wives on the news and confused children. It is a firestorm of mayhem. Samson basks in the mess he orchestrated and then heads to the den.

His parents sit around the television in their den, watching the media frenzy. "That makes the third CEO that has stepped down today," Manoah remarks.

"I think they are all quitting before this gets worse," Hazel assumes.

"I saw some of the photos," Manoah replies. "I don't know if it can get any worse." Samson finds himself smiling, pleased with the results of his actions. "Sam, why are you smiling?"

"I'm just in shock, that's all," he replies, feigning concern for the men.

"The entire situation is utterly mind-boggling," Hazel remarked. "I wouldn't be surprised if an extensive investigation were launched to take down those corrupt public officials, and amazingly, their Philistine-like conduct remained shrouded in secrecy, hidden from public awareness."

Timnah citizens are in an uproar, asking questions. *Where did the media get the pictures? Who were the women involved?* They have to be a part of something bigger. *Were the men targeted at random?* People have their doubts.

The local detectives begin their investigation by questioning individuals who were present at the club and the women captured in the incriminating photographs. They probe deeper, asking whether anyone had orchestrated this situation or if financial incentives had been involved. Despite the mounting pressure, none of them are willing to implicate others. Each woman asserts her innocence, adamantly denying any external involvement. However, the seasoned detectives can sense a different truth lurking beneath the surface.

Over fifty of Timnah's high-level public officials, CEOs, and business owners meet on the top floor of a downtown office to minimize the risk of being caught. Each sneaks away from families, and the reporters secretly hang around their homes to meet.

"I'm not sure if bribery will do the trick," Judge Malroy conveyed. "These women either possess an unwavering loyalty to the mysterious figure behind this or are deeply concerned about their potential involvement." Despite various enticements, the women remained silent.

The mood in the room is ominous. The men scoff and shift in their seats. Beads of sweat appear on some of their foreheads. Ideas are tossed around the room like frisbees.

"I have an idea," a pastor speaks up. He is furious about pictures of him snorting cocaine. He not only lost his family that day but was forced to step down from the pulpit—the church his father and grandfather preached before him. "These women are in it for the money. Let's offer a substantial amount of money for a tell-all book. Wiley Wilton's publishing company can front the offer."

"I agree," Wiley says. He owns one of the largest publishing companies around and is also livid about all the damage these photos are causing. "It would look like a legitimate offer."

It doesn't take long for the women to come forward once the offer is made. Dollar signs entice them to sign the fake book deal and tell the Philistines everything they want to know. When they learn who'd set them up, they are enraged.

Surveillance is placed on Samson's ex-wife's home to make sure their entire family will be present when revenge is exacted. Nothing would crush him more than this. At three in the morning, men in black masks spring into action. They place chains on the house doors to keep anyone from escaping. They pour gasoline all around the house and light it on fire, starting with the front and back doors. They circle the house, throwing Molotov cocktails through each window, setting every inch of the brick home aflame.

Neighbors hear screams and run to call the fire department. The flames rise, and the roaring flames can eventually be heard as the house crumbles.

Chapter 14
JUDGES 15:7-8

Samson stares at the television. He isn't sure if he's heard the story correctly.

In the news this morning, a Timnah family was barricaded in their house last night and set on fire by arsonists. Two family members survived but are fighting for their lives at County Hospital. The father, a local talent agent who owned MMS Modeling, and his eldest daughter died in the 2-alarm blaze.

He changes the channel and checks another news station. He watches as the reporter details the night's events:

The fire started sometime during the night. Neighbors say they heard screams but could not enter the house because of the size of the blaze and the chains on the doors. Once firefighters arrived, they could break down the door and pull two people out. We are told the mother and youngest daughter are in Timnah Medical Center in critical condition with third- and fourth-degree burns.

Samson's gaze remained fixed on the television screen, his emotions plunging into an icy abyss. Yet, amidst the chilling despair, a surge of anger ignites and snaps him back to this harsh reality.

The tragic loss of the father and the newlywed eldest daughter proved insurmountable for the valiant efforts of the fire department. In response, the compassionate neighbors rallied, their unwavering support manifesting in a vigil spanning the police station, hospital, and local TV station, where they tirelessly aided the ongoing investigation.

Samson stormed into the garage, seizing his helmet. He wiped away his tears with the back of his hand before securing the helmet firmly upon his head. Today, his sorrow has to take a backseat to an urgent mission. His destination: Timnah. Fortunately, his parents were absent when he departed, sparing him from their attempts to dissuade his furious pursuit. As he revved his bike's engine, a conflicted thought gripped his mind: *I can't go to Timnah and let my rage consume me.*

Samson rides to Lilith's neighborhood and stops one house over from the charred remains of her family home. He can't breathe for a moment; all the air sucked out of his lungs. The thought of them trapped in the house with fire and smoke filling the rooms makes him nauseous. He tries to shake it off and stay focused on why he is here: he needs information.

One of the neighbors is sitting on his porch drinking coffee. Samson approaches the man. "I lost someone in the fire," Samson explains, "and I need any information you can provide." The man turns away, walks back into his house, and closes the door.

Samson continues door-to-door, trying to talk to the neighbors. The woman watering her lawn pretends not to hear him. He walks further down the street and tries to stop a man jogging with his dog, but he continues to run right past Samson. Some neighbors peek at him through their curtains but hide behind their doors. Those who opened their doors to listen to Samson's well-practiced speech didn't say much.

Deflated, he almost knocks down an older man reaching for his morning paper. "I'm sorry," Samson apologizes. "My name is Samson." Samson extends his hand to the gray-haired gentleman. The older man looks at the extended hand, nods, and stares at Samson. "It was my…," he pauses, "…friends that were killed in that fire last night."

The man glances up but doesn't respond. "I know you may be afraid to talk, just as some of your neighbors are, but you must care about what happened last night.

Someone can do something like this and get away with it. This was someone I loved, someone that meant a lot to me. I need to know who did this."

"I understand why people don't want to talk," the man counters, "but I'm not scared. I've lived in this city too long to let someone run me off or scare me into allowing something like this to happen without consequences." The man kicks at a weed and spits in disgust. "I don't know what you will do with this information, young man, but just know they won't go down without a fight."

Samson nods, not wanting to interrupt. The older man looks around and then continues. "I saw unfamiliar cars in the neighborhood 4 nights in a row. They stood out because the people just sat in them for hours. That is not normal for this part of town." When the older man finishes recounting the events of the night before, Samson thanks him, gets on his bike, and heads towards the police station to wait for the Chief.

Samson pulls into a convenience store a block away from the station – he can watch the station while he pretends to fill his tires with air. When his cell phone rings, he debates whether or not to answer. He doesn't want to be distracted and miss the Chief, but it is his mother.

Her voice is broken. "I heard, honey. I'm so sorry. How are you doing?"

Samson swallows against the rise of pain. "I'm good. I'm in front of the police station. I was thinking about turning myself in for speeding. Is everything okay with you?"

"What?" Hazel says, panicked. "What are you talking about?"

On second thought, "I'm kidding, mom. Don't worry."

"We should be together right now, Sam," she whispers, her voice carrying a lingering plea. "Please come home. I need to know you're okay."

"I'm okay," he remarks, scanning a group of officers walking out of the building. "I have to go, but I'll see you later tonight or in the morning."

"I'm praying for you, okay? Love you."

"Love you, too, Ma."

Samson slides his phone back into his pocket. Fifteen minutes later, the Police Chief leaves the station and climbs into his white, city-issued SUV. The Chief makes a right out of the parking lot and heads north. Samson puts on his helmet and speeds up to avoid losing him. The pursuit ends sooner than expected. The Police Chief lives only 2 miles from the station, on a long, narrow street off the main road. The area around his house is covered with shrubbery.

Samson rides past the yellow and white cottage-style home as the sunlight fades. He parks his motorcycle in an alley around the corner and walks through alleyways to the Police Chief's back fence. Using a knothole in the fence, he spies on the Police Chief.

The Chief walks around the kitchen, talking on the telephone. Samson grabs the top of the fence, vaults over, and lands softly. He reaches into his back pocket for his knife. It isn't there. He peers through the fence into the alley and sees it on the ground. He shakes his head in disgust and is about to climb back over the fence when he hears the back porch door open. Samson freezes.

"I can't make it tonight, but I'll come through tomorrow." The Chief is still on his phone. He walks toward a shed in the rear corner of the yard. Samson squats to hide behind the brush in the corner; the Chief is now in the woodshed, fiddling around. Samson creeps closer and can hear him on the phone.

"Hold on one sec... Hello?" Samson ducks, thinking he's been spotted, but the tone of the Chief's voice changes. "I told you I had to come home first and change. I'm coming. What time is it now?"

Samson listens to make sure the Chief remains in the shed. He examines the yard for another weapon and spots a brick beside the fence. He tiptoes over, but once he comes upon it, he realizes it is a small pile of dirt. His presence causes the neighbor's German Shepherd to bark. "Shut up, you mutt!" the Chief bellows.

With his knife on the other side of the fence, still weaponless, Samson scans the well-lit yard again. If the Chief comes out in the dark, he can approach stealthily and take the gun-toting man down. Samson creates noise to keep the dog barking, then jumps up to knock out the light.

"Where are you? Have we crossed paths there before? My memory's fuzzy. Third and Market. That rundown neighborhood? Can you give me the exact address? It's Three fifty-five Market Street, a red brick two-story house with a basement. Alright, noted. Give me until around 8:30 or 9. Maybe push it to around 10-ish."

The Chief emerged from the shed, glued to his phone screen. But before he could react, Samson charged forward, unleashing a mighty blow that sent the Chief sprawling to the ground. The phone went airborne, sailing out of the Chief's hand, skidding across the lawn, and disappearing into the darkness.

Samson rushes into the small entryway of the shed and searches for a weapon. He grabs a Phillips head screwdriver out of an open tool chest while the now bloodied Chief scrambles to his feet and comes at him. They tussle in the darkness as the Chief tries to gain possession of the screwdriver, but Samson is too strong. Samson throws the Chief back onto the shelf, causing him to fall to the ground once again. The unstable, hand-made tool shelf rocks before landing on top of the Chief, the contents pinning him to the floor. He wails in agony.

"Who are you? What do you want?" he cries out. He tries to free his legs before eventually giving up, lying motionless on the floor, squinting to focus his eyes in the dark.

Samson's dark shimmering locks and the right side of his face shine through the open door in the moonlight as he steps closer. "Hmm...Samson," the Chief grumbles, recognizing him. "I knew eventually you'd come. Why don't you kill me now and put me out of my misery?" he taunts, becoming more brazen as he speaks. "Kill me like I killed your girl."

"I will, but I want you to die slowly. That's how my wife died, isn't it?" The image of the charred house plays in his mind, and then an image of Asher's gray eyes flashes, and the pain threatens to knock him over. How many more of his people lived with this vicious, unrelenting ache?

"She was Philistine!" His throat feels like gravel. Revulsion fills him. "If you could murder one of your own, is it any surprise that you've been stealing from, killing, and ruining the lives of millions of Israelites all these decades just for the fun of it?"

The man's thin lips curl, a mask of wicked humor. "Guess not."

Samson's breaths come out in ragged chops. It takes everything in him to keep from smashing the man immediately into the concrete abutment beside them.

Suddenly, the smell of gas fumes fills the air. He looks around and realizes a can of gasoline spilled on the floor next to the shelf during the commotion. Samson watches as the gas begins to run under the Chief's legs. At that moment, he knows how this is going to end.

"Do what you have to do," the Chief says confidently, jamming his hand into his pocket and pulling out a crushed box of cigarettes. Samson watches as he empties the box of cigarettes, looking for his lighter. They both noticed it on the floor about a yard away. Samson kicks it to him, allowing the Chief to indulge in this last wish. With a scrunched face, the Chief lights his cigarette and takes a long drag. "I could hear your wife begging us to let them out."

Samson struggles to keep his composure. "Keep digging your grave."

"You're going to kill me anyway." The Chief shrugs his shoulders and sighs as he puffs on his cigarette. "What does it matter?" The longer Samson stares at his face, the angrier he becomes. The Police Chief is smug and unrepentant. Samson walks over to the small window and cracks it open. "What are you doing? Just kill me already," the Chief cajoles, inhaling deeply.

"Oh, I'm going to, but you aren't going to die fast. I want you to suffer and feel what my family felt as they burned. I want you to smell your flesh burning and feel the fire penetrate your skin."

Samson yanks the cigarette out of his mouth and drops it into the gasoline on the floor. "You should have come for me instead."

Quickly, it goes up in flames, and the Chief lets out a piercing howl, agony filling the air as his legs catch on fire and the flames move up his thighs, eagerly consuming every inch of the man's skin.

Chapter 15

JUDGES 15:7-8

"Will that be all, sir?" the cashier asks, briefly glancing up.

"Yes," Samson replies.

"Your total is $12.56…out of $20." She counts his change out of the register and hands it to him. "Thank you. Have a nice night."

Samson throws the sack into his solo saddlebag. He inhales the crisp night air as he speeds toward his destination with his long, dark locks blowing in the wind.

"Study long, study wrong," grumbled a man with a worn ball cap, his salt-and-pepper beard catching the dim light. A solitary overhead fixture cast a soft halo around the card table as rock music hummed in the background. A gentleman in a sleek black cap tapped his fingers impatiently, his steel-gray eyes locked on the player across from him, who scrutinized his hand of cards intently.

"Hurry up and play," the man in the worn ball cap and salt-and-pepper beard urged, his impatience palpable.

"I fold," sighed a bespectacled man, pushing his luck by leaning his wooden chair precariously on two legs, nonchalantly discarding his cards onto the table.

"You knew you were folding ten minutes ago," jested a third player, his eyes concealed beneath a crimson baseball cap. "That's why I detest playing with you."

"Just shuffle the cards," retorted the man in dark-rimmed glasses, gesturing for the others to follow suit in discarding their hands. "When's the Chief showing up? My stomach's growling."

"Don't think you can change the subject just because you're losing," one of the men countered.

Samson's bicycle carries him onto Market Street, and he steers it with a purposeful gaze, scanning both sides of the road. His eyes flit from one building to another, seeking the telltale street numbers. The sun's golden rays playfully dance on the storefront windows, casting dappled patterns on the sidewalk as if nature acknowledges his quest's gravity.

Finally, his determined search is rewarded when his eyes lock on the sought-after address. He eases his bicycle to a stop, pulling it up to rest three houses from the target location. The neighborhood exudes an air of quiet familiarity, with houses lining the street, each harboring its secrets. Samson's chosen parking spot is right in front of a house marked by a "For Sale" sign, the words promising new beginnings and endless possibilities.

He pulls three sodas and two bottles of pure acetone nail polish remover from the plastic bag. After a glance around, he pours the soda out of the glass bottles onto the street and then fills the bottles with acetone, leaving one bottle half-full. After taking a rag from his back pocket, he tears it into strips and stuffs them halfway into the bottles, exposing half of the strips. Samson grabs matches from his bag and places them in his pocket. He walks across the lawn to the red brick two-story house with a basement. A light shines inside the home. There are no curtains on the window; Samson can see a man in front of the refrigerator pulling out a handful of beer cans. "How many do we need?" Samson hears him holler.

Samson doesn't see anyone else in the room. He watches as the man takes the beer and walks downstairs into what appears to be a basement. Once Samson sees no one else is on the main floor of the house, he tries the windows, but they are locked. He turns the knob on the front door, and to his surprise, it opens.

Confident the coast is clear, he moves in. Music blares from the basement. Samson turns off all the upstairs lights and sets the three bottles down at the top of the staircase. He takes the bottle of acetone and pours the remaining liquid around the house. Opening the basement door, he starts down the stairs. He has a bottle in each hand and is heading towards the remaining men involved in his wife's murder.

He only tiptoes halfway down the stairs when he reaches one that betrays him. Heart pounding, he freezes, hoping they don't hear him. "About time you got here!" one of the men groans in Samson's direction. "Bring down more beer. I hope you brought snacks, Chief."

"Hey, you guys smell that?" one of the men asks, noticing the smell of nail polish remover.

"I don't smell anything. You're going crazy." They all laugh.

"No, I smell something," the same guy insists. "You don't smell it?"

"It's probably something you stepped in outside." They all laugh again.

Samson pulls out his lighter and lights the rags. He now jogs down the remaining stairs, taking two at a time, until standing at the base of the steps.

"About time," another man says without raising his head. When Samson doesn't respond, all at once, everyone's gaze meets the flames coming from the bottles in his hands.

Without a word, Samson throws the two flaming Molotov cocktails in his hands onto the middle of the poker table. They explode, and fire rains down on the men. Everyone shrieks in fear. As they jump out of their seats trying to put out the flames, Samson stands quietly, watching as they panic. Satisfied, he runs back up the stairs, locks the door behind him, and slides a chair from the kitchen under the doorknob. Samson lights the final bottle and tosses it in the kitchen. The bottle crashes against the tile, and the flames quickly spread across the floor.

Stepping out the front door, Samson returns to his bike, the cool night air embracing him. He kickstarts the motorcycle, its engine purring to life, breaking the eerie silence of the neighborhood. A profound stillness prevails, interrupted only by distant traffic sounds that echo in the emptiness.

As the adrenaline surge of the night gradually subsides, Samson's mind replays the Chief's murder. Doubts and fears creep in as he rides through the dimly lit streets, his racing thoughts tormenting him. Should he go home? The realization strikes him that they'd first search his parents' house if he's discovered. It's a risk he can't afford to take.

His searching eyes land on a dilapidated motel as he enters the part of town known as Etam. Samson eases his motorcycle into a parking space in front of the motel's office. He enters, pays for a room, and accepts the key from the manager, the weight of his choices settling upon him in this dimly lit sanctuary.

After showering, he glances at the digital clock on the nightstand—3:44 a.m. *I can't believe it's almost four in the morning. I need to get some rest.*

He pulls back the dingy comforter and lays on the cool sheets of the queen-size bed. Whenever he closes his eyes, images of the flames covering the men's faces at the poker table haunt him. *Did I go too far?*

Chapter 16
JUDGES 15:9-10

"**M**y dog was barking a lot, so I knew something was wrong."

The Chief's neighbor is outside, providing the information she can to the police officer. "I glanced outside to see what he was barking at, and I saw someone in the Chief's backyard down in the grass."

"Did you get a look at his face?" the Deputy asks her. But before the woman can answer, the officer notices the onlookers getting too close to the caution tape. "Hey! Please step back." The Deputy walks in the direction of the crowd, pushing them back. Many of the Philistines believe the fire on Market Street is drug-related but find it too coincidental that the Police Chief also died in a fire the same night on the other side of town. The police question everyone in both neighborhoods.

Most people don't want to talk or get involved, but one of the Police Chief's neighbors is happy to tell what she saw when the Deputy returns. "No, I couldn't see his face, but he had long, dark dreadlocks," the elderly woman recounts.

The Deputy jots down notes. "Do you remember anything else? Any strange smells or sounds? Do you remember seeing anyone else in the area around the same time?"

"Well, I heard a loud noise, like an engine or a hot rod."

"Like a motorcycle?" the officer offers.

"Yeah, like a motorcycle," she nods.

Sounds like Samson, the Deputy thinks, as he smiles and thanks the woman for her time.

Back at the station, the Deputy gathers his men to plan a massive search for Samson. They go to his parent's home and visit his friends and neighbors. They checked local businesses he frequented and the track in Timnah where he practiced when they failed to find him.

Reports are all over town that the police are looking for a man dressed in a black hoodie with long dreadlocks. A local truck driver says he saw Samson on his motorcycle near Lehi. The police raced to Lehi and set up a base camp. They prepare to question everyone until they find him, searching cars randomly as they enter the town.

After days of searching, the people of Lehi became frustrated. No one understands how one man keeps an entire town from living in peace. The Lehi police stepped in after angry phone calls by citizens came to the local police and city government. The mayor calls a meeting. "We have been more than accommodating, allowing you to come into Lehi and set up roadblocks to search for your suspect. Now, you're upsetting our residents. We can't have that," the mayor complains.

"We have assisted you, gentlemen, in every way we can, but this is ridiculous," the sheriff agrees.

"I think you're forgetting one thing, gentlemen. Samson is a powder keg that can blow at any minute," the Timnah Police Deputy warns. "Samson must be found. The Philistine mob protestors are unpredictable. Who knows what they will do? We ensure they don't destroy your property or harm your residents. We will if you want us to leave, but we can't say what will happen. You saw the fire they set in Timnah that killed the father and daughter."

The residents of Lehi don't take his threats lightly. They know their cooperation is keeping their city and residents safe. If they don't allow the Timnah police to continue, their present situation could worsen. There have been small fights around town and minor vandalism complaints, but nothing the city can't manage.

After the meeting, the mayor instructed his sheriff to do everything possible to assist the Philistines. They need to get them out of their city. "I don't care how you do it, but we must find Samson. We don't want them to think we aren't doing our part to help in their investigation."

The Sheriff sets his men into action. They talk to people at local bars, restaurants, and around town. They spread the word that a reward is available for information about Samson's whereabouts. His men follow each tip.

Days into the search, an anonymous tip shows that Samson is staying in a motel in a part of Lehi called Etam. The Lehi police department descended onto Etam like angry locusts.

Chapter 17

JUDGES 15:11-13

S amson's room is filled with worn, dingy furniture at least two decades old.

There is a faint, musty smell of mothballs and dust, but he isn't concerned with the décor or the odor. It is cheap, and it leaves him alone with his thoughts. He needs time to think to make his next move.

As the sun begins its routine descent behind the Etam landscape, Samson lazily flips through the channels on the television. The last week has been a difficult one. He'd been alone and couldn't go home. To make matters worse, all he has been able to think about was watching those men die, the horrific scenes playing trapped in his head. He knows it was wrong to kill them. He feels no solace as these heinous acts have not brought back his ex-wife and her father. He desperately wants to call his father to help him figure out what to do, but he can't involve his parents. He won't.

With its creaky floors and paint-starved walls, the motel hunkers on the outskirts of town next to the railroad tracks. Two Lehi officers sit in their government-issued van in the parking lot, keeping their eyes on the motorcycle registered to Samson.

"I think we should go in and get him," one officer muses to his muscular partner. "We were here first anyway. We can't let someone else come and make the arrest."

"You're right," the muscular one replies, pounding his fist on the dashboard. "Do you know how great it would look if we were the ones to bring him in? I'll call the captain." The officer calls his superior to get the approval to bring Samson in.

"But wait until backup arrives before you attempt it in case there is a problem," the captain commands. The officers smile and thrust their fists in the air as if they've won a prize. To them, Samson is a prize. The type of prize that will ensure a promotion. All they need to do is reel the big fish in. "Let me know once you have him secured."

"We will, sir!"

"Good. When you've got him in custody, call me back."

"Yes, sir!" They grin, hanging up with their captain.

"Dude, do you realize how popular we will be?"

"Trust me, I know. We'll get promoted to Sergeant."

"I don't care about being a Sergeant. I want to be a detective."

The headlights of another squad car cut through the thick woods. The officer driving the car cuts the lights, and the vehicle coasts until it stops next to their van. The backup officer, who doesn't look old enough to have a driver's license, exits the squad car and approaches the passenger side window of the muscular officer's vehicle. "Heard you boys needed backup," the pimple-faced officer murmurs. He is small and thin and wouldn't have posed a threat to a band of senior citizens on his own. "Finally, I get to use these new cuffs."

The two officers sitting in the van don't bother replying. They are determined to make this call on their own; a pimply skin officer is just a form of insurance as far as they are concerned. The headlights of more cars approach, lighting up the tree line. Without warning, the muscular police officer grabs a bullhorn and exits the van. He stands next to his vehicle and barks into the bullhorn. "Samson, come out! We know you're in there, Samson! We know you can hear us!"

Samson tosses and turns, thinking the voices he hears are in his dream.

"Samson!" As he continues to hear his name being called, his eyes shoot open, and he jolts out of bed. He uses the heels of his hands to dab the sleep from his eyes.

"*Samson!*" Samson's head is on a swivel as he searches the room's dark corners. It isn't until he hears his name called again that the mental fog lifts enough for him to realize that the person yelling his name is outside.

Samson staggers to the window. He parts the dusty curtains to see the motel parking lot, blinking, wiping his eyes, thinking it must be his imagination. He sees what seems to be thousands of men outside in the parking lot, all shouting his name. Some men wield nightsticks; others have guns.

"Samson, we can do this the easy way or the hard way. The choice is yours!" Samson knew he would eventually have to face what he did, so he opened the door and glanced out over the crowd.

"We need you to come with us! The Philistines are in our town tearing the place to shreds!"

"Yeah, this is all your fault!" another officer chimes in.

"Calm down," Samson replies. "Why don't you tell them to get out of your town and go back to where they came from? I only did to them what they did to me. Kick them out."

"Kick them out?" the bull-horned officer asks rhetorically. "Did you forget they run the country? You can't run the government."

"They weren't too smart. The big, bad government couldn't find me. They had to use my people against me."

"Samson, you know why we're here. They're threatening our families."

"You're going to sacrifice me for your family?"

"Our problem isn't with you. We won't hurt you, but you need to come with us." Samson thinks about it. He knows what they are capable of, but what choice does he have? He reluctantly walks out with measured steps, holding one hand high and using the other forearm to shield his eyes from the blinding headlights.

The muscular police officer cranes his neck to see his partner. "Don't forget to call the captain."

The rookie takes out his cell phone. "I know what to do," he growls before phoning the captain. "Captain, we got him." The officer listens intently. "Yes, sir. Okay, will do."

Placing the bullhorn on the hood of the van, the muscular officer races over to Samson so that he can slap the cuffs on him before one of the others does. He then escorts Samson back to the van and shoves him in the back. Climbing into the driver's seat, the officer pants slightly, his adrenaline causing his heart to race. He eyes his young partner. "Well? What did the captain say?"

"I don't want Samson to hear." The rookie glances at Samson. Frown lines streak across his forehead as he runs his fingers through his hair. "I'll tell you the plan once we get there."

"Dummy, the glass is soundproof. He can't hear you." They pull the vehicle onto the road and head back toward Lehi.

"He wants us to take him to the meat packing plant up on the hill. He said he would send someone up there to meet us. We will leave the car and return tonight and pick it up."

"Wait, I thought that place closed down?"

"It did. The local food safety and inspection service had a sting there a while back and found out they were mixing ground beef with horse, donkey, and mule meat and selling it."

"Oh yeah, I remember that."

"They had to shut their doors."

"If the place is closed, there's no electricity, water, nothing. Why take Samson there?"

"Captain said they had someone turn on the electricity for the day. Everything else will remain off. The lights will be all they need."

"Why did they pick that place anyway, and who will meet us there?"

"You ask too many questions."

Samson sits in the back of the van, unsure what is about to happen but knowing it won't be good.

The officer turns off the main road and drives down a long street, passing rows of loading docks. Following the winding road, he turns and pulls up to the service garage in the far-left corner of the cul-de-sac. His partner hops out and lifts the roller door of the old warehouse building so they can pull the police van inside. As they make their way to the bottom of the ramp, six all-black SUVs pull up to the building, followed by a stream of never-ending lights. A slew of men dressed in all black and wearing shades step into view. The muscular officer elbows his partner, speculating. "Who are they? The Secret Service?"

Chapter 18
JUDGES 15:14-19

Samson's heart races as the van comes to an abrupt halt. He strains to hear any clue about his destination, but the silence is stifling, only amplifying his fear. His eyes dart around the confined space, searching for any sign of escape, but despair settles in as the men exit without releasing him.

Desperation fuels Samson as he leans forward, scanning the empty front cab. Minutes tick by ominously. The absence of police intensifies his dread, prompting him to frantically fidget with his handcuffs in a futile attempt to break free.

In the distance, a foreboding rumble grows, accompanied by eerie chants. Samson squints out the window but sees nothing.

As the voices approach, Samson's pulse quickens. He shuts his eyes, a silent plea for deliverance. Summoning every ounce of strength, he strains against the handcuffs. To his astonishment, the chain snaps. Through the window, he glimpses a man shouting to someone beyond sight.

A cacophonous banging on the van echoes like thunder. Panic surges through Samson, his body twitching at the assault on his senses. Voices demand his surrender, their threats reverberating. Samson retreats to a defensive stance, prepared for a confrontation as the van's doors rattle under the men's assault.

As the door opens, Samson explodes forward, hurling himself at it. The doors swing wide, sending the men tumbling. Samson seizes one door, tearing it off its hinges, wielding it like a Spartan warrior.

Two more assailants charge, but Samson, still handcuffed, leaps onto the pavement, becoming the aggressor. Shielded by the door, he retaliates. The dust clears in less than a minute, leaving Samson the last one standing.

He spots a looming building connected to the warehouse in his peripheral vision. Time is scarce. His downed attackers groan but aren't out of the fight. Samson sprints to the building's door, but it remains closed. With night's eerie sounds surrounding him, the door mocks his feeble attempts.

Samson grasps a nearby rock, smashing the glass above the door handle, gaining entry. The abandoned lobby is filled with old furniture and scattered papers. Panic urges him to find a hiding place or a weapon. Surely, there has to be something he can use for protection.

As expected, his pursuers regroup and approach. Samson hears their menacing voices. An arrow points him to a slaughterhouse, and he rushes toward it. The door yields to his frantic push. Samson scours each room for a weapon inside, but only broken tools lie on a metal table.

Near a conveyor belt, a pile of animal bones catches his eye. Samson sifts through it, finding a jagged jawbone, his makeshift weapon. He hurries out of the room, seeking an escape route down a long corridor flanked by locked doors. Frustration boils over as he jiggles each handle, muttering in the hope of a miracle, *"I've got to find someplace to hide."*

He comes to the final door, and it flies open. Behind it is a staircase with emergency exit signs. Samson ascends four flights, taking two steps at a time, nonstop, until he hears the door slam behind him and more voices calling out. "He's in the staircase!"

On the fourth floor, Samson sees a sign that reads *Exit to Warehouse Roof.* He pushes the door open and finds himself on the roof of the connecting warehouse. Even an infant could tell the roof was an accident waiting to happen. Pieces of sheet metal and wood are used to cover up the rotting spots. The areas that aren't covered with debris feel like mush—Samson wonders for a moment if he is walking on a foamy surface.

While sprinting to the other side of the building, dodging the gaps he can see, he misjudges a step, and his leg falls through a spot in the roof. A shark had never bitten Samson, but he would bet all he owned that those metal sheets slicing through his flesh felt similar to a shark bite. "Ugh!" Samson growls, his quivering lips stifling the wail that begs to be unleashed. "C'mon, Samson. You can't stop. They'll be on this roof any second now."

Samson carefully extracts his mangled leg from the hole. The gash on his leg resembles a gaping wound, oozing crimson liquid like a ruptured artery. The searing pain surges through him, but he knows he must postpone addressing it for now.

With a grimace, Samson surveys the remainder of the rooftop. His trained eye identifies a potential route. Hopping on one leg, he makes his way to a corner he deems structurally sound, gingerly tapping his foot to confirm its ability to bear his weight.

The roof door swings wide, revealing an ominous sight. "There he is!" Four men armed with pipes and bats approach Samson, ready for another confrontation. However, with his leg hemorrhaging blood like a ruptured vessel, Samson is in no shape to oblige their desires.

Samson glances over the rooftop's edge, then back at the menacing men. "Don't jump!" one of the men sternly commands.

Once more, Samson peers down at the ground below, the distant sounds of their heavy boots approaching echoing in his ears. The men behind him slowly pursue, and he senses the walls closing in. He's run out of escape routes. For a moment, an eerie silence envelops the rooftop. Samson understands he has no choice but to confront the impending threat.

"Get 'em!" The ringleader commands, and his comrades charge forward, wielding their weapons with menace. Their mouths are wide open, releasing primal shouts reverberating through the night air. They resemble characters from a poorly choreographed action movie, too caught up in theatrics to notice the fragile rooftop buckling beneath their collective weight. Blind anger has clouded their judgment, and the roof gives way, swallowing them whole in a chaotic collapse that unfolds with breathtaking speed.

Samson, closer to the edge, peers through the hole. He's met with a surreal scene: a pile of motionless bodies, debris, and swirling dust. The rooftop's structure now lies in ruins. Without wasting a moment, he hops back across the edge of the remaining structure, gingerly opens the door just enough to ensure no one remains, and slips back into the safety of the stairwell.

As he descends the staircase, the faint voices of the remaining men below reach his ears. These are the ones who hadn't ventured to the rooftop, and Samson's heart continues to race as he inches further away from the perilous scene above.

Come on, Samson, think ...think...THINK! His thoughts race like he had on the racetrack. Samson leans his back against the wall, breathing deeply while he debates his next move. Then, he comes up with an idea. "I've got to get out of this stairwell," he mumbles.

Emerging from the dimly lit stairwell onto the third floor, he hobbles towards a pair of elevators and inserts his trembling fingers between the tightly closed doors. With every ounce of his dwindling strength, he strains against the unyielding metal.

Finally, the doors relent, revealing the elevator shaft's stark emptiness stretching above and below. The car rests silently at the lowest point, but his keen eyes catch the faint grooves etched into the wall, a sign of a downward alternative path.

Aware that time is not on his side, he doesn't hesitate. He slips into the elevator shaft, clinging to whatever footholds he can find, a one-story climb away from the elevator car below. His pulse quickens as he descends, each movement measured and deliberate.

However, as he lowers himself, the distant voices of another group of men reach his ears from above, an ominous reminder that he's not alone in this perilous descent.

"He's in the elevator shaft!" In his haste to escape, Samson forgets that he is bleeding like a stuck pig. A blind man could've tracked him.

One by one, the men climb into the elevator shaft while Samson descends toward the bottom as fast as possible. When he reaches the basement, he opens the hatch on top of the elevator and drops inside. Their voices and steps grow closer, so Samson does the only thing he can think of—he pushes the elevator button with hopes that the electricity is still on.

It is.

A smile creases Samson's exhausted face as the elevator creeps upward, and the men start to yell.

"It's moving!"

"Go back up!"

"Hurry up, it's going to crush us!"

Doom hangs heavy in the air. The anguished yells of the men assail Samson's ears, their desperate cries echoing through the confined space. Each guttural scream is followed by ominous thumps and crashes reverberating through the elevator's confines.

As the elevator finally grinds to a halt, a sense of anticipation fills Samson. He's now granted a precious moment of respite, free to hobble around within the confined space. He fashions a makeshift tourniquet for his injured leg. The fabric binds tightly, stemming the flow of blood.

Samson's eyes scan the dimly lit elevator, searching for signs of an exit. The agonizing moments of uncertainty weigh heavily on him; his instincts alert him to the possibility of danger lurking nearby. He clings to the fragile hope that, for now, he remains untouched, but the looming unknown keeps him on edge.

More voices come from his left. "My God, how many are there?"

He turns away from the sound and faces a passage with two adjoining halls. He chooses the hall that has only one door, which is locked. He turns around and retraces his steps down the other hallway; two doors are at the end. The first door is also closed. Samson's heart pounds as he hears the footsteps of the men coming closer. He notices a small crack in the other door and enters the room. There is no exit. As the footsteps and voices grow nearer, he knows it is his only option. If he goes back out, he will run right into the men.

Samson positions a desk firmly behind the door, its legs scraping softly against the carpeted floor. He clutches the jagged jawbone tightly in his right hand, taking a defensive stance in front of the makeshift barricade. Despite the pain throbbing through his injured leg, he knows this is his best vantage point. The approaching men can only enter directly in front of him and can do so only one or two at a time.

They begin to trickle into the room, cautiously pushing the desk aside just enough to enter one by one. Samson wields the jagged jawbone, striking each man as they enter. The room becomes a gruesome battleground. With every swing, the jawbone connects, splattering the room with blood as the assailants fall one by one. Their bodies pile up, effectively barricading the doorway.

Samson's heart pounds in his chest, the rapid rhythm drowning out the shouts of his attackers. His adrenaline surges, sweat pours off him, his resolve unshaken. Despite his injured leg, he climbs onto the desk, sliding a ceiling tile to access the adjoining room. He leaps to the floor below, using his good leg to propel himself forward.

He peers out the door into the hallway and sees more men still trying to push the door open. At that moment, one of the men sees Samson and alerts the others.

"I'm tired of running, fellas," Samson sighs, his body slouched and chest heaving mightily from long breaths. "Let's end this once and for all."

Samson is ready to confront each man who advances towards him. They approach in waves. However, the reality of the situation is far from cinematic. As the skirmish unfolds, it's clear that these are not superhuman foes.

After an intense struggle, Samson stands exhausted, sweat-soaked, and battered. He scans the hallway, anticipating another attacker to emerge, but there's nothing but eerie silence. The once tumultuous scene has given way to an unsettling calm. There are no more approaching footsteps, no more voices, and no more shouting. Everything remains quiet, leaving Samson in a state of uneasy anticipation.

A cold half-smile stretches across Samson's lips. "With the jawbone of a donkey, I piled them in a heap." He mutters. "With the jawbone of a donkey, I put them to sleep."

His celebration is short-lived. Although exhausted, he knows he must leave before more police arrive. He navigates through the bodies, pausing to pat and search the pockets as he works his way through them.

The van, he remembers.

Samson rushes outside and frantically searches his car's glove compartment, visors, and drink holder. His blood-soaked leg shows signs of coagulation, but the persistent ache serves as a painful reminder. He pushes through the discomfort, scouring the interior for his keys.

With growing urgency, he examines the floor and checks beneath the seat, his arms starting to cramp from the effort. The ordeal leaves him parched, his thirst gnawing at him, but he persists in his quest for the elusive keys.

When was the last time I had something to eat or drink? He wonders, pausing long enough to glance down the road and back at the building. Samson tears into that van like a savage beast. Eventually, he finds the keys to the handcuffs underneath the passenger floor mat. Samson pauses to rub his parched throat. His temples throb, and he starts to feel light-headed. *I need water badly.*

He returns to the building in search of a faucet. He glances in rooms and down hallways with every ounce of energy left, desperately seeking water. Finally, he returns to the slaughterhouse and into a clean room with sinks and worktops. He staggers around the room, turning on the faucets. The water is off; not even a sound comes out of the pipes. Samson braces himself by leaning against the dirty concrete wall.

I don't even know where I am. He sighed and looked around for a clue to his location, and then a thought occurred to him. *I need to find a cellphone.*

He staggers back into the room where bloodied bodies are sprawled on the floor to rummage through pockets in search of a phone. He finds two that are unlocked. He tries the GPS, but neither has a signal. Samson walks toward the exit, holding both phones in the air to get at least two service bars, but it doesn't help. Once he is back in the night air, he tries again, walking toward the street, but there are still no bars. He pushes the navigation app on one of the phones, hoping it will somehow work, but it doesn't.

Nothing is going my way. I was kidnapped, tied up, beat up. Did I survive all that to die of thirst? He starts across the grass in front of the road. *God, I need your help.*

"Ahh!" Samson yelps as he trips over something in the tall grass, bringing him to his knees. With his toe now throbbing almost as much as his leg, he reaches back to grab the rock he thought tripped him – he is shocked to find a spigot. He twists the rusted knob of the faucet and prays for water. He hears a dripping sound; then, a splash hits his leg. Water pours into the grass.

Samson cups his hands and sips the water on his dry lips. He chugs it down so fast he has to take a moment to catch his breath. Nothing has ever tasted so good.

When he looks down, he notices blood on his arms and hands. He washes off as much as he can and stands up. It's time to try phones again. He waves them above his head while walking up and down the sidewalk, but still, he can't get a signal. Samson suddenly pauses when he realizes he can't call a cab from here even if the phones work; that would link him to all those men in the warehouse.

Samson shoves one phone in each pocket and starts down the road.

Chapter 19

JUDGES 15:20

After years of hiding, Samson cautiously ends his constant running and returns home. He chooses to cut ties with the relentless news cycle. The reports of further acts of destruction by the same perpetrators only serve to deepen his sickness and depression, opening up festering wounds he's desperate to heal.

With time, Samson understands that no surviving witnesses can link his face to past crimes. The police have no case against him, and this realization allows him to breathe a sigh of hope for the first time in what feels like an eternity.

As Samson steps into the gym's locker room, he finds it nearly deserted. His eyes scan the space, hunting for an unoccupied locker. Settling on one situated along the back wall, he peels off his shirt, revealing the toned physique beneath.

Over the past two weeks, the gym has become a sanctuary for him, a refuge from the tumultuous past events. Here, he blends into the anonymous crowd of dedicated gym-goers, finding solace in activities like basketball and the occasional yoga session.

The soft rock music pumping through the speakers does not work for him. He is exhausted and wants to go home but changes into his black basketball shorts anyway. Pulling on a white V-neck, he shuts his locker and heads to the door. If he doesn't get moving now, he might leave.

Samson makes his way to the club's basketball court and stretches while he waits for the current game to finish. "Who's up next?" one of the players calls out. Samson throws up his hand and runs out onto the court.

After the game, he sits on the sideline to catch his breath. In between sips of water, a fellow patron walks up to him. He has seen the man here many times in the last few weeks, and although they have spoken, he doesn't know his name.

"You're Samson, aren't you?" The stranger's voice carries a note of admiration. "Great game out there. You left your competition in the dust."

Samson manages a weary smile, his thoughts drifting to the aftermath of his encounter with the Philistines. The stranger's praise is a bittersweet reminder of his fierce battles, the cost of his strength, and his choices. Despite it all, he appreciates the irony of the compliment.

"Those guys put up a good fight, though." The remainder of the men who'd played in the three-on-three games, along with Samson, give him high-fives and fist pounds on their way out.

"We are all wondering," one begins, as he exits, "how are you that strong when we never see you work out? All we see you do is play basketball and go to the yoga class with the women. Are you using steroids?" All the men stop and laugh as they wait for Samson to respond.

"See, that's the problem. You're worried about me. What you need to worry about is your lady taking a yoga class with me. I've noticed her checking me out. Must be the long hair." As they leave the gym, the men laugh and tease the man who asked the question. The door shuts behind them, leaving Samson and the man who walked up to greet him standing alone. Samson rubs the towel across his forehead to wipe the sweat dripping into his eyes.

"My name is Steve Russom," the man introduces himself, extending his hand. "I hear slaughtering the competition is something you do often, even outside the gym."

Samson gives a small laugh. *Does he know about the meat packing plant?* "I don't know what you're talking about, Steve."

"Let's just say a little birdie told me about you. You're a man who has no fear and stands up for your beliefs. You stop at nothing to win. The fact you're willing to stand up to the Philistines when most people would cower says you're just the kind of man we need for mayor."

Samson laughs, assuming the man is making a joke. "What do you mean by 'we'?"

The elder's voice resonates with solemnity as he addresses Samson. "Pay close attention, my young friend," he says. "We are witnessing your tremendous potential unfolding. You're garnering the respect and admiration of your peers and those with greater life experience. I'm here to offer my guidance to you, securing their respect. Samson, our community is in dire need of a courageous, authentic champion."

"And how do you know I'm not afraid?"

Steve leans a little closer and lowers his voice. "I know the Chief of Police in Timnah was not an accident. I know you aren't afraid."

Samson is speechless.

"I'm not judging you. I respect you for the things you've done. We need more men like you. Take your time. Think about it. Here is my card. Call me and let me know what you decide. I can make it happen; I will get you into office."

The man walks away. Samson sits, toying with the idea. *Me? As a mayor? Am I even old enough? Do I even have what it takes? All I want to do is start a race team, not sit in an office all day.* The voice of one of the gym's trainers steals him away from his thoughts. "Sam, I didn't know you knew the senator."

"I'm sorry, what did you say?" Samson asks frown lines creasing his forehead.

"I didn't know you knew the senator."

"Oh, I don't. I guess I do now, though."

Chapter 20

JUDGES 15:20

S amson's palms are sweaty, and his mouth is as dry as the desert.

He isn't shy by any means, but this somehow feels different. He has never been responsible for anyone other than himself, much less an entire city. He pulls his shirt cuffs down past his suit jacket and starts to remove the flashcards from his pocket but immediately decides against it.

If I don't know it by now…

Loud applause erupts as the curtains of the high school auditorium part. Samson steps out onto the stage, waving to the crowd. The high he feels makes it hard to contain his smile; it's as if he has just won the championship again. He looks presidential in his dark blue suit, white shirt, vintage cufflinks, and red tie. He makes his way to the wooden podium.

Looking out over the packed crowd, Samson soaks it all in. "Thank you. I appreciate your support." As the applause subsides, so does his anxiety.

"In my pocket, I have a stack of flashcards about this thick," he says, holding up his index finger and thumb three inches apart, "of hard questions I hoped you wouldn't ask me." The audience laughs. "Questions like, *aren't you too young to be in politics? He knows nothing about my struggles; he's never had a job.* This evening, I would like to address those concerns and any others you may have." He noticed there weren't any empty red seats in the packed auditorium.

"We find ourselves in a city at a critical juncture, a community facing significant challenges. Our plight stems from the insufficient involvement of young men and women in politics. When the implications of today's laws and policies become apparent, it's often too late. What I implore you to do is to join me in shaping a future that we can secure together."

The crowd enthusiastically applauds, and their approval echoes with determination and hope.

"I've never worked for anyone, but I had a job. I'm an entrepreneur, like my mother. When you are a grassroots racer, you don't get paid for just showing up. There is no prize for 10th place. If I didn't produce a positive result, I didn't get paid. This is the only way I know how to operate. If you know anything about racing, you know you don't get the number one plate by running one or two fast laps. You don't earn a championship by winning one or two races. You can only hold the trophy over your head if you are consistent. I didn't win every race, and I didn't always have the fastest laps, but I was," Samson pauses again for effect, "consistent." The crowd unleashes more thunderous applause. When it finally dies down, Samson continues.

"Tonight, I can promise you this and *only* this...consistency. I will consistently work to get our young people interested and involved in politics and what is happening in the communities around them. I will consistently work for budget transparency so that you know how your taxes are used. And I will be consistent in holding the police accountable.

"Too many times, the Philistine police have tried to explain away their use of racially biased deadly force with the statement, *I feared for my life.* Then, they are caught when video surfaces, showing an unarmed victim who had their back to them or, worse, walking away. At that point, the officers hide behind their blue walls and claim they need more training. You can't train out racism. How are you afraid for your life when you have a gun, taser, body armor, and extensive training against someone in a tank top and flip-flops walking away from you?"

Samson comes to an abrupt halt, his breaths ragged and heavy. The weight on his chest suddenly intensifies and grips him like a vice. His voice trembles as he speaks.

"Asher Jonas," he begins, the name carrying the weight of cherished memories. "One of the finest people I had the privilege of knowing—my best friend—was murdered. And I, too, came close to sharing his fate because of a mindless display of power, the same evil that tore him away from us."

A somber hush falls upon the gathering. The injustice hangs heavy in the air, leaving those present grappling with the enormity of the loss.

In the silence that follows, a question lingers unspoken, gnawing at the edges of their hearts: Is healing even possible in the face of such senseless brutality?

Samson takes a deep breath, dispelling the angry lump lodged in his throat, determined to hold back the tears threatening to surface. His voice is firm as he addresses the attentive crowd.

"We all share stories like this—a brother, sister, friend, parent, entire families, businesses, homes—all lost to the irrecoverable damage inflicted by their wicked hands."

But his tone shifts, raising his voice with conviction. "No more! We cannot stand idle forever. If you can't perform your duties or fulfill your responsibilities, you should be removed from that role."

Cheers resound throughout the audience, echoing the collective willpower for change.

"Finally," Samson continues, his gaze sweeping across the expectant faces, "I pledge to remain unwavering in my commitment to self-improvement, to be the best mayor I can be for all of you."

As he points out to the audience, people rise to their feet, applauding enthusiastically. Samson lifts both hands high into the air, declaring victory.

Women are drawn to Samson because of his quick wit, charisma, and undeniable good looks. But with every interview he gives, women (along with men) realize that Samson isn't just a pretty face; he is someone who understands the real issues of his constituents.

Throughout his campaign for the mayor's seat, Samson focuses on the essential things to him while trying to balance an appeal to the people's issues. He goes on to win because of this strategic platform and because he is just so personable.

Beloved by his constituents, Samson served as mayor for five consecutive four-year terms. During this time, Samson makes sure to accomplish, or at least set in motion, everything he promises the people. As a child, his parents instilled in him the significance of being healthy, so he tackled childhood obesity. He also executes a plan to help underprivileged students receive scholarships to colleges. He creates a strategy to assist small business owners in growing their businesses, thriving in the community, and creating more jobs. He knows companies like his mother's shop can start small and develop into corporations.

His goal for the Israelites is financial stability: earning money and living comfortably. With the help of his father, Samson created a program to help criminals re-enter the workforce and become financially independent. When his time in office ends, Samson can say, with a straight face and head held high, that he made a difference in people's lives.

"Do you need help cleaning out your office?" offers the janitor who has been cleaning the building Samson has worked in for the last twenty years. They often chatted on the nights Samson worked late and have established a healthy rapport.

"No, I've got it," Samson says, flashing a warm smile.

"Well, good luck, Mr. Mayor," the janitor replies. "God bless."

"God bless you too."

With a large box in his arms, Samson pushes the exit door with his back and leaves the office for the last time. He gazes up to look at the full moon. It is a beautiful night, with no clouds in sight, just endless blankets of stars. The cool night air blows his hair as he walks through the parking lot.

When he reaches the truck, he braces the box between the side of his vehicle and his leg to unlock the door. His phone vibrates in his pocket while he is shoving the box in the backseat. By the time he is finished, the phone stops ringing. He glances at the screen, a missed call from his mother.

"Call me as soon as you get this message," the voicemail instructs him. His mother's voice is shaky as it echoes, leaving him wondering what noise he's hearing in the background.

Frowning, he calls her back. "Ma, is everything alright?"

"No, your father is in the hospital. We are at Zorah General."

"I'm on my way. What happened?"

"We will talk when you get here."

"Ma, what happened?" he pleads, but his mother has already hung up.

Moments later, Samson screeches to a halt in front of the emergency room entrance, his heart pounding in his chest. He leaps out of the truck, urgently propelling his every step through the automatic sliding doors. Panic is etched into his face as he approaches the first nurse he encounters.

"I'm looking for my father. Manoah," he stammers, his voice trembling with desperation. His eyes darted around the bustling hospital corridor, searching for any sign of his father.

Before the nurse can respond, Samson's gaze locks onto his mother, Hazel, who stands a little farther down the hallway, engaged in a hushed conversation with a doctor. Fueled by mixed emotions, Samson rushes to his mother's side.

Hazel steadies herself and introduces her son with a tremor in her voice, "This is my son."

The doctor, momentarily caught off guard by Samson's sudden arrival, hesitates for a moment before he continues, his tone grave and compassionate. "Okay," he begins, choosing his words carefully, "I was just explaining to your mother that your father, at this point, shows no signs of brain activity. It's the ventilator that's keeping him alive. Your family faces the decision of when to consider withdrawing life support."

"But what happened?" Samson continues to probe. His stomach is in knots, and he hears himself breathe.

"Your father had a stroke, and his brain was oxygen-deprived. The ventilator is breathing for him now. It is out of our hands at this point."

Samson stands with his mouth agape and eyes fixed on the doctor. He can't wrap his head around what he just heard. His chest starts to hurt; he blinks to fight back the tears.

"Thank you, doctor," Hazel whispers.

"I'm sorry. Please, let me know if you need anything," the doctor replies before walking away.

"Sam…Sam…Samson," she says, slipping her hand into his. "Let's go see your father."

Without uttering another word, Samson obediently followed the nurse into the room; the sterile hospital air clung to his senses. The sight is both disquieting and heartbreaking.

His father, Manoah, lies motionless amidst a labyrinth of machinery. Tubes and wires connect to him, a web of lifelines binding him to a world he seems detached from. A breathing mask, stark white against the pale backdrop of the room, covers his nose and mouth, feeding precious oxygen into his fragile body.

As Samson walks closer, he is struck by the paradox of his father's appearance. Despite the chaos of medical intervention, Manoah appears serene, as if he's embraced the inevitability of his situation. But Samson's own emotions tell a different story. Numbness spreads through him like a bitter chill, and a heavy lump lodges in his throat, making each swallow arduous.

In the periphery of his vision, Samson glimpses his mother, Hazel, standing by the bedside. Her grief is palpable; tears cascade down her cheeks, marking the cruel passage of time in this room. It's as if the weight of their collective sorrow has caused Samson's heart to beat slower, ponderous. His legs tremble beneath him, and his eyes betray the unshed tears that well up.

Unconsciously, his hand extends itself, reaching for his father's fragile grasp. It's a touch laden with love, a desperate attempt to bridge the chasm between the living and the fading. In that touch, Samson expresses all the words he cannot say, all the emotions too overwhelming to articulate in the face of this harrowing moment.

"I guess God decided his work on earth is done," Hazel laments.

But Samson doesn't hear her. All he hears is the sound of the ventilator pushing oxygen into the tube. He watches his father's chest rise and fall.

Hazel leans close to her husband, her lips forming silent words of love and farewell. Tenderly, she gently kisses his forehead, a final embrace of their shared life. With measured steps, she turns away, heading towards the nurse, the bearer of their agonizing decision.

Time seems to stretch in those moments, and there is an unending pause before the nurse reaches out to disconnect the lifeline. The machine, a relentless guardian of life, emits a single, heart-wrenching beep that stretches into an agonizing eternity, a deafening symphony of finality.

Hazel turns her tear-filled eyes toward Samson as the sound echoes through the room. The weight of their shared sorrow becomes too much to bear, and she collapses into her son's arms. His embrace, firm yet tender, provides the only semblance of solace in this world turned upside down as they share the profound grief of bidding farewell to a beloved husband and father.

Chapter 21

JUDGES 16:31

O ver the next few days, Samson stays in Zorah with his mother. Intent on assisting Hazel in preparing for his father's funeral, Samson is relieved to discover that his parents had already taken care of most of the necessary arrangements as they'd grown older. This unexpected foresight on their part grants him a bit more breathing room than he had initially anticipated. Hazel's dearest friend from college, Carina, also steps in to lend her support, joining the effort to finalize the funeral preparations.

Samson supports his grieving mother, all the while disregarding his own grief. He is still numb, going through the days like a spectator watching someone else's life. He can't come to grips with the realization that his father would no longer be around to lounge in his favorite recliner, work on his crossword puzzles, or sit outside in his garden.

On the day of the funeral, Samson arrives at the church without remembering how he'd gotten there, his muscle memory leading the way. He hasn't been to the red brick building since childhood; it seems much smaller than he remembered. Both Hazel and Manoah's extended families stand in front of the church. He greets them with half-hearted hugs and very few words. This is not the family reunion anyone ever hopes for.

He trudges up the brick steps through the maze of friends and family, past the faded white wooden doors leading into the main sanctuary. Glancing around the wood-paneled room, he makes his way to the first pew where his mother sits. Carina rubs her friend's back while she cries, but two men are sitting nearby, and they are unfamiliar faces to him as he approaches his mom. Shoving it to the back of his mind, he sits next to his mother and places a soft hand on her knee, her frail hand covering his. *How have I not noticed how much she's aging?* Samson wonders lost in thought.

The sun shines through the vibrant stained-glass windows, giving the solid oak pews a polished glow. A deacon plays the organ as ushers direct people down the aisle to their seats. Men and women dressed in maroon and white robes file in to fill the choir stand. Not far behind them, the pastor makes his way to the pulpit.

One of the ushers walks up to the casket and adjusts the pastel flower arrangement on top. Samson and Hazel had decided on a closed casket with two large pictures, one at the head and one at the foot, to speed up the service proceedings since they were unsure of the number of attendees. Manoah had already buried many of his friends, colleagues, and classmates.

The pastor, suited in dark blue, stands, and the music fades. "Thank you for joining us today to honor this beloved man. If anyone would like to speak, please step up to the microphone." He motioned toward the left side of the casket. "Out of respect for time, please keep your comments to one minute. Thank you."

Samson removes his arm from around his mother and stands. She lovingly gazes up at her son. Placing his hand on her shoulder, he squeezes it in quiet acknowledgment. Samson walks to the microphone to face the congregation. He scans the crowd, steadying his voice, further pushing away thoughts about who these two men are watching him. "There are a lot of people here today. I know I sound surprised, but I'm not. But how many of you are here to pay your respects, and how many are here to make sure it is Manoah lying up here?"

An awkwardness descends upon the solemn church, its hallowed halls filled with hushed whispers and mournful glances. Then, as if sensing the heavy atmosphere, a comforting voice breaks through the silence.

"It's alright; you all know Pops would've had a good laugh at this," Samson reassures the congregation. After a collective exhale, laughter ripples through the pews. Even Samson's mother, her face etched with grief, cracks a small smile as she fondly remembers the countless lawyer jokes Manoah had once delighted in sharing. At that moment, amidst the sorrow, there's a spark of warmth—a tribute to the humor and light their beloved Pops had brought into their lives.

Samson takes a deep breath. "I have been to funerals, sitting out there where you all are," he says, pointing, "but I have never been up here in this position. I've sat where you are sitting. I viewed the body, hugged the family, ate the repass, and then continued my life as normal. Everyone knows this day will come, but it still sneaks up on you. I always thought I knew how I would react."

Samson looks out into a sea of familiar faces attached to bodies stiff as mannequins, the two strangers sitting there motionless among them. "If I have ever attended a service for one of your friends or family members, I would like to take this time to say I'm sorry. I didn't know." He hangs his head as he starts to choke up. "I'm hurting right now." He takes a long pause and a deep breath to compose himself. "I want the world to stop spinning."

He pauses again, gazing up at the ceiling as he reflects, blinking back tears. "I'm about to bury my father," he finally manages, his voice wavering. "I have learned *so much* from this man. This man gave me the shirt off his back and the shoes off his feet. I told him I thought they were cool, and he took them off and gave them to me." The audience laughs and nods their approval.

"Let me tell you a story about when my Pops made me 'lie' to him," Samson jokes. "Early in his career, I'm sure my dad put his time in at work, but by the time I started school, it seemed like he was *always* at home." Everyone laughs. Samson rolls his eyes. "I know, right? Poor me. I remember having to pry him away from the house to do anything. That's why it was so strange to me that when we did go out, everybody knew him. And I do mean *everybody*.

"It would take forever to get in and out of stores with this man. From the bread store to the hardware store. But the worst part was that he wanted *me* to know them, too! He would point out individuals, and I would tell him I don't remember them. Then he would insist that I did."

Samson waits until the laughter calms down. "Then he would set off on a quest to make me remember. He would say they lived down the street from Mrs. So-and-So. Or, they had a red pickup truck," he says, throwing his hands up and giving the church a bewildered look. "Finally, I would just say, *yes, Pop, I remember them*. But most of the time, I didn't." Laughter erupts in the congregation. "Hey, don't judge me; have you ever tried arguing with a lawyer?" Samson jokes.

"But seriously, if my dad gave you free legal advice, raise your hand." Many people slide their hands into the air and then put them back down. "Please, keep your hands up," Samson requests, raising his hand as well. "If you have used my dad's truck, or if he helped you move something in his truck, raise your hand." More hands raise.

"If my dad helped you fix your car, truck, or lawnmower, raise your hand." Samson pauses as more hands go up. "Or, if you have eaten anything from my father's garden, please raise your hand." He pauses again, allowing additional hands to ascend.

"Now, take a look around."

Everyone in the church has their hand in the air. "Thank you for helping me realize my family will not miss him alone. With your prayers and support, we will not go through this alone. God bless."

Samson returns to the pew, glancing again toward the unfamiliar faces. Within that split second, he notices a striking resemblance to his father that catches him off guard, causing him to take a second look. *Is it possible? How could this be?* Filled with more questions than answers, his mind reels with the possibility of having brothers he knew nothing about.

Hours later, alone with Hazel, he finally asks, "Can I ask you a question?"

"Of course, dear, you know that you can ask me anything," she replies in matching hushed tones.

"There were two men there today that I can't recall seeing around town growing up, and I … well, I noticed –" he begins, but before he can figure out how to complete his thought, she finishes his sentence.

"You noticed they looked an awful lot like your Dad, huh?" Having seen them, too, she knew it would only be a matter of time before he asked; Samson was always such a curious child.

Without meeting her gaze, he nods, confused that she seems so nonchalant about the whole matter. "Do I … do I have …," he stammers, unable to say the words aloud.

"Yes," she offers. "You have two older brothers. Your father already had them when he and I met, and he was heartbroken when they moved away. He wanted to be a part of their lives growing up, but their mother didn't allow it. Samson, you...you are our miracle. I tried for many years to fill in the hole their absence had left in his heart, and just when I was ready to believe it would never happen, you came along. Oh, he was too nervous to get excited when we heard from an angel that we would have you after all the disappointment that had washed over us with each miscarriage. But God kept his promise and delivered you to us. Your Dad never took that for granted, Sam. He loved you incredibly, but he also loved how much you let him be involved in your life. That's all he had ever wanted, to leave the world a better place than the way he found it. And in you, he was able to do that." Her eyes brimming, the tears finally crash upon her cheeks as she blinks and sets them free to roll down her face.

Samson lifts his hand to wipe away one of the tears gently. "Why didn't you all ever talk about them? How did I grow up not knowing I had brothers?" he asks, trying to wrap his head around what his mom shared.

"It's complicated, Sam, but please know we always make moves in your best interest. You'll have to trust that this is what your father wanted. They abandoned him when they were old enough to make their own decisions, following in their mother's footsteps. Then he had you; you were enough for him."

As a man learning to maneuver through his choices, Samson understands what she is saying. For the first time, his perspectives shift to allow him to see them as adults, not just parents.

Dad, I wish you would have shared this part of your life with me. I would have understood, I promise. There is nothing you could have done that would have let me down. Please stay with me as I continue to grow and am forced to face my own decisions; guide me and be here for me. I know you see me as your miracle, but Dad, you are mine. I love you.

Chapter 22

JUDGES 16:1-3

Hazel watches her son climb down the stairs with her heavy luggage.

After the descent, Samson sets it down at her feet. She glances at his face; he has bags under his eyes and looks like he hasn't slept in weeks. "Are you sure you will be okay?" she worries.

"Yes, I'm going to get out of here, too. Where are you going?" he inquires flatly.

She places her hand on Samson's chin, turning it so she can look into his eyes. They lack their customary twinkle when he speaks to her, but things are returning to their routine. No more life insurance agents, funeral homes, or friends are calling in shock at the news, and Hazel's crying spells are less frequent. But even with all these positive things happening, she can tell her son feels beat down. He needs time off as much as she does. She pulls his face toward her to kiss him on his cheek.

"Carina and I are going on a cruise," she replies. "Go, take a break. Don't worry about your mom. I will be fine."

Samson picks his duffle bag up off the chair and kisses his mother on the forehead. "Okay. But if you need me, call me."

Hazel stands to hug her son. The two exchange heartfelt smiles, and Samson walks outside. She watches from the doorway, giving him a small wave as he looks back.

Samson tosses his bag into the passenger seat and heads to Gaza, a relaxing town with crisp blue ocean views within a moment's drive from most of the city. This is his little slice of heaven when he needs a moment to breathe without the worries and stress of the world. The sun seems brighter today than he remembers seeing it in a long time. As he drives along the coast, he rolls down his windows and lets the sun dance on his skin. The spring flowers bloom, and he can feel the cool breeze from the ocean. The smell of the ocean air calms his soul. He heads to downtown Gaza to check out the vintage shop for unique cufflinks to add to his collection.

Later that night, he finds the restaurant/bar where they hold Salsa lessons in the evening. He has heard many locals rave about the live band and wants to see it. Strolling in, he adjusts his eyes to the dim lighting.

"How many, sir?" the host asks behind a yellow podium.

"Just one."

"Bar, table, or booth?"

Samson glances around the room. The music in the restaurant is energetic, and the band has people on their feet, dancing on the small wooden dance floor. Soft orange light bounces off the blue and yellow stucco décor. People are singing and dancing as if they didn't have a care in the world.

"The bar is fine," Samson replies, smiling. He can see why the place is so popular with the locals. It isn't fancy but has good music and a vivacious atmosphere.

"What can I get you, sir?" the bartender asks, approaching Samson before he even sits down. The young man has sweat running down his temple and wipes it with his shirt sleeve.

"I'll just take a glass of water."

The bartender pulls a glass from a rack above his head, flips it into the air, throws a scoop of crushed ice, and fills it with water. "Here you go, and here's a menu. I will be right back," he says, hurrying away to serve another customer as they arrive.

Samson locks eyes with a beautiful woman sitting across the smoky restaurant. She is at the other end of the bar, her long legs crossed, wearing a short multi-colored sundress. Her dark hair sways back and forth to the music as she nods along, mouthing the song's words.

As she becomes conscious of his gaze, she looks down at her near-empty glass. Suddenly nervous, she begins to swirl her Merlot, disturbing the beauty reflecting back at her. She glances back up in time to see him talking to the bartender and pointing in her direction.

"The lady at the end of the bar – can you get her another glass of whatever she is drinking?" Samson requests.

The bartender nods and holds up a bottle of wine before refilling her glass. She traces the rim of her glass with her right forefinger. When her gaze meets him, she raises her glass and nods in appreciation.

Samson stands and walks in her direction. As he approaches, he can smell her perfume. Fresh lilac and jasmine fill his nose. Her features are stunning: chestnut eyes, mahogany skin, glossy lips.

"Thanks for the drink. Please, sit down," she motions.

"I'm Samson," he reaches out.

She extends her hand.

Samson searches the room for the bartender and signals him. "Chips and salsa, please."

"Yes, sir. Anything for you, miss?"

"No, I'm good," she answers, winking at him. Then she eyes Samson head to toe. He is in jeans and a pressed white shirt adorned with silver cufflinks. "I love the music here."

"Would you like to dance?" In a single motion before allowing her to respond, he guides her down from her stool and leads the way to the dance floor.

Once they reach the middle of the floor, music cuts through the crowd's voices. His hands slide around her waist, and he pulls her in closer, her head finding its way to the center of his chest. She glides her arms over his broad shoulders until her hands find each other again at the nape of his neck. Closer now, his cologne masks the smell of smoke in the room. She shuts her eyes and melts into him. Her head moves against the rhythmic breathing of his chest while her hips swivel to the music with his hands on her waist. Although unspoken, they both know they will spend the rest of the night together. For now, they are two strangers giving in to the rhythm of lust.

The music shifts to a slower, jazzy tempo, and he seizes the moment. His hand finds its place on the small of her back, drawing her closer into the intimate embrace of the dance floor.

Their skin brushes together, and he leans in, his voice a sultry whisper in her ear, "How about we find a quieter spot?" He's not ready for the night to conclude just yet; he wants to know her on a deeper level. She exudes an allure that captivates him, and he senses that she might be the perfect antidote to his evening—exquisite and tantalizing.

"How badly do you want to leave?" she teases, licking her lips.

The lead singer croons on; their bodies continue to sway. Samson leans in, leaving his hand on the small of her back. "It's whatever you want." He caresses her bare shoulder.

She chuckles and pulls her body closer to his, her breath on his cheek. "It's going to cost you."

"It already has," Samson laughs. "These drinks are expensive."

She leans closer to him, whispering, "It'll be the best money you ever spent."

"Let's go," he grins without a second thought. Samson returns to the table, pulls cash out of his wallet, and lays it down. "You never know; you might want to pay *me* after I teach you some things to help you make more money," he winks, walking her toward the door. She laughs, intrigued by his cockiness. Samson smirks to himself.

At the entrance to the gated community, her car pauses in front of the guard booth. Samson watches from his truck as the guard leans toward her open window. He sees him look back in his direction, and then the metal gates swing open, welcoming both cars into the community of custom homes.

She lives in a residential subdivision named *The City*. It sits atop a hill with a spectacular view of downtown Gaza. Samson pulls his truck in front of her home while she parks in the driveway. She climbs out of her cherry-red sedan and opens the door; Samson follows her inside.

"Have a seat while I change into something a little more comfortable," she offers, pointing to the black leather sectional in the corner.

Samson sits and flips through a magazine lying on her coffee table.

"You thirsty?" she calls from the bedroom.

"No, thank you. I'm good," he replies, glancing around her place, accented in black and silver.

Moments later, she reappears, standing in the entry to the living room, wearing a pink and black lace negligee. She beckons him with the curl of her index finger. "Come to bed."

Samson does as instructed, eager to see if it will be the best money he ever spent.

Samson is jarred awake and sits straight up in the bed.

He glances around the room, realizing he is still at the woman's house. Flipping back the covers, he slides out from the sateen sheets, trying not to wake her. On his way to the bathroom, he notices movement outside the window. He lifts one of the wooden blinds and spots two men walking around his truck, trying to look inside: one in a police uniform and the other in jeans and a t-shirt.

From the window, Samson can also see the guard station at the front of the subdivision. The guard watches the men for a moment, then wraps chains around the handles of the front gate and places a padlock on them.

Here we go again.

The burly guard, stationed at the entrance to the suburban neighborhood, casts an appreciative eye over the vintage truck as it pulls up.

"That truck is a classic. I haven't seen one of those in a long time," he remarks to the approaching men. "I saw you eyeing it."

"It looks familiar. A guy I knew back in the day had one just like it. Did you see who was driving it?" inquires Buddy.

"I did, Buddy," the guard confirms. "He had dreads. Looked familiar, but I can't place him."

"I bet it's who I think it is, especially with those dreads," Buddy ventures. "Samson."

"That's right. The former mayor, Samson," the guard acknowledges.

"There's no mistaking that truck. You don't see these on the road anymore. It matches his bike from his old racing days."

Buddy takes a moment to recall a time when Samson seemed to effortlessly glide through life, basking in the glory of fame, beautiful companions, and the prestige of being a long-standing mayor for over two decades. Buddy's life hadn't enjoyed the same favor, leaving him to wonder why. What was it that set Samson apart? He couldn't help but feel resentment, even though he wasn't even a Philistine himself.

With the unmistakable truck now captured in a snapshot on his cellphone, Buddy starts making late-night phone calls.

"Why are you calling so late?" a groggy voice grumbles on the other end.

"You won't believe who's parked in my neighborhood," Buddy begins, launching into the astonishing news about Samson's unexpected presence. He shares the revelation with acquaintances he knows will find it intriguing. Then, returning to the guard, Buddy conveys his final, firm instructions.

"Whatever happens, do not let that truck leave. I have unfinished business with him." The night is charged with suspense, with questions about what might prompt this long-delayed confrontation with the man who has been a public figure for two decades, living in plain sight yet somehow eluding Buddy's grasp until now.

Once the man was gone, Samson peered down at the security guard; the guard was fast asleep in his booth, his head leaning against the wall. He glances back at the bed to confirm she is still sleeping. When he sees she is, Samson grabs his keys and shoves them into his pocket, heading out the door.

He walks past his truck and to the front gate for a closer inspection. He cannot drive out of the neighborhood with the gates locked. He goes to one side of the gate, squats down low, and grabs the steel post with both hands. As Samson stands up, the concrete around it begins to crack, and the post begins to give. The veins in his neck are protruding from straining. Samson takes a deep breath once the earth relinquishes and releases the gate.

One down, one to go.

The other post is a bit more stubborn, but once again, he pulls as hard as he can and breaks the concrete underneath. With one final jerk, the post breaks free. Samson turns around to see if the guard heard any commotion, but surprisingly, he is still asleep.

Samson lifts the gates into the air and scans the area for a place to put them down. In the distance, a colossal hill overlooks The City's homes. He hikes to the enormous hill facing Hebron. Sweat pours off him and drips into his eyes, but he is determined to show these Philistines that they still can't get over him, although he is older.

Once he reaches the summit, Samson throws the gates down, kicking up dirt and grass. He pauses to catch his breath, resting his hands on his knees. He can see the sun peeking above the horizon behind the hill, back toward Hebron. He needs to get out of this town before everyone wakes up. He takes off at a full sprint toward his truck.

Chapter 23

JUDGES 16:4

Photographers stand behind velvet ropes, snapping pictures as celebrities, socialites, and athletes parade across the red carpet. The circular drive is lined with black limousines and exotic sports cars. Samson has been invited to the grand opening of a new development company. Because he is in the market to purchase a new home, the invitation allows him to check out the newest and best builders.

The Valley of Sorek was a wonderful place for Samson's new home. He arrives wearing a tan summer suit, a baby blue shirt, a plaid pocket square, and cufflinks.

"Samson, say hi to the fans," a photographer coaxes. Samson waves, smiles, and walks inside. He feels a little old for camera attention. This was one of the reasons he was ready to buy a new place; he wanted out of the spotlight of the big city.

The fourteen-story brick structure might not command attention from the exterior, but as he steps inside, it becomes instantly clear why the owners chose this building. The grand atrium stretches up to four stories, a cathedral of space and light. The building's front features expansive windows on three sides, inviting the outside world to intermingle with its interior.

At the heart of the entryway, a monumental fountain takes center stage, standing at least a story tall. The floors beneath his feet are bathed in the lustrous elegance of cream-colored marble. Nickel-plated wall sconces punctuate the walls, complementing the silver vases brimming with orchids that grace the space. The ambient lighting is subdued, casting a gentle glow on the touches of silver that adorn the interior.

Off to the right, a gifted artist wields his brushes and paints, and a mesmerized crowd forms around him. Their collective awe becomes a part of the unfolding scene in this architectural masterpiece.

"Champagne, sir ?" a waiter asks Samson.

"No, thank you," Samson says, shaking his head.

A pianist is playing on the other side of the atrium. Near him, Samson spots the men who had invited him. He walks over, grabbing a hors d'oeuvre as he walks by another waiter. He says his hellos and makes small talk, but his conversation is interrupted by a man who stands at the center of the atrium holding a microphone.

"Excuse me, ladies and gentlemen," the speaker announces, stepping onto the spiral staircase where everyone can see him. "This stunning building you are standing in was created and designed by Valley Custom Builders. Valley Custom Builders has been involved in many phenomenal projects here in the Valley of Sorek, including the children's museum, the aquarium, and the theatre. It is my pleasure to introduce the head of the design division," he motions to an exotic, dark-haired woman standing near the fountain, "the beautiful and talented Delilah."

Samson watches as she walks across the room, wearing a long, hip-hugging black dress and thong stilettos that peek out with each step.

"Thank you, Steve, for being such a gracious host tonight," she gushes, kissing him on his cheek. "Good evening, everyone. We are here tonight to celebrate the opening of Valley Custom Builders' new home office. Our offices will occupy part of the first floor, but we plan to make this building a mix of retail stores, commercial businesses, and luxury apartments. Please feel free to look around. This is just a taste of what you can have when you join us here at *Stonebrook Tower*. I'm glad you could make it, and I know this will be a great beginning."

"So, that's Delilah," a woman near Samson remarks to her friend.

"I heard she thinks she is a bit of a local celebrity," the friend gossips.

"How do you know?" The women laugh together.

"I have my ways. Let's find a server. I need another glass of wine."

Samson turns back to his friends to continue his conversation, but his mind is on Delilah. He has to meet her. He watches her mingle with party guests and decides to introduce himself. Excusing himself, he heads in her direction.

Samson approaches her while she is speaking to a well-known banker and a beautiful young woman. The banker introduces his girlfriend to Delilah. He talks excessively about how they met. Samson watches Delilah's face. She isn't interested but politely smiles at them as they speak and maintains eye contact.

"I'm sorry. Can you excuse us for a moment?" Samson interrupts, stepping between Delilah and her guests. Samson places his hand on her back and moves her away from the couple. Delilah eyes him for a moment but doesn't speak. "You're welcome," he says.

"For what, exactly?" she retorts.

"Saving you from that bore of a conversation."

She laughs, flashing a beautiful set of white teeth. "He wasn't talking about business; he wanted me to meet his new girlfriend. I'm about business tonight."

"Samson," he says, extending his hand.

"Delilah," she replies, tickled by his boldness. "Thanks for saving me, Samson, but I have to go now." She walks away without another word, leaving Samson standing there in surprise. He isn't used to that – it intrigues him even more.

This may be harder than I thought. "Wait a second, excuse me," he calls, but the crowd and the music drown him out.

Delilah is on a mission—she needs tenants to fill the building and bring in revenue for her company. She doesn't have time to stand and talk unless it is about making money. Her company is stretched as thin as possible, and while she would prefer for someone to come in and buy the whole building from her outright, at this point, she will take what she can get.

Samson is on a mission—he makes tracks around the party with his neck stretched and, at times, standing on the tips of his toes, trying to find the dark-haired beauty. He strategically plants himself where he can see the bar and restrooms. After standing there for thirty minutes, he worries that he is starting to look creepy. He makes one final unsuccessful stroll around the party, then leaves, feeling dejected.

Chapter 24

JUDGES 16:4

S amson searches his phone for Olivia Driscoll's number and dials.

"Hey Olivia, Samson here. I'm hoping you can help me with something."

"Of course. Anything for you," she says.

"I'm looking for a home," Samson starts. "I have narrowed my area down to the Valley of Sorek, but I'm having a tough time finding the right home. I'm beginning to think building a home is the way to go, but I don't know any builders. Do you have any recommendations?"

"I have the perfect builder for you, and their home office is in the Valley of Sorek. The company has been around a long time and has an excellent reputation for their homes' quality and attention to detail. Plus, the owner and I went to school together and know they will take good care of you. If they don't have it, they can design and build it for you."

"That sounds perfect." Samson is ecstatic.

"I will set an appointment for you."

"Okay, any day this week before noon would be great," Samson confirms as he checks the calendar on his phone.

Olivia called him later to let him know his appointment was at ten the following morning. Samson adds it to his calendar and then changes to his bedroom. He suddenly feels like a bike ride and fresh air.

Samson wakes early the next day to the sound of his next-door neighbor playing loud music on his patio. As he steps out of bed, he is reminded that this is one of the reasons it is time to buy a house. He is relieved that his lease agreement on the quaint 1500-square-foot condominium is set to expire soon.

The cold, polished concrete floor jolts Samson as he steps off the rug beside his bed. He adds wood floors with radiant heat to his mental checklist and opens his groggy eyes wide. After walking down the blue hallway into the retro, black-and-white-tiled bathroom, he starts the shower. Today, he throws on jeans and a white V-neck t-shirt when he's cleaned up. A quick breakfast of oatmeal and fruit completes his morning routine, and he heads out the door.

Traffic is congested because of construction in Sorek; he makes it to the Valley Custom Builders' office with just minutes to spare. Samson sinks into an oversized, brown leather chair in the waiting area. Displays of house floor plans and available features are mounted on the walls.

After a moment, a woman comes out to meet him, carrying a stack of paperwork. "You must be Samson. I'm Sarah, the design assistant—nice to meet you", she introduces herself and hands him the booklets. Realizing it was missing additional material, she left floor plans for Samson to look at while retrieving them.

There are six available options ranging from 900 to 2,700 square feet. Samson is interested in the most extensive floor plan, a three-story brownstone with stained maple hardwood floors and a rooftop terrace. The neighborhood is positioned on a hill overlooking the city's beautiful skyline. This home is the first part of his plan for his new life after office.

 The design assistant enters the waiting room, and a woman's voice follows her. "Excuse me, Sarah. Did you get the plans for the building on Third Street?"

Delilah walks into the room. Samson looks up as she stops short.

"Oh, I'm sorry. I didn't realize you had someone with you," she says, glancing at Samson. "I apologize. I will come back."

"Please go ahead," Samson insists.

"Are you sure?"

"Please."

Delilah shifts her attention back to Sarah.

"They're on my desk," Sarah says, rushing to retrieve them.

Delilah walks into the room and extends her hand. "Hi. Delilah. Again, I apologize for interrupting."

Samson looks her up and down. Her long, black hair is lying on her shoulders, and she is wearing a grey pantsuit, pink blouse, four-inch heels, and pink polish on her toes to match her shirt.

"Samson," he says, standing to greet her.

"Very nice to meet you," she replies.

What? We met a week ago. She must be playing hard to get, he ponders, *or maybe she doesn't recognize me without my suit on, or this is an act because she is working.*

"Sarah taking good care of you?" she asks, snapping Samson away from his thoughts.

"She is, thank you," he says, returning to his seat.

"If you need anything, please don't hesitate to let us know." With a quick smile, she turns and heads back toward her office.

An appointment for 10:00 a.m. the following day is made for Samson to view the brownstone. Outside, he hands the valet his ticket to bring his truck around. As he waits, he can't help but notice the line of cars out front: Mercedes, Range Rover, hybrid Escalade, and a convertible Bentley GT. Samson loves bikes, but like his father, he also has an affinity for fine automobiles.

When his vehicle arrives, he rubs the dashboard of his faithful truck with his hand.

Don't worry. You will always be my first love.

Traffic heading into Timnah's furniture district is usually congested. Several cars turn off the main road down the side street. A black convertible Bentley GT zips between his truck and the one ahead of him and disappears down a side street. He catches a glimpse of long, dark hair blowing in the breeze. Is that the same car from the builder's office?

A couple of days have passed since his appointment at the homebuilder. He takes out his phone and their business card.

"Is Delilah available?"

"May I ask who is calling?"

"Samson."

"This is Delilah."

"Delilah, good morning. This is Samson. I'm having a little trouble deciding on floor plans."

"I understand. They're all fantastic. I'll grab Sarah, and she can assist you with that."

"Can *you* help me? Over lunch."

There is an awkward pause before Delilah replies. "Sure."

"Sure, you are free?"

She chuckles. "I'm free to help you, and I haven't eaten. Let's meet at the steakhouse on Fourth."

"Perfect. I'll see you there."

PART III: DELILAH

One year before the explosion

Chapter 25

JUDGES 16:4

Delilah remembers Samson's face from the office.
His hair is pulled back into a ponytail that sways when he walks. She didn't remember noticing his hair before, although she hadn't paid much attention to him. Nice-looking men come into the office daily, and work is just that: work, not a place to find a man.

She greets him with a sincere smile, wondering what his angle is. Is this about his home purchase, or is he only interested in her? She catches Samson looking her up and down, even though he tries not to stare. The fitted black pencil skirt she wears looks like it's been painted on. The ruffled fuchsia blouse, four-inch fuchsia stilettos, and black nail polish on her fingernails and toes are further proof that style is something she doesn't lack.

"I think I'm a little underdressed," Samson admits.

"Don't worry about it. You're with me."

"Delilah, how lovely to see you, my dear," the maître d' beams as he opens the door for them. "Your table is ready. What is your preference for wine today?"

"You know what I like. Surprise me," Delilah smiles back, patting the man on the arm. As they head to their table, a man sitting with his wife glances in Delilah's direction and nods.

"Good afternoon, Delilah," a server at their table says, waiting to push in her chair.

"Hi, Ryan, how are you today?" She and the waiter make small talk as he places her napkin in her lap, then leaves without acknowledging Samson, who gives Delilah a smirk. "What's that look for?" she asks.

"You seem to know everyone here."

She smiles. "I come pretty often."

Samson notices a man in a dark navy suit eyeing Delilah from a booth in the restaurant's corner. He is alone—pretending to be looking at the menu in his hand—but his wandering eyes keep zeroing in on Delilah. The man catches her gaze and smiles, but Delilah doesn't smile back. Instead, she averts her eyes and smiles at Samson.

I may have to keep an eye on this one, Samson notes. "This isn't a place I normally frequent, but I've heard about it. I'm more of a taco stand, food truck kind of a guy," he jokes.

"Don't get me wrong, I enjoy that too, but this is how I normally do it." Delilah laughs. She pulls a packet out of her bag. "So, you're having trouble deciding which floor plan to go with?"

"Why don't we eat first? I don't like to talk about business on an empty stomach."

"Okay. Tell me something about yourself. Something that you don't share with people."

"Is this an interview? You want a list of strengths and weaknesses, too?"

Delilah laughs. "That's only if you get called back for a second interview."

Pretty face—check. Athletic body—check. Quick wit—check. Nails perfectly polished—check. "You tell me something," Samson says. "Tell me about your lawyer boyfriend."

"What lawyer boyfriend?"

"Word around town is you are with an attorney."

She laughs again, this time louder. "Every time I stand beside an attractive man, everyone thinks we are dating."

"Were you attracted to him?"

"He is nice looking, yes."

"If he is so hot, why wouldn't you want to date him?"

"Dating someone trained to argue sounds like a headache waiting to happen."

"I'll go with that answer."

"Your turn," she says. "Tell me something you don't share."

"I have never cut my hair. I'm a Nazirite. I don't drink or eat anything unwholesome."

"So, what *do* you eat? With processing plants and factories, is any food clean?" Samson laughs at her witty remark. "Where do you get your protein?" she asks, tracing the outline of the muscles in his shirt with her eyes.

"From beans, nuts, grains, and leafy vegetables. The strongest mammals in the world are vegetarians."

"Well, lions aren't exactly known for their vegetarian diets," she challenges playfully, her hand gracefully resting on her chin, a gleam in her eye.

"True, but lions aren't the strongest mammals either; they just have the weapon to kill."

"That's good to know."

"Your turn," Samson says, smiling at her.

"I have three kids—and they all have the same father." Samson laughs nervously this time. "No, I'm kidding…let's see." Delilah says in her best pageant voice, "My name is Delilah. I was born in the Valley of Sorek to a young couple named…" They laugh in unison.

"How about you tell me how you started building custom homes?" he offers.

"Valley Custom Builders was my father's business, but I grew up working with him. Once I was old enough, he taught me everything about the business so I could take it over one day. When he became sick, I took over the reins. I have to say that my true passion is fashion, though. From an early age, I watched my mother make jewelry. She was the most fashionable woman I knew." Delilah smiles as she remembers the days she sat in her mother's bathroom, playing in her jewelry box. "I used to sketch designs for clothes and handbags. When I showed my friends, they all went crazy. After that, I started taking orders and sewing bags in Home

Economics to make a little cash. Now I design scarves and sell fashion handbags and accessories part-time."

"What kind of scarves?"

"All kinds: silk, wool. I mean, if it feels good against my skin, I use it."

Their conversation is seamless, and they never revisit the home purchase discussion. There is a cool breeze blowing when they leave the restaurant.

"It's a perfect afternoon to put the top down," Delilah mentions. They each hand their ticket to the valet. The roar of Samson's truck's V8 engine shakes the ground underneath their feet before it appears.

"That's my baby," Samson says.

Delilah giggles.

"This is me…all day, every day."

"Aww, I think you need me to upgrade you," she teases. She purrs after touching his chest, "I got you. Don't even worry about it."

"What? My truck is a classic," he feigns.

"Oh, it's a classic, all right," she laughs.

"I don't have to be flashy to be classy, unlike *some* people," he jokes, staring at her car as it comes around. "You're a speed demon."

"Why do you say that?"

"Oh, I just know." His memory flashes back to her whipping through traffic.

"You think the Bentley is flashy? I toned it down a bit for you."

"All show and no go. Such a waste," Samson says, hoping it would hit a nerve.

As he walks past her car to get to his truck, Delilah starts her engine and pulls close to Samson's driver's side window. "I can show you better than I can tell you. This car has speed."

"Speed? What do you know about speed?"

With a tilted head and raised eyebrow, Delilah replies, "I know I can leave you and your broken-down truck in the dust."

Samson starts his truck and yells over the rumble of his engine, "Just remember, I tried to save you from this." He strokes the dashboard lovingly and whispers to his truck, "I don't know why people always underestimate you?"

"You're not scared, are you?" she smirks. "Let's race."

I hope she isn't serious.

Delilah motions with her hand for him to follow her as she weaves through parked cars in the driveway.

I guess she is.

They both turn right and head toward the interstate. At the light, Samson pulls up beside her. Her phone rings. She rolls up her windows to drown out the street noise. A minute later, she rolls it back down again.

"It's your lucky day. Something just came up. I can't play with you today, but rain check."

Samson concedes as the light turns green.

Chapter 26

JUDGES 16:5

"**W**hat's on your agenda for tonight?" Samson inquired as Delilah answered the call.

Delilah's voice carries an undertone of excitement. "I'm headed to a soirée at the lakeside mansion of an investment banker acquaintance. His wife is a renowned figure in the fashion world, and my mission tonight is to persuade her to invest in my exquisite collection of scarves."

Samson, ever the supportive companion, extended his willingness to accompany her. Their bond blossomed over the past few months, marked by shared adventures in cycling, hiking, and go-kart races. Delilah reciprocated by immersing Samson in her world of culture, treating him to enchanting concerts and theater performances. Together, they had crafted unforgettable memories.

A faint sigh escaped Delilah's lips as she gently declined Samson's offer. "As much as I'd adore your company, I plan to keep the evening concise: scout for new fabric sources, glimpse the latest fashion trends, and then make a discreet exit. I'm too drained for anything else."

Samson knows that feeling all too well. There were many nights as mayor when he wanted to stay home and watch racing instead of mingling with politicians.

"What is that noise? What are you doing?"

"Nothing...stop being nosey," she says, laughing.

"Are you in the bathroom while you are talking to me? You're nasty," Samson jokes.

"What? You're silly. I would never do that. I don't even know what you are talking about," she says. "Hey, don't forget about the party on Friday. I have a fashion show to attend in the new shopping mall in the design district. I want you to attend *that* one with me."

"I'll put it on the calendar you bought for me," Samson mocks. "Okay then, have fun."

"Thanks, I will. Goodnight."

"Goodnight."

Delilah adds the finishing touches to her jeans and cashmere sweater ensemble and heads out the door. When she arrives at the lake house, Delilah heads inside to grab a glass of wine. She stops periodically as she works her way through the crowd, speaking to other designers she knows.

Delilah spots someone she'd been avoiding for the past few months through the sea of people. She searches for an exit, but the man in the dark blue suit is on her heels before she can escape. "My, don't you look beautiful today?" the man says in a menacing voice.

"Thank you," she says. "How have you been?"

"Wonderful, especially now that I've seen you. It's been a long time. I've called you. You haven't returned my calls."

"A long time? I saw you in the restaurant not long ago," she chuckles, though unamused. "Seriously, I'm trying to come up with the money, but it's taking me longer than I thought."

"Well, you better produce something, Delilah. In case you lost it, here is my card again."

Delilah takes the card out of his hand, slides it into her clutch, and watches him walk away.

"Sounds pretty serious, Princess," says someone from behind her. "Are you in trouble?"

Annoyed, she turned around to see who was eavesdropping on her conversation. For a moment, she stares at the man standing before her, looking at his features. He stands at about eye level with a scar on his cheek. He is wearing a tailored suit, flashy watch, and shiny shoes—the ensemble suggests he has money—but still, she does not recognize him.

"You don't recognize me. I'm hurt."

"I'm sorry," she says, shrugging her shoulders. Then it hits her. *It can't be.* "Thaddeus, is that you?"

It has been many years, and he is still the handsome man he was when she was a child. As the sound of him calling her by a nickname he used all those years ago repeats in her head, she unequivocally knows it is him.

"What happened to Uncle TP?" he says, extending his arms. "Why so formal, Princess?"

Thaddeus Phillips was her father's good friend and business partner, but he disappeared when she was younger. Delilah remembers her father always keeping pictures of him in the office and at home. She never knew what had happened to him; her father told her he moved away.

"Oh, my goodness," Delilah says, hugging him. "What are you doing here? Where have you been?"

"I'm looking for investors, the same as you."

Delilah doesn't correct him. "You just caught me. I was about to leave."

"Come on, I'll walk you out." He motions with his hand toward the door.

There is a chill in the air. Delilah tightens the scarf around her neck and secures her wool pea coat. A sheet of snow covers the grass.

"What are you smiling about?" Thaddeus asks.

"I was just thinking about Daddy. The holidays always make me think of him."

"I'm sorry I didn't make it to his funeral, Princess," he says, watching Delilah. She is a beautiful woman. He watches her hair move in the winter breeze against her cheek. He remembers her father sending him pictures of the family years ago, but the pictures did her no justice. She reminds him of her father in her mannerisms, but her features are those of her mother.

"What happened to you, TP?" Delilah asks. "You were around our family daily, and then poof—gone."

"I went to prison," he replies.

"What did you do? I mean," she pauses, now embarrassed, "what happened?"

"I was accused of money laundering, fraud, and falsifying records. I did my time, and now," he says with a sheepish grin, "I'm searching for new opportunities. Opportunity doesn't always come knocking. Sometimes, you have to chase it down and knock on its door. If it doesn't open—kick down the door."

"What are you talking about?"

"It isn't important. What's important is that it's all behind me now, and we can all move on. Your father made sure I was well taken care of for my efforts. He was an honorable man. I wouldn't change the decision I made." He stares into the sky to pay his respects to her late father. "I wish I could have been there to say my goodbyes."

Thaddeus continues to tell her about the years he served in prison and what it was like. Much to Delilah's surprise, he doesn't sound upset or bitter for serving numerous years, but she can tell when he discusses how the company was sued that it is a sore subject for him.

"It was a setup. An Israelite company we were working with suddenly claimed that our company was trying to avoid paying them and had us investigated. It opened up an assortment of problems. You know how the Israelites have always hated the Philistines." He rambles on about the Israelite company, their lawyers, and how, eventually, they would all pay for sending him to jail. Delilah doesn't pay attention. Prison would make anyone bitter and angry at the world.

"Tell me," he asks, "why did your man let you come alone tonight, especially as beautiful as you look?"

"Come on, you are making me blush. Who said I had a man?"

"You don't think people know you and Samson are together? People see you all over town walking around with that long-haired Israelite. What's the deal? What do you see in him?"

"I still didn't say we were dating. He's a friend." Delilah laughs.

"You know you could do better."

Delilah's brow furrows.

"It's the uncle in me. I can't help it," he says, gently patting her arm like a child. "Tell me, why is he so strong?"

"What do you mean? He works out and eats right. Don't drink," she says. "Where is this going?"

"I don't mean like that. You obviously don't know who you are dealing with."

"A gorgeous Israelite?" she teases. "Why don't you tell me who I'm dealing with?"

"The Timnah Police Chief some years back – burned to death in his shed. Your man did that."

Wasn't he a dirty cop? How do you know it was Samson? It could have been anybody."

"Trust me, it was Samson. That isn't the only incident. Killed thousands in a meatpacking plant."

Delilah laughs uproariously. "Did you say *thousands*?"

"Yes, maybe more. You don't know this man."

"And you do?" She folds her arms. "Not everything on the Internet is true. Did you have the Internet in prison?

"Ha-ha," he replies. "I know people, and I hear things."

"You sound like you've had too much to drink. Why don't we talk about something else?"

"Why don't we talk about your debt?" Her facial expression completely changes. "I told you – I know people, and I hear things."

Defensively, she rebuts, "I'm not having this conversation with you."

"Why not?"

"You've just been released from prison. I know you don't have any money."

"No, what I don't have is debt. You would be surprised how fast a thousand can turn into a million when you can't spend it. Interest is a beautiful thing. Let me help you." He touches her arm. "All you have to do is discover the secret to Samson's strength."

She glances at the people leaving the party, averting her attention. She is embarrassed that they overheard her conversation.

"Let's be candid, Princess. Can you afford *not* to?"

"Why do you want to know? What are you going to do with the information?"

"Does it matter? Do you think you're in love?" Delilah stares at him. "When you are done playing with your boy toy, the bills will still be here."

"I'll bite," she says, hoping to learn why Thaddeus is so interested. "How much will you pay me?"

"Twenty thousand," he responds, smiling.

She chuckles. "I'm sorry. You misunderstood me when I said, *'Show me why this information is important.'*"

"Fine, Delilah. Forty thousand dollars."

"Come back to me when you offer *real* money, Uncle Thaddeus. I have grown-up problems, and 40,000 dollars is play money." She kisses him on the cheek and says goodbye.

He slips her his card. "Keep in touch, Princess."

Delilah struts out the door. It has been a long day, and she needs a hot bubble bath. But the more she thinks about it, the more concerned she becomes. *Why is Thaddeus so interested in Samson?*

Chapter 27

JUDGES 16:4

"**A**re you ready? The wine party starts in twenty minutes," Delilah calls out.

She is standing in front of the floor-to-ceiling mirror in her bathroom, applying her makeup. Out of the corner of her eye, she sees Samson stroll into the bathroom, pull down his pants, and sit on the toilet. Surprised by his comfort level, Delilah rushes out of the bathroom and shuts the door.

Samson chuckles, shaking his head. "Come back in and finish. It won't take me long."

"I can't be in the bathroom while you *go*," she squeals. "We will never be *that* close."

Samson laughs, saying, "I thought you wanted to be together. This is what happens when we become one."

"How is the home-buying going?" she asks.

He shrugs his shoulders nonchalantly. "Fine. Still narrowing it down to what I want."

She wonders if he thinks about her when considering his home plans, but she doesn't ask.

As she slips on her eggshell empire-waist dress, her cell phone rings. She glances down and sees that it is Thaddeus. She is growing sick of his pestering. She had debated whether to file for bankruptcy, but she couldn't fathom it. Everyone would know, and she has a reputation to uphold. Delilah sends the call to voicemail and thinks about his offer to ferret out Samson's secret. Her curiosity is getting the better of her. She knows about Samson's family and upbringing but little about his past. When Samson strolls out of the bathroom, she returns to finish her makeup.

"Getting to know your question," she says, lining her lids with liquid eyeliner and applying mascara. "I heard rumors of a man who caused mayhem back in the day, setting fires, fighting in warehouses, killing a lot of people in the process. Was that you?"

"Where did you hear that?"

"Around. Why? Is it true?"

"I don't know what you're talking about."

She knows he is being evasive anytime he responds to a question with that statement. "Samson…"

"Where did that come from anyway?"

"I was just curious."

"Shouldn't you be getting dressed?" He walks by her, smacks her on her bottom, and heads toward the door. "I'll be outside pulling the car around. Don't believe everything you hear."

His avoidance of the question only intensifies her desire to know the truth. *Why is he so cagey about it?*

The following weekend, Delilah stands alone on the beach's white sands, watching the ceremony, wishing she could step closer to the cool water creeping up to reach her toes as the tide rolls in. She recognizes that this will serve as the backdrop for the beginning of her life with her future husband. She closes her eyes and sniffs the salty breeze of the ocean. She can imagine herself standing in a pile of sand outlined in a heart. Rose petals are sprinkled on her bare feet, and her dress sways in the wind. A man stands in front of her, mouthing his vows.

"I hereby renew your vows and pray that the next ten years will be even better than your first. Please, kiss your wife," the pastor says, bringing Delilah back from her daydream.

The bride, Delilah's close friend from high school, kisses her husband and turns to face the small crowd gathered around them. She raises her bouquet of white hydrangeas, and all her friends and family cheer. Delilah claps and whistles with everyone else, but she can't help but think about her situation. Months have flown by, and she and Samson are progressing in their relationship. Delilah has given Samson a key to her house in case of emergencies; to her surprise, he didn't run away. He hasn't given her a key to his house in return, which disappoints her. *She reminds herself that men are leery of letting go of their precious keys until necessary.*

She can't help but feel resentment every day that he doesn't factor her into his housing plans. Even after all this time, he still hasn't mentioned the possibility of moving in together. He isn't like the men her friends date; they all get married and have babies. Every time he gets down on one knee to tie his shoe, her heart rises into her throat before dropping back into her chest when she realizes this isn't it. *Why is he so hesitant?*

Delilah knows she is ready to take it to the next level. Although she isn't *in love* with Samson, she is convinced it will come with time. Samson is fun to be around; he makes her laugh, and they enjoy many of the same things. But to her, none of those things are as crucial as feeling secure—and she knows Samson can provide that.

Nevertheless, Delilah is unsure of how Samson feels. He does seem concerned about her feelings and what is going on in her life. *But is he in love?* she wonders. She doesn't know. However, she does know that a candid conversation needs to be had. Tumbling headlong into a dead-end relationship is not in her plans. Delilah is ready for a long-term commitment that promises a life-long marriage. She decides she will face the situation and talk to Samson once she is back in town.

After arriving home, Delilah goes to Samson's house for dinner. Her phone lights up in the cup holder of her car. It is a bill collector calling again. She sends the call to voicemail.

Delilah pushes the button to close the roof of her car, taking one last look at the beautiful night. The stars dance in the night sky. She enters the unlocked front door and finds Samson sitting on the couch. "So, I was thinking…" she starts.

Samson sighs aloud. It is never good for a man when a woman starts conversing with "So" or "Hey." Bracing himself, he asks, "How are you? I missed you."

"Hey, sweetie," she says. She kisses him on his lips before sitting down.

"So, I was thinking," she repeats.

"Yes?"

"Where are we going, relationship-wise?"

"What do you mean? We already decided we were together." His knee bounced impatiently.

"I mean, we are, but I want to eventually get married, buy a bigger home, things like that. We are on the same page with that, aren't we?"

"I thought we were good," he says, frowning. "What's the benefit of that, anyway?"

"What? Are you scared?" She glares at him.

"No, but the leading cause of divorce these days is marriage." Samson raises both eyebrows to keep the conversation light.

"Samson."

"What?" His voice shoots up three octaves.

"You haven't brought up living together. You are buying a house and are not including me in your plans. How do you think that makes me feel?" Before he can answer, Delilah sits on her leg, turns her body to face him, and continues, "Don't you like spending time with me?"

Samson tries not to pause too long; he doesn't want to fuel the fire. "Yes, I love it," he says, touching her leg. "But we enjoy spending time together because we still have a choice. Living together takes that choice away."

"You could just say you're scared."

Samson defends his point. "I'm serious. When we see each other, it's because we want to. When you live together, you are in each other's face, even if you don't want to be."

"I know you're serious. That's what makes it so sad." Delilah scoots forward to lift herself off the sofa, deflated. "Before your father passed, were your parents together?"

"Yes, I told you that," Samson answers.

"And I remember hearing that," Delilah counters. "You would think someone with such a great example of marriage wouldn't be so terrified of it."

"Wait…I'm…I'm scared the Philistines will kill you," Samson finally admits.

"What are you talking about?" Delilah asks.

"I was married before, well almost… anyway, she was killed."

"Did you say *killed*?"

"Yes, killed," he replies, with a blank face.

She doesn't know how to respond. Stuff like that happens in the movies, not in real life. "I'm sorry to hear that, but that was long ago. I don't think it would happen to me." Delilah moves back to be closer, placing her hand on his. Samson's hand tenses up underneath. "Seriously, can you see yourself marrying me?"

"One day," he answers, shrugging his shoulders.

"That's saying nothing." She snatches her hand off his.

"I'm afraid I can't provide a conclusive response, Delilah," he admits. "I find myself unprepared, uncertain. It's as if there's a chapter of my life I've yet to explore fully."

"I'm sorry. Is life going to end when you marry?" She pushes back into the cushions, crosses her arms, and stares at him. Her eyes pierced through him.

"I'm not suggesting that," he begins. "It's just that I need to achieve a particular state in my life before I embark on the journey of marriage once more."

"So, let's live together."

"I want to get all the fun out of my system before settling down."

"So, now you are saying we can't have fun?"

"That's not what I said…ugh…The movie is coming on. Let's talk about this later."

Delilah is too fired up to postpone the conversation. "We can have fun. Life doesn't end when you marry, Samson."

"I'm not saying that. I like you and want to be with you, but I'm not ready yet."

"What are we? Five? You *like* me?"

"You know what I mean."

"I'm not sure I do. I mean, I *love* you," she lies to Samson. "Isn't that how you feel, too?" Truth be told, she doesn't think she loves him. She doesn't even feel love has anything to do with marriage.

"You know how I feel. Why are you acting brand new?" he says, chuckling.

"I'm serious right now. I *love* you," she lies again. "I want to be with you, and I don't see why we can't get married. Tell me we're headed down that path. How long do I have to wait?"

"I've had a long day, Delilah. I'm tired. Let's talk about this later." Before giving her the chance to respond, Samson starts the movie.

She is appalled. *Did he just blow me off?* The longer the movie plays, the angrier she becomes.

"Is there something on your mind, Delilah?"

"Oh no, I wasn't talking about anything important when you shushed me and started your movie."

"I told you we would talk about it later."

"*You told me?* Okay, Daddy, we will discuss this when you feel the time is right. I didn't know everything was about you and what was on your schedule. I'm going home." She gathers her things.

Samson sits and stares at her. "All right then," he says.

"*All right then?* We need a break. Call me when you are ready to grow up and talk to me like an adult."

"You think all this makes me want to live with you?" he calls out as she flies out the door.

Delilah is fuming.

After her last relationship, she vowed not to allow any man to string her along. She slams his door and peels out in her car, leaving skid marks in the driveway.

Delilah drives with the top down, the wind blowing through her hair, but the cool air isn't helping to extinguish her irritation. She isn't angry with Samson. Yes, it bothers her that he isn't ready, but her anger stems from all the other issues going on in her life: her new business hasn't taken off the way she wanted, the company has been slow with her home designs, and her credit cards are now maxed out. She initially had so much going for her, but now it is all crumbling down.

"Hello," Delilah answers hesitantly. She is too tired from her long day to argue with Samson.

"I've been thinking about our conversation. Although I'm not sure I'm ready to walk down the aisle *today*, I shouldn't have dismissed your concerns. How about we figure out our finances and move toward our future together?"

Delilah sighs. "I think that's a good idea. I have a client call, but we can discuss this later," she says, ending their conversation but expressing her delight.

Chapter 28

JUDGES 16:5

What am I going to do? She wonders. Delilah knows this could be a deal-breaker for Samson: she has heard him say he wouldn't marry someone with huge debt or who couldn't manage her finances. She is turning into that person.

But what *can* she do? Purses, scarves, and jewelry aren't selling fast enough, and her other company is suffering in the recession. *It is time to go into action.* She admits that this is one of those moments where she has to get off her behind.

She scrolls through her call log to Thaddeus's name. "Delilah, to what do I owe this pleasure?" he asks, smug.

"If I give you the information you want, how much are you offering? Let's try to come up with a better number this time."

"Oh, did you forget that *you* called *me*?" He clears his throat. "We will give you–"

"*We?*" she interrupts.

Thaddeus slows his cadence. "My five business partners and I will offer you 50,000 dollars."

"Make it $200,000 each, and you've got a deal." She isn't sure who needs who more, but she's willing to bet that he would pay much more than he's been offering.

"Wait, *what?* That's a big jump."

"Do you want my help or not?"

There is a long pause. Thaddeus takes a deep breath. "$75,000."

"150,000," she volleys right back to him.

"110,000, Princess. That's the best I can do," he resigns.

"From all five partners."

"*Each?*" he asks, sounding defeated.

"If you want the information, I'll give you the account numbers to which you can wire the money."

"Fine," he concedes after a long pause.

"I can't have this come back on me. I'm in a relationship with this man."

"Of course not."

"What are you going to do with the information? You aren't going to ruin his reputation, are you? Our livelihood depends on that."

"Don't worry, your pretty little head, Princess. I promise I won't touch a single hair on his head."

"Give me two weeks."

"You can roll with me or get rolled over. The choice is yours," Thaddeus barks into his phone while parking his red SUV. "Soon. That's all I can tell you. Don't ask me again."

He enters the crisp night air, noticing two police officers talking near the street. Watching them, he makes his way into the construction site trailer. "Who are those two?" he asks, nodding to the street.

"One is my wife's cousin, Kashton," the supervisor replies. "The other is his partner, Ally."

"Do you trust them?" Thaddeus asks. "I need people I can trust."

"With my life," the supervisor reassures him.

Thaddeus walks back outside to talk to the officers. "How's it going this evening, gentlemen?" he asks, shaking their hands, then turning up his jacket collar to protect his neck from the chill. "My name is Thaddeus. You guys work here overnight?"

"Yes, we do security to make extra cash," Kashton answers, blowing warm air into his hands. "I have a kid in college."

"Me, too. I have a new baby," Ally says, laughing. "Diapers are expensive."

"I have a proposition. I need some guys to do a simple pickup and delivery for me," Thaddeus says.

"What are we picking up, and where are we delivering it?" Kashton questions.

"I'm still working out the details, but it will be a nice supplement to your income. Are you in?"

"How much money are we talking about?" Ally probes.

"I'll get back to you," Thaddeus replies. "We will talk about the money then."

The officers glance at each other. "You're not giving us much to work with here. You look like a well-connected man. Why do you need cops to make a delivery? You know the uniform is extra?" Ally speaks up.

Thaddeus nods in agreement, silently validating their concerns. "You will just have to trust me on this. It will be worth it." A sly smile slides across his face.

"I'm in," Kashton confirms. "Because I only got a three percent raise for doing a great job."

"Me, too," Ally cosigns.

The three shake hands to seal their deal.

Chapter 29

JUDGES 16:6

"Hello?" Samson sounds cautious when he answers.

"I know things have been a little tense lately," Delilah says on the other end, "but I have a new penthouse suite on the twenty-fourth floor with a stunning water view. I would love for you to spend some time with me."

"Well…"

"No talk about marriage, no arguing; just hanging out and spending quality time together."

"Okay, that sounds good," Samson says. "I have functions planned this weekend, but I can come this evening and stay with you."

"Great, I can't wait."

Delilah settles into the suite given to her by her client, James Wilson, owner of the five-star *Wilson Hotel* chain. He has chosen her to design their new resort in Timnah. This is monumental for her company; it could be the stepping-stone she needs for more significant projects. She is shooting for the Governor's contract to revamp all the government buildings and the urban revitalization project. She will have financial breathing room if she wins the job bid. In the meantime, the money Thaddeus has promised her will at least help stop the bleeding.

Mr. Wilson wants her to get a feel for his attention to detail and that certain *je ne sais quoi* that goes into all his hotels—hence the complimentary suite. She figures she can use the three weeks in the suite to think in peace without concern with cooking, cleaning, or any of her chores at home. Plus, she is determined to use the time to make up for the fight with Samson and get their relationship back on track.

Samson pulls out his leather duffle bag from the top shelf of his closet. He has mixed feelings about visiting her; nevertheless, he continues to pack.

I think I'm going to call her back. I don't feel like fighting with her, and I know that's what will happen. It would be much easier to say no if she didn't look so good. Samson checks his watch and continues to pack. *I had a packing list somewhere; it might be on my phone.* As Samson is lost in thought, it dawns on him: *I wonder if she left me a key?*

He whips his phone and texts her: Did you leave a key?

Delilah replies before he can set his phone down on the dresser: No need. Done with meeting. I will wait for you in RM # 24-825.

Samson texts: On my way.

Back at the hotel, Delilah is feverishly working to assemble the most unforgettable outfit ever. She checks and rechecks herself in the hallway mirror, becoming more anxious by the second. *Should I wear studs or hoops?* She ponders, adjusting the thermostat for the third time. *I don't want to have to redo my makeup.*

Samson arrives at the hotel. He parks his truck and makes his way toward the lobby. He isn't walking at his usual quick pace; it is more like a soldier trying to avoid landmines.

"Sir, can I help you with your bags?" the bellhop asks.

Samson smiles. "No, I got it, thanks."

Dressed in designer jeans, a white T-shirt, and flip-flops, he is surprised anyone notices him. He strokes his five o'clock shadow while his head swivels, searching the beautiful lobby for the elevators. It is modern, with bright touches of lavender and silver. A vast, polished crystal chandelier is floating in the center of the lobby. It sparkles as the glowing sun seeps in through the floor-to-ceiling windows.

He drifts in the direction that most people are traveling. There is already a group waiting when Samson arrives at the elevators. Three young girls, all chatting on their smartphones; a man on a business trip; two small kids with a younger couple; and an elderly couple, undoubtedly on vacation, all decked out in their tourist gear.

Ding. The elevator doors open, and the herd of people pack in. Samson holds back to ensure he isn't caught in the commotion.

A woman waves him in, "There's room for one more."

"Thanks, but I'll wait," Samson responds. He isn't in a rush, and he's starting to second-guess his decision. *I hope she understands the meaning of the word vacation because I'm not in the mood; he* is thinking when the ding of the elevator snaps him back to reality.

Chapter 30

JUDGES 16:6-7

Delilah, delicately aiming the perfume bottle upward, released a fragrant mist into the air, creating a seductive prelude to the evening. The sweet droplets settled upon her body and clothing, enveloping her in their delicate embrace. Taking one last scrutinizing look in the hallway mirror, she confirmed her allure from head to toe.

However, beneath her poised exterior, a gnawing question tugged at her thoughts like an insistent undertow. "How am I going to get him to tell me the secret of his strength?" she pondered. She harbored no illusions that he would willingly divulge such a guarded secret. After all, it was just a question.

Interrupting her contemplation, a knock at the hotel door brought her back to the present. "Ma'am, your sparkling grape juice," the bellhop announced, breaking the spell of her thoughts. Delilah replaced the seductive look she had summoned for Samson with a friendly smile. "Come in," she warmly called out.

The bellhop promptly placed the ice bucket on the nearest countertop and exited the room. Delilah scanned the room, ensuring every detail was perfect for the evening.

"Boo!"

Her heart leaped, and Delilah gasped in surprise as Samson materialized with uncanny stealth, entering just as the bellhop exited. "Don't scare me like that, Samson," she playfully chided, swatting him on the arm with mock annoyance.

"Is it my birthday?" Samson inquired as he retrieved the sparkling juice from the ice bucket. Setting it aside, he opened his arms invitingly. "Don't be mad. Give me a hug and a kiss."

Delilah couldn't resist his magnetic presence and happily obliged, her laughter mingling with his. Moments later, she stepped back and performed a slow twirl, her eyes locking onto his. "Do you remember this dress?"

"I do, but it doesn't fit the same," Samson cheekily remarked, his fingers tracing a playful path along the contours of her dress, teasingly exploring its snug fit.

"What did you say?" Delilah queried.

"I mean, it's a little tighter right here," Samson replied with a playful grin, punctuating his words with gentle touches in various places.

Delilah couldn't help but laugh, her playful retort hiding beneath her amusement. "Ha, ha. Come on, we have to go. We have reservations."

"I'm not hungry yet," Samson protested half-heartedly.

"Trust me, you will be. The restaurant in this hotel is world-renowned and known for its vegetarian dishes. The chef is a star in his own right, and I can't wait to see if the food lives up to the hype."

With some reluctance, Samson dropped his bags in the bedroom and took a quick shower. He was in the process of putting on his socks when Delilah reemerged.

"Which shoes should I wear, Samson?" Her mouth curled into a seductive grin as she showcased her footwear options. One foot was adorned with a silver sling-back sporting a four-inch heel, while the other boasted a black peep-toe with a silver four-and-a-half-inch stiletto. Delilah knew well that both pairs were Samson's favorites from her extensive collection.

"Dee, you always know how to distract me," Samson smirked. Their flirtatious banter heightened the charged atmosphere in the room.

"I guess I'll choose then," Delilah purred, embarking on a sultry model-like spin before departing the room, leaving a trail of intrigue in her wake.

"Without a doubt, going with the black," Samson muttered behind her. He had donned a light-gray suit, a crisp white shirt, and gray shoes, adding a white and purple pocket square to complement Delilah's elegant earrings.

With their preparations complete, they rode the elevator down to the hotel restaurant. The host graciously ushered them to their seats and presented them with menus just as their waiter appeared, ready to describe the evening's specials and catch-of-the-day.

Sitting quietly as the waiter departed, an awkward silence hung over their table, threatening to eclipse the evening's promise.

"Let me tell you how the project is going," Delilah ventured.

However, Samson's impatience and hunger grew as she began to speak. "Where is our waiter? Have we ordered?" he interjected, his agitation palpable.

"Yes, Samson, don't you remember?" Delilah replied with an amused glint, recalling their earlier exchange.

Just as Samson was about to retort, the waiter reappeared, their plates in hand. "Our chef asked me to let you know he made this vegetarian delight, especially for you, sir," the waiter announced as he served their meticulously crafted dishes.

Samson's anticipation surged as he eagerly anticipated the first bite.

As the waiter departed once again, Samson acknowledged the chef's culinary skills and sent his compliments. Yet, an undeniable tension lingered over their table, manifesting in the pregnant pauses between their exchanges.

"I mean, all these muscles," Delilah teased, lightly tracing Samson's arm. "Come on, don't play dumb. I never hear you say you're going to the gym. What's your secret?"

Samson leaned in slightly, his eyes locked with hers. "There is no secret. Stay active and eat right," he responded, his tone light. "Are we going to have the protein conversation again?"

Delilah couldn't help but chuckle. "No, I'm trying to get to know you better," she admitted, taking a bite of her salad. "Fine, tell me something else."

"Let's see," Samsom started. "I haven't owned a television in thirty years."

The revelation prompted a curious look from Delilah. "Who doesn't have a TV?"

Samson's conviction shone through as he explained his perspective. "I don't see why I need to watch someone else's life when I have my own. Plus, I only have twenty-four hours and want all of them."

Delilah considered this for a moment. "How do you watch sports, then?"

"I go to a sports bar. It gives me a chance to get out," he shared.

The memory of a previous movie night at Samson's house suddenly resurfaced in Delilah's mind. "Wait, we watched a movie at your house."

With a sly grin, Samson clarified, "That was on a projection screen."

Their laughter bubbled up once more, an echo of their shared connection. "You are unique, Samson. I have never met a man without a TV."

Their laughter continued as they delved deeper into their meal, yet a subtle tension remained beneath the surface.

"Are you ready to go back upstairs?" Delilah inquired once their plates had been cleared.

"Not yet. Let's take a walk."

They ventured through the hotel, strolling side by side, the muted ambiance of the hotel corridors offering a cocoon of privacy.

Clearing her throat gently, Delilah needed to address a different matter. "I have to admit, I was wrong for coming at you like I did. I didn't mean to make you feel like I was giving you an ultimatum." A faint blush tinged her cheeks, revealing her embarrassment. "I've been with men who strung me along, and I ended up investing years into relationships that ultimately went nowhere. I assumed you were the same. I'm getting older and ready for something long-term and stable. I apologize."

Samson responded with a reassuring smile, acknowledging her sincerity.

"Feel free to own up to your mistakes as well," Delilah playfully prodded, her raised eyebrow an invitation to share his side.

"Who, me? I wasn't wrong. You went crazy on me while I was watching a movie," Samson teased, his demeanor light and playful.

"Samson, you're going to let your guard down eventually. It's okay to be vulnerable sometimes."

A mischievous glint sparked in Samson's eyes as he posed a counterquestion, leaning in ever so slightly. "What will you give me if I let my guard down?"

Delilah playfully hung her head and continued walking, her voice carrying a hint of allure. "Samson, what are you so afraid of?" she inquired softly.

"I'm afraid of bowstrings," Samson replied with mock seriousness.

Delilah's laughter rang out, partially masked by her incredulity. "Are you serious?"

"Yes, I'm serious," Samson maintained, his playful demeanor unwavering. "There's something about fresh bowstrings that causes an allergic reaction. I become nauseated and weak. Sometimes, my throat swells, and I can't breathe."

"There must be something you can take for that," Delilah suggested.

"If there is, I haven't found it," Samson mused, lighting the mood with a gentle pinch to her chin. "Now, wasn't that being vulnerable?"

Delilah rolls her eyes with a smirk, "If you say so. At this point, I'll take what I can get."

Their laughter echoed down the hotel corridor as they continued their leisurely walk, savoring the moments of connection that bound them ever closer.

Chapter 31

JUDGES 16:8-10

"The pictures for the site are saved on the desktop in the folder labeled *Images*," Delilah says, walking past Samson and putting on her earrings. "I'm taking you on a romantic dinner cruise tonight."

"Sounds good to me," Samson replied, his gaze unwavering from the glowing computer screen.

"I will stop by the concierge to set it up after my meeting," Delilah continues while shaking her head gallingly. She has grown used to him being distracted while he works. Samson is one of the most driven men she knows. "Thanks for working on the webpage for me. I will be back after the meetings." Delilah leaves to attend her meetings, giving him a quick peck on his cheek as she scurries out the door.

Hours later, she scrambles back to the room to change before the cruise. "I'm back," she calls out, kicking her heels off at the door. "I'll be ready in five."

Samson puts on his shoes and grabs his sports jacket just as Delilah emerges from the bathroom wearing a red and black sweater dress with black leggings. They stroll to the lobby to wait for the harbor shuttle. It is quiet on the shuttle, with light jazz music playing in the background. Minutes later, the driver announces, "We're here. Please watch your step and enjoy your evening."

Ten couples file into the boat, shoulder to shoulder, as if embarking on Noah's ark. "Your name, sir?" asks the host, holding a list.

"Delilah, party of two," Samson replies.

"Right this way, sir."

As they step on board, a dark-haired greeter places a lei of purple flowers around Delilah's neck.

"Glad you're joining us this evening," he says with a smile.

"Thank you for joining us this evening, sir," a slender brunette says to Samson. She pulls a larger lei of white flowers from a different stack and hands it to Delilah to place around Samson's neck.

"I see they found something that can actually fit over all that hair," Delilah remarks, twirling a piece of his dark hair around her finger.

"Jealousy is the only thing that doesn't look good on you," Samson teases.

Delilah winks at him. Samson and Delilah almost loop around the ship when they hear the captain over the loudspeaker.

> *Ladies and gentlemen, I welcome you aboard the Paradise Oasis. This 60-foot power catamaran accommodates eighty passengers, but for your ultimate comfort, we never take more than thirty reservations. The cruise is two hours long. Life vests are located under the benches on the deck. Life rafts are on the portside stern. The water is choppy, but we will smooth the ride. Grab yourself a glass of wine and enjoy the beautiful view. Thank you all for coming aboard.*

Jazz music once again drifts from the speakers. Samson looks over the crowd. There are couples holding hands and admiring the water, families standing and talking amongst themselves, and ladies chatting while sipping their champagne. In a corner, two men scan the crowd.

"Kids, stop running!" a mother says to a group of kids as she chats with friends. The children, who are six or seven years old, continue as if they don't hear her.

Delilah takes a glass of wine from the handsome waiter walking by and pulls out her camera.

"Would you like me to take a picture of you two?" the waiter asks.

"Please," Delilah says, slipping her arm around Samson's waist.

The waiter snapped a picture and returned the camera to her. After thanking him, she takes a quick picture of Samson by himself. "This view is gorgeous," Delilah says, snapping photos of the hotel as they drift away from the dock.

Samson watches Delilah step further away.

"Great view. The hotel looks amazing from here," Delilah mumbles from behind the camera.

He shrugs his shoulders and looks for a server to order a bottle of water. He thought this trip might be an opportunity to reignite their romance. He cares for Delilah and wants to make the best of this mini-vacation, but with all her work, it isn't turning out to be as romantic as he'd hoped. Delilah has nothing but work on her mind most of the time.

"No running," a staff member tells the children while playing.

Samson sits on the bench to watch the sunset while waiting for his water. Suddenly, a wave crashes into the side of the ship. Samson leaps from his seat as the boat rocks back and forth in a fight to remain level.

"Jimmy!" someone screams several feet away from Samson. "*Jimmy!*"

People scramble to the edge of the boat. Jimmy had been climbing one of the ship's flagpoles when he was thrown over the rail by the force of the wave. The frantic passengers yell and call out to the boy, who is now bobbing in the icy water, waving his arms.

"I can swim," he responds through chattering teeth, "but the water's too cold!"

His mother cries out hysterically, the blood draining from her face. "Someone, please, *help him!* I can't swim." she whimpers, her eyes wide like saucers.

"Grab the life preserver!" The crew yelled at Jimmy's father. 'Kill the engines and drop the anchor!" With a hopeful look, Jimmy's mother starts to help her husband coach their son to safety.

As Jimmy swims to meet the white and red lifesaver, a second wave crashes into the boat. This time, everyone aboard the ship tried to brace themselves. Several passengers shriek. When the movement slows, all eyes return to the side of the boat. Jimmy is no longer in sight. Jimmy's father, a massive man over 300 pounds, climbs the railing without hesitation.

"Jimmy, Jimmy!" the mother squeals, searching the water for her child. Jimmy's father leans over to jump in the frigid water just as she tries to stop him. "Don't!

Your pacemaker!" she pleads. When she reaches for her husband, she catches him by his pant leg, causing him to fall awkwardly over the side of the ship. His legs slam hard against the boat, breaking instantly as he falls into the water. Jimmy's father groans in pain.

"*Please*, try to stay calm, ladies and gentlemen," one of the crew members pleads. Other crew members try to move the crowd away from the side of the boat to allow room for the others to attempt to get Jimmy—and now his father—back aboard.

"Are you alright? Talk to me!" the wife yells, clinging to the edge of the vessel.

Her husband is out of breath, taking in mouths full of water. "I can't tread water. I think I broke my legs."

"I see him!" screams a crew member. He spotted Jimmy floating about fifty yards away.

Samson can't stand by any longer; he *must* do something. So, he removes his shoes and shirt, grabs a life vest from under the deck seat, and dives into the water. Samson reaches the father first.

"Please, get my son," he begs, swallowing more seawater.

Samson glances in the boy's direction. The waves have taken him too far from the boat to throw a rope. Samson hands over the life vest and swims toward the boy with the father floating behind him. The crowd watches from the deck above in sheer amazement.

Once he reaches the scared little boy, he grabs him and swims back to the boat. Samson calls for the crew to throw down a rope. They drop the rope into the water, and within seconds, the crew pulls the boy up to safety. Samson hooks the father up next and watches as the crew tries unsuccessfully to pull him up. They can't do it. The force of the waves slamming into the massive man is holding him back. They try again in unison, but he is too heavy for them.

Exhausted and defeated, Jimmy's father starts to cry. "What's your name?" Samson asks. The man only sobs. "Grab onto my shoulders. I will carry you up."

"It's impossible. All those men can't even lift me. I'm too huge!"

Samson ignores his comment. "You ready?"

"But, wait," the man shudders.

"Wait, for what, a shark? We don't have time to wait," Samson snaps, turning his back to the man so he can grab ahold of his shoulders.

Samson clutches the huge chain attached to the anchor and starts climbing up the side of the boat with the three-hundred-pound man on his back. Gasps come from the crowd. Samson grunts as he climbs, grasping the chain so tightly that his knuckles turn white from the strain.

When they finally reach the top, the father collapses in exhaustion. Hunched over, Samson stands with his hands on his knees, trying to catch his breath. His pants cling to his water-drenched body. After a minute, he lifts his head to scan the faces for Delilah.

"Samson, are you alright?" Delilah gasps, emerging from the crowd of spectators.

"I'm fine," he lets out slowly.

"Thank you so much. You saved my family today," the mother says, kneeling to hug her husband.

Samson gives the woman a slight smile. "No problem." He pats Jimmy on his head and takes his shirt and shoes from Delilah.

"Sir, here is a towel," a crew member says.

The captain completes an incident report while the crew returns to the dock. With the dramatic turn of events, the cruise ends early. Delilah is strangely quiet once they dock and return to the shuttle until they reach their room.

"Why would you lie about that?" she asked suddenly.

"About what, Dee?"

"I thought you were allergic to bowstrings?"

"I am. Why?"

"The lei you were wearing was made from seven fresh bowstrings."

Samson raises his hands in frustration. "Is this how you want to end the evening?"

"Don't change the subject."

Much to his surprise, she hadn't yet mentioned the boy and his father, who'd almost *died* that evening. "I don't know, maybe the strings weren't fresh. Maybe they used shoestrings. *Wait, were you* testing *me?* How do you know they were made from bowstrings?"

"No, Samson, all leis are made from bowstrings."

Samson gives her a blank stare and sighs. "Why does it even matter?"

"I just found out," she defends. "When I was taking pictures of the hotel, the captain came by on his rounds to greet passengers."

"Don't change the subject," Samson interrupts.

"I'm serious. I asked him why you received a different lei than mine. He explained market research showed some men don't like wearing them because the fit is too tight and the color selection is feminine, so he had some specially made. I'm surprised he didn't ask you how it fit."

"No, he didn't," Samson replies flatly.

"I apologize for snapping at you. Give me a hug and a kiss," she teases. "I received a free voucher for a spa. Why don't you take it tomorrow and have a massage? When I finish my meeting, we can hang out by the pool. It will be a short day for me."

Samson stares at her, unimpressed.

"Hello…yes, I don't know why. I know. I will keep trying." With a small sigh, Delilah hangs up the phone. She tosses it on the lounge chair and walks to the pool steps, where she slowly enters the chilly water.

"Jump in and get it over with," Samson calls to her from the water.

She smiles at him but continues to walk in. "Getting to know your question," she says when she finally reaches him.

"Here we go," Samson mumbles.

"Come on, don't be like that," she smiles. "Tell me something embarrassing about you."

Samson rolls his eyes in response. She gives him a disapproving stare until he finally cracks. "Okay, okay. When I was younger, one of the games we played involved the other kids finding stuff to tie me up with to see how long it would take me to break free. One time, they tied me up to a tree with a brand-new rope and left me there. Everyone thought I would break free like I normally did, but I couldn't. I peed all over myself. To this day, I have a mental block when it comes to rope. Those guys teased me for years."

"With that story, I'll let you off the hook. The torture test is over."

Samson pulls Delilah closer and places his hand on her back. She puts her arms around him, kissing him gently on his lips. She runs her fingers through his hair.

"I should have put it up. Could you braid it for me later?"

"Of course." She smiles and moves his hair off his face.

He watches her, her skin glowing in the sunlight, hair soaked. Delilah notices that he is staring at her. "What's wrong?"

"Nothing. I forget just how beautiful you are sometimes."

Delilah blushes. Her phone rings from the table near the cabana.

"I think your phone is ringing."

"Let it ring. I'll get it later," she says, kissing him again.

"Where are we going?" Delilah asks as they ride down the coast. The top is down on her convertible with Samson behind the wheel. Her hair blows in the wind, the sun giving her skin a glow.

"Just a ride." Samson places his hand on her thigh and flashes a huge smile. "But here is a hint: it's a place you have been begging to go."

Fifteen minutes later, they arrive at *Rock & Waves*, an outdoor rock-climbing facility close to the beach with a beautiful view. People jog, play volleyball, walk their dogs, and play in the sand along the coast.

"Looks like they rent surfboards, too," Delilah points out as they enter the small building to sign in.

At the counter, they discover that the last group for rock climbing for the day has just left. If they get done fast enough, they are told they can still make it. They complete the legal paperwork and then rush to catch up. They reach the group outside just as the guide is telling his story.

"How many of you have rock climbed before?" Only two people raised their hands. "Everyone here looks athletic. How do you all stay in shape?" Sporadic voices speak up.

"I lift weights."

"I run."

"I like hiking."

"In hiking, you mostly go up zero to seventy degrees slopes. In running, you are getting from point A to point B. When you are rock climbing, you're going straight up a rock or a cliff, and you may even climb inverted at a degree greater than 90, as you can see here to my left." He points. "You have no gear to assist you in climbing up the rock, just your hands, feet, and the rock. That's why it's the perfect sport. The gear you carry is for support so you don't fall. Rock climbing involves strength, control, and finesse. Using the muscles in your arms and legs to pull yourself up a sheer rock face takes strength and control. Using your brain to know where to place your hands and feet so that your muscles can do their job, now *that's* finesse."

"The basic premise behind rock climbing is straightforward," he continues. "You are trying to climb from the bottom to the top. However, if that were all there was to it, you would need nothing but your body and a good pair of climbing shoes. The other part of the sport comes from knowing how to protect yourself should you slip."

"First and foremost, never climb alone. Starting out, you need someone to belay for you. This is a harness. It's what you clip all your gear onto and run the rope through." The guide explains sizes and then passes out the appropriate harnesses. "This is climbing rope; it is one of the most important pieces of gear. It is the main thing keeping you from falling and breaking your face. I need to know your weight. And ladies, don't lie because this determines which rope you use. We'll all know you lied anyway when the rope snaps."

All the men laugh while the women stand there unamused. When it's Samson's turn, and he shares his weight, the instructor tells him, "I have a brand-new rope for you." Another assistant passes out the other ropes while the guide returns to directing his group.

"This is the belay device. You hook this to the front of your harness and run the rope through it to belay for the person who is climbing." He walks over to the wall. "This is a crash pad. It's a large piece of foam laid on the ground where you climb. I hope you never have to use this, but it's nice to know it's there." The instructor scans the crowd. "Since we have an odd number of people, I'll help belay. Who wants to go first?"

Delilah decides to go first. She braces one foot on the lowest rock and pulls her body up the wall, reaching for the next handgrip as she moves along. Halfway up the cliff, her forearms ached. She let go of the wall and allowed the guide to float her down to the crash pad.

"Sir, your turn." The instructor motions for Samson to step up.

"How does this work again?"

"You want to climb with your legs. Don't pull yourself up with your arms."

"No wonder my arms hurt," Delilah sighs, massaging her forearms.

"Does the cliff get more difficult as you go from left to right?" Samson interrupts.

"That's right. You want to start somewhere in the middle."

Samson looks up and down the wall. "Let's go all the way over to the right."

"We don't let beginners start on the hardest wall."

"You have a crash pad. The worst that can happen is I fall, right?"

The guide stands in silence.

"Belay me, and let's do this." Samson starts on the back wall. He climbs to the ceiling and across the cave with ease. Once he reaches the front opening of the cave, he swings his foot around to get over the lip. With that, he scales the rest of the cliff to reach the top of the rock. He comes down with a cocky smile, the instructor and the others on the ground staring in awe. "Are you ready to go back up, Dee?"

"Yes, but don't think I can do what you did."

Samson and Delilah take turns until her arms can't handle it anymore. "Use your legs, not your arms." Again, she only makes it halfway up the rock before getting ready to come down.

"At least go to the top. Take a rest, I got you," Samson calls.

"I'm too tired," she says, letting go of the wall.

"I'm not letting you down until you go to the top," he says playfully.

Delilah swings for a moment, thinking he is playing a practical joke. After realizing he isn't going to let her down, she shouts, "Fine!" She musters up all her energy and climbs to the top.

"Good job!" Samson gives her a high-five when she's back on the ground.

"Let's get out of here," Delilah starts to pull off her harness.

Samson laughs and removes his harness as well. He glances at the people around him and notices two men sitting on jet skis near the shore. He thinks that it's odd they are motionless in the water. He remembers seeing them in the same position when they arrived.

Delilah says on their way to her car, "I thought you'd never done this before?"

"I haven't. That was my first time."

"Looks like you got over that new rope phobia, too."

Samson doesn't know what she is talking about at first. Then it clicks, "That was a long time ago."

Delilah rolls her eyes.

Chapter 33

JUDGES 16:13-15

"Dee," Samson says as he gently shakes her.

Delilah rolls over and looks at him with partially open eyes. Samson is standing over her. "I went out to pick up dinner while you were asleep. Why don't you go take a quick shower, and we'll eat?" Without a word, she stands and gathers her clothes. Samson grabs her hand to pull her close to him, staring at her for a moment.

"What, Sam?"

"Are you alright?" he asks.

"Yes, I'm fine."

"Give me a kiss. I will not let you go until you kiss me," he says, tickling her side. She tries to break his hold and not laugh, but he keeps it up. Finally, a smile crosses her face.

"Okay, okay." She kisses him on his lips.

"Not feeling the love; try again."

"Samson," she pleads as he tickles her neck. Delilah laughs and kisses him again. Samson releases her, and she turns on the shower. She wraps her hair while waiting for the water to reach the correct temperature. As the bathroom mirror fogs, letters appear in front of her. She stands there, trying to make them out.

Time is almost up.

She gasps. Someone wrote that while she slept. Were they *here*? Inside the room?

The next day, Samson and Delilah eat dinner at the hotel restaurant, then head upstairs to watch a movie.

"You want me to braid your hair while the movie is on?" Delilah offers. Samson moves to sit between her legs, resting his head on her knee. She sections his hair into seven segments. He closes his eyes as she starts braiding. "Are you sleepy?" she asks.

"No, just relaxing."

Delilah kisses him on his neck and continues to braid. "Rock climbing was easy for you like you've done it for years."

"Nah, I was a late bloomer."

"What are you *not* good at?"

He laughs. "Losing."

"You can't be this strong all of the time."

Samson points at the loom across the room Delilah uses to make scarves. "If you wove my hair into the metal part of the loom, I would be weak."

"Now you think I'm a fool?"

"No, really. It's the metal screws and bolts in the loom that causes me to lose my strength."

"Samson," she says.

"You asked; I gave you an answer," he replies, turning his attention back to the movie.

Delilah continues braiding his hair. It sounds unbelievable: weaving his hair into a loom. But what choice does she have *but* to believe him? It has been weeks, and she is no closer to giving Thaddeus the information. Time is running out. She needs the answer soon.

Samson dozes off. The longer she braids, the deeper he sleeps. She stares at the loom. *Just try it, Delilah; you never know. You don't have much time.*

She looks at him sleeping peacefully, then slowly slides her leg out from under his head, bracing it between the couch and a pillow. She quietly rolls the loom near the sofa and sits beside it. When she finishes the final two braids, she intertwines his hair into the steel bar of the loom. She eases her way out from behind him again, pacing around the room.

The room is eerily quiet; the movie has finished. Samson sleeps soundly. She hears a scratching noise on the other side of the wall. She stands quietly, listening to see if she can hear it again. The note on the bathroom mirror has her on edge, giving her the feeling that someone is watching them.

Suddenly, there is a loud bang on the sliding glass door. Startled, she screams, and Samson jumps up. The steel rod of the loom breaks; Samson is groggy, so he doesn't notice.

"What's wrong?" he yells.

"I don't know." Her breathing accelerates. "I heard a loud noise. Something hit the balcony door."

Samson scrambles to investigate the noise. As he goes onto the balcony, there is a sharp knock at the door. Delilah snatches the door open and sees two Philistine men. She knows Thaddeus sent them. "No, thank you, we don't need more towels," she roars, swiftly shutting the door before Samson can see them.

As he enters the room again, Samson begins to realize that something is in his hair. Delilah watches him. He is as strong as always. "What is this?" he yells, pulling metal from his hair.

"You lied *again*!" she screams, balling her fists.

"Were you *testing* me again? *Seriously?* What is the point of all of this? If I told you I had a peanut allergy, would you put peanuts in my food and wait to see if my throat closed?" Samson pulls pieces of the broken loom from his hair and throws them on the floor.

"Of course not, but why do you keep lying to me? You keep making up stories, trying to make a fool of me. How are we ever going to get closer if you keep lying? You don't care about me."

"What are you talking about? What does my strength have to do with anything?"

When the shouting ceases, Samson is still oblivious to Delilah's motives, and Delilah is still oblivious to the source of Samson's strength. The only thing they are both sure of is that neither can trust the other completely.

Thaddeus sits in his red Mercedes-Benz G-Class, waiting for the light to turn green on the corner of First and Center Street. He taps the top of the steering wheel with one hand and holds his cell phone with the other. "Are you *sure* everything is in order? I want to make certain there are no mishaps," he barks.

A horn blows behind him to remind him the light is green. He throws up the hand from the steering wheel and waves, annoyed at the person behind him.

"I'm here," Thaddeus returns to his phone. "Everything had better be perfect. Do you understand me? This will be one of the biggest events this town has ever seen. There is no room for error."

He ends the call and dials another number. "It's Thaddeus. How is the guest list coming along? I want to make sure everyone is there to see him."

Chapter 34

JUDGES 16:15-17

As Samson gets ready for bed, he and Delilah are silent. The air in the room is thick, the tension palpable. Samson is irritated, angry, and tired. He strips down to his boxers and lays down. Delilah climbs into bed beside him and puts her arm on his shoulder. He doesn't move for a moment, but she pulls her body closer and wraps her arm around him. Samson leans back into her.

"Sorry," she whispers.

At first, he didn't speak. He is still bothered by her persistent need to test him. Finally, he asks, "Why is this so important to you?"

"I know I seem pushy and nosy, but I'm trying to get to know you. I've told you so much about me, but I feel like you won't open up about yourself. I don't feel like I know you at all."

"Is my strength all I am to you? All the things we've done, all the places we've been, all the time we've spent together, doesn't that mean anything? You act like I know everything about you."

"You *do* know everything about me. I'll tell you everything."

"Because you don't know this one thing, you don't know me? When did you take your first baby steps? I don't know that. Does that mean I don't know you?"

"You know what I mean." A tear rolls down her cheek. "I feel like you don't want to get close like you're keeping things from me."

Samson sighs. The conversation is going nowhere. He undrapes his arm from around her and turns over. With his back to her, he closes his eyes and drifts off to sleep.

"Are you awake?" Samson whispers after a thirty-minute respite.

"Yes," Delilah growls.

There is no way she is going to let this go. He finally caves; he tells her the secret of his strength.

"My hair," he finally says. Delilah doesn't speak, and he is confused by his reply. "My power is in my hair."

She is emotional, but surely, she isn't crazy enough to try and cut it, he tells himself.

"The hair on your head?"

"Yes. If you were to cut my hair, I would lose my strength. No razor has ever been used on my head," he explains to her. "Because I have been a Nazirite dedicated to God from birth. If my head is shaved, my strength will leave me. I would become as weak as any other man."

After all this time, Delilah is surprised at his answer, but something in Samson's tone tells her it is real this time. "Thank you," she whispers, pulling herself closer to him.

Samson turns over to face her, kisses her forehead, then turns back to his side. She turns over, puts her back to his, and drifts off to sleep.

Their stay in the hotel is now over. Samson is anxious for a break from Delilah. He cares about and loves spending time with her but also needs time.

Chapter 35
JUDGES 16:16

Going home without his father being there is strange for Samson.

He is still adjusting to life without him. Although he and his mother are close, he misses talking to his father.

Samson rolls down his windows and turns up the radio as the trees fly by. Glancing into his rearview mirror, he watches the city grow smaller behind him. He pushes the arguments from the last few weeks behind him as well. He is tired of fighting with Delilah; they are so far from marriage right now. It's hard for him to believe that Delilah thinks they are ready.

"Ma, you here?" Samson calls out as he enters the foyer and removes his shoes. "Ma!"

"I'm upstairs," she answers.

Samson jogs up the steps and enters his mother's room. She is lying in her bed watching soap operas. She looks delicate, different from the last time he saw her. It was as if she'd aged years.

Samson kisses his mother next to a small scar on her forehead and climbs onto the bed. "What are you watching?"

"I don't know, some show. There is nothing on right now." Hazel looks at her son from head to toe. "What's wrong? You look like something is bothering you."

His mother could always read him. "I was just wondering why you are upstairs watching TV when there is a big TV downstairs. You are going to hurt yourself walking up those steps," Samson announces. "Looks like I'll have to sell the house."

"You will *not,* and don't repeat it. You grew up in this house. Your father built this house."

He has no intention of selling the house, but he knows it will get a rise out of her. "Okay, Ma, I won't talk about selling the house, but I need you to stop coming upstairs when you're alone."

"This is my house. I will go where I want."

Samson laughs a little. "Are you still mad about the car?"

"No, I'm not mad you took away my freedom," she replies, crossing her arms.

Samson keeps a straight face. "Ma, are you really playing the victim? You've wrecked *four* cars."

"One of those wasn't my fault."

"I didn't count that one," he laughs.

"And don't forget, no one was hurt."

"That's true. However, someone—I'm not mentioning any names—survived four accidents without a scratch, then hit her head on the curb getting out of the car." After an awkward pause, they laugh together. Samson falls back against the pillows on her bed, still laughing. "Do you remember that time you were lost for five hours?"

"You would be lost, too, if it wasn't for GPS," she says with a frown.

"What do *you* know about GPS?"

"I'm cool. I'm hip."

"You watch too much TV. Are the housekeeper and chef doing an excellent job? Does the van service come on time?"

"Yes, yes, and yes. Enough about me. How are things with you?"

"I'm fine," he replies, not wanting to involve his mother in his relationship drama.

"Women problems?" she asks, patting him on the arm.

He smiles at his mother but changes the subject. "It's gorgeous outside. You look like you need some sun. You and I are going shopping tomorrow."

"That sounds like fun. I haven't been downtown to the boutiques in a while. Are you hungry?"

"Starved. What did the chef make today? Feels like I haven't eaten in days—not a good home-cooked meal anyway."

"Check the freezer. She usually makes meals and freezes them for me for the week. How long are you going to be here?"

"I don't know. Until the end of the week."

His mother gives him a serious look. "Have you prayed about it?"

"Huh?"

"Samson, I want to talk about your father, Manoah. I know you've heard me say this before, but I genuinely believe God can answer prayers for strength and wisdom. Your father is a perfect example of that.

"When I met your father, he was everything to me. He was fun-loving and carefree, but his lawyer side was suspicious of everything and everyone. Your father told me many years later that he knew he loved me but wasn't sure he wanted to marry me. So, he asked God for wisdom.

"We had been dating for about two or three years when your father took me to a fancy restaurant. When it was time to pay, he said he forgot his wallet at work. I volunteered to pay for the dinner; I didn't think much of it since he'd paid for everything since we started dating. Your father said that was the sign he needed to show him I would be beside him for richer or poorer.

"I just wanted to share this story with you because it shows how your father's faith in God helped him make a crucial decision. It's a reminder that we should always pray for wisdom and guidance, especially regarding matters of the heart."

Samson interrupts. "I get it, Ma. If I had girl problems, that would be good advice." He smiles and kisses his mother on the forehead. "Since I don't, let's discuss our plans for tomorrow."

Chapter 36

JUDGES 16:16

Delilah sits in the middle of her bed, reading stacks of contracts and looking over the final additions for the hotel. She fell asleep around 2:15 a.m. and has been up since 5:00 a.m., unable to fall back asleep. She looks over at the clock: 9:27 a.m. Delilah rubs her eyes with the back of her hand, gets out of bed, and stretches. Slipping on terry cloth slippers, she heads into the kitchen to make coffee. The smell of the coffee beans renews her energy. While the coffee brews, she places a bagel into the toaster and walks to her bedroom.

Picking up her cell phone, she checks for any missed calls. Samson hasn't called her back since last night. She can't stop thinking about him. She wants to ensure he isn't still upset about their fight. He said he wasn't before he left, but she could see in his eyes he was lying to her. As she went to leave her room, her phone rang. She smiles and rushes back to the phone in anticipation. But it isn't Samson. She rolls her eyes.

"Hello." The tone on the other end is impatient. "Why haven't I heard from you?"

"Because I have nothing to tell you. When I do, I will call you."

"The party is coming up."

"I know. I said I would take care of it. You will be the first to know."

"You better," he growls and hangs up. Delilah stands there, staring at the phone.

Samson walks through his front door, drops his keys on the end table, and removes his shoes. It feels good to be home. Replaying his conversation with his mother, he knows she is right. After praying about it, he finally admitted that Delilah wasn't the one for him. There is just too much she has done and said that he couldn't get past, like her controlling, manipulative, deceitful, and hostile attitude. These are not the traits he wants in his partner. Lost in his thoughts, he wonders why it is *so hard for me to leave.*

He feels like he'd been on the go for the last few weeks and barely remembers being home for the previous month. Sitting on the couch, he begins to go through the stack of mail he picked up on his way in. He also pulls out his phone. *Wow. I've missed a few calls. Delilah is one of 'em.*

Samson knows he needs to tell her how he feels. He considers telling her over the phone but decides it is a conversation better suited for face-to-face. In the long run, she will see how breaking up is best for them both. He knows it will not be easy because he genuinely does love her. As if she is reading his thoughts, Delilah calls.

"Hey, what are you up to?" she asks.

"Relaxing. I just got in from my mom's. Now I'm going through the mail."

"It would be nice to meet her one day."

"Dee…" he starts.

"Calm down, I was just playing." Delilah giggles. "I'm on my way to grab dinner. I had a taste for a good wedge salad."

Samson thinks about telling Delilah that he wants to talk, but he knows she won't let the subject drop until he tells her everything. He decides against it. "What do you have planned for the weekend?" Samson asks. "I thought maybe we could get together Saturday or Sunday."

"I'm working on building plans and running errands, but I can work around your schedule. I have nothing definite."

"Okay. I'll let you know closer to the weekend."

They are both silent for a moment. "Are we good?" she asks.

"What do you mean, *Are we good?*"

"Just asking. I'm not trying to start anything."

"I'll call you tomorrow," he says.

Chapter 37

JUDGES 16:18-21

Samson knocks on Delilah's door and hears her call out that it is open. Maybe he should have done this in public, but he is here already. He enters the kitchen, where Delilah holds an ice-cold ginger beer in her hand, one of his favorite drinks.

"Where did you find that? I didn't know they still made those."

"I ordered it, especially for you." Reluctantly, he takes it. "Come sit down," she says, patting the seat of one of the bar stools in front of the island.

"No, I'll stand." He takes a sip of his drink, closing his eyes. *That is good.* "What is that smell?" he asks, noticing a hint of a flavorful aroma wafting in the air. She pulls a green bean casserole from the oven. "That's one of my favorites." She smiles knowingly. "I need to tell you something," he says somberly.

"Before you do, follow me first."

"I think we should talk."

"We can talk, but first, I want to show you something." She walks Samson out to her patio. There is a table with two place settings, soft candles, and his favorite band's music from an outside speaker. "I know things have been strained lately. I thought we could have a romantic dinner but with a twist." She turns on an outdoor projector. "I recorded some motorcycle races you said you didn't have time to watch."

"That's sweet, thank you," he says, shocked. Delilah makes him a plate. A stunned Samson sits down at the table.

She fidgets from side to side as she rubs her palms together. "Samson, sometimes I'm a drama queen and act spoiled. I'm not always honest, nor do I say or do the right thing. But my intentions are good." He looks at her, searching for a sign like his own father had asked for. "You may not believe it, but I don't like arguing or fighting with you. I sometimes act the way I do because I fear losing you." She strokes her hair and twists a dangling strand around her finger. "I love you. I have lost too many people I loved over the years. I can't take that hurt again. I want to be with you. I want to be happy. You make me happy, and I couldn't ask for anything more than that. You make me better. You make me want to be better. I want you to help me be better," she says, reaching out across the table and placing her hand into his.

Delilah notices his empty drink. "Let me get you another one, and I'll start the races for you." She turns on the recording and then heads towards the kitchen. While she's gone, she checks her phone. One unread text message appears: The package was delivered. It's in the garage.

Samson glances at the TV, at the food, and his specially imported ginger beer. He doesn't want to ruin the moment. *I'll tell her after dinner. What if she's trying to change? What if she's telling the truth?* It's hard for him to stay focused – on top of the ambiance, the great food, and the recorded races.

When she returns outside, she hands Samson his drink and pulls her chair around the table to be closer to him while they eat and watch the races. Moving closer, Delilah lays her head on his shoulder, gently stroking his arm. "I'm glad you came over," she whispers, running her hands through his hair. "When was the last time you had your hair braided?"

"I don't know. It's been a while." He glances at her from the corner of his eyes.

"Let's go into the living room." Delilah stands and transfers the race to the TV. Entranced, Samson follows her inside, where she takes off her shoes and sits on the couch. She pats her lap and smiles.

"How are you going to braid it?"

"Maybe cornrows, not sure." She jumps up to fetch oil for his scalp. When she returns, Samson sits on a pillow on the floor and rests his head on her lap. Delilah gently caresses his hair and methodically runs her fingers through it. Samson closes his eyes, letting out a deep breath. She sections his hair into seven equal parts. Samson's lids become heavy as she braids, his breathing slows, and he drifts off to sleep. Delilah continues until the last braid is complete, then leans forward and watches him sleep peacefully. Slowly, she slips her leg out from under his head and gently places his head on the couch.

Delilah tiptoes to the garage and opens the door quietly so as not to awaken Samson. She stands there for a moment, scans the room, and then turns on the light. Stepping into the garage, she heads to the back of her car. She stops and checks underneath it when she gets there, only to be confused when she finds nothing. *Maybe he was wrong?* she wonders while standing up and dusting off both knees. The sudden appearance of a light inside her car causes her to jump backward with a yelp.

"Don't do that," she scolds, barely above a whisper. "You scared me." Kashton and Ally lean back on her black leather seats and simultaneously exit the vehicle. "Coming straight from work?" she questions, eying the police uniforms they wear.

"You should learn to lock your doors," Ally warns with a menacing look, sending a cold chill down Delilah's back.

"Follow me and be quiet. He is asleep." They stealthily return to the living room, and she is relieved that Samson hasn't woken up. Kashton begins walking around the room and moving furniture, searching for an outlet for the clippers he holds. "Wait! He will hear that and wake up," she whispers. Motioning for the men to hold off, she sprints to the kitchen and returns with cooking shears. "Quickly, before he wakes up."

Kashton puts down the clippers and accepts the scissors. He picks up the end of one braid and starts to cut without the sound of the scissors waking Samson from his sleep.

"Move, let me do it," Ally demands. He snatches the shears and finishes the first braid with a quick snip—his pace quickens. In a matter of seconds, all seven braids are severed from Samson's head.

Delilah stands there, expressionless, watching the men. As they finish, she confirms, "Are you ready?" Both men take their stances, ready to snatch Samson off the floor – they have heard about his strength and hope that she got it right this time. When they nod, she cries out, "Samson! The Timnah police are here."

Startled by Delilah's scream, Samson opens his eyes to see the men hovering over him. Surprised, he tries to scramble to his feet but instead falls back onto the couch and knocks over a lamp. They lunge at him, but he manages to get free. "What's going on? Why are the police here? Dee? Where are you?"

In a calm voice, Delilah answers, "I'm here."

The officers corner Samson, approaching him from either side of the dining room table. As Samson turns to face Delilah, the men lunge again to tackle him. Missing, they crash into each other and break Delilah's centerpiece.

"What are you arresting me for? What did I do?" No one answers. Kashton begins to shake a spray bottle he has pulled from his pocket. With Delilah in Samson's line of sight, he yells to her, "Dee, call the police!" He's delirious and forgets that it is the police who are assaulting him.

Samson manages to flip the table over towards the officers. Buying him a sliver of time, he uses it to scan the room for an exit. He begins to run for the back door but nearly immediately stops. He is nauseated. Discovering his long, glorious hair in a pile on the floor next to a pair of kitchen scissors, the magnitude of the situation becomes clear. His chest tightens, and the officers take advantage of his halted movement, quickly wrestling him to the hardwood floor.

"Has the money been transferred?" Delilah's words bring Samson's struggle to a standstill. His eyes darted toward her.

"Dee…how could you?" he asks softly. Samson tries to break free again, yanking his arms and kicking the officers, but it is no use. His strength is gone. The officers pulled Samson to his feet and handcuffed him.

"Take a good look," Kashton chides, "because hers is the last face you'll see."

Samson prepares to give it one last fight. He looks for an escape route, but before he can put a plan into motion, he feels something sprayed into his eyes. "Ahh!" he yells in agony. He thrashes his head back and forth, continually blinking to no avail.

"It burns!"

"I'm sorry. I thought you liked to play with fire," Ally quips.

The laughter is cut short by Delilah. "He isn't leaving this house until I have my money."

Her frustration simmers a product of her impatience with the man who had, in her mind, wasted her precious time.

Her father's advice reverberated in her mind: 'No one will take care of you but you.' She had to seize control. The mounting debt and the moral cost of her decisions were becoming overwhelming.

Samson's heart shatters hearing this. How could he have been so stupid? The pepper spray leaves him unable to see, but her sharp words leave him unable to feel. As he struggles again to open his eyes, he feels a blow to the back of his head and loses consciousness.

"Do you want me to pull the car around to the alley?" Kashton asked.

"No, we can take him out through the front," Ally replies.

"Somebody might see," Kashton argues.

Ally cuts his eyes over to him in disbelief. "We're the *police*," he reminds him.

The two police officers lift Samson's limp body and carry him out the front door, down the steps, and through the grass to the black unmarked police car parked on the side of the house. Ally drops Samson's left arm, opens the trunk, and throws him in like a rag doll. "I'll drive; toss me the keys."

The two officers are on the highway before Kashton breaks the silence with a nervous question. "You know who will be happy we finally got him?"

"Who?"

"Everyone." They both chuckle.

"Let's just kill him," Kashton muses.

"How about we not, but say we did," jokes Ally. "He's not worth anything dead."

"All of the bad he's done to people? People *you* know, people *I* know. I don't even care about the money anymore," Kashton snaps back at him.

"Speak for yourself." Ally grabs his cell phone and dials. When a voice on the other end of the line speaks up, he asks, "We have the package. We want to know if you had a plan or if we could just kill him ourselves?" The person on the phone yells. He pulls the phone away from his ear. "Okay…all right…see you in a few."

"What did he say?" Kashton asks.

"He said we can have him later. For everyone to be paid right now, he has to be alive."

"He doesn't have to know. We can just do it."

"Did you just say no one would know if we killed Samson?" Ally laughs in response. "Tempting as it is, let's get the money first."

Seated at his desk, Thaddeus struggles to maintain an air of calm despite the unease brewing within him. Eight faces stare back at him from his computer screen, their expressions somber and unwelcoming. These are his partners, representing various businesses essential to the functioning of a city – contractors, roofers, interior decorators, plumbers, and more.

Clearing his throat, Thaddeus ventures, "Does everyone want their money back?" He studies the faces on the screen, but there's no hint of a smile, only a prevailing sense of discontent that weighs heavily in the virtual room.

A woman among them speaks up, "Thaddeus, you promised to double our money, and it hasn't happened." Thaddeus can't help but release a loud sigh; his disappointment is evident.

"Why do you seem annoyed?" she presses, her curiosity bordering on frustration.

Thaddeus leans back in his chair, struggling to choose his words carefully. "I'm not annoyed. I'm surprised and slightly disappointed that seasoned entrepreneurs and veteran businesspeople can be so short-sighted." He looks around the virtual table, meeting their skeptical gazes. "But I think I know what this is about. Please don't let pride get in the way of the bigger picture.

"Yes, I've been to prison. I know the last thing you want is to be hustled by an old, washed-up, uneducated convict. Let me lay it all on the table for you: I have much more to lose. Remember, I'm the one with a record. Each of you has ten times the amount you gave me on your accounts receivable books, and you're riding my back?

"I'm guaranteeing all of your business for the next four years, and—"

"You didn't deliver on your first promise. Don't try to feed us this mess," a bald man in the top-right corner of his screen interjects, his voice firm and uncompromising.

Unperturbed, Thaddeus rises from his seat but maintains his composure. "I can give you your money back, and you can put it towards advertising or bonuses for your overpaid executives. You can invest in the future of your companies and your families. The choice is yours." Leaning against his desk, he locks eyes with the individuals on the screen, allowing the uncomfortable silence to linger as his unspoken challenge.

"Since you already have the money, I guess we can be a little more patient," another man concedes on behalf of the group.

Buoyed by this small victory, Thaddeus can't help but mock the man, "You guess? This isn't a loan. You aren't doing me any favors. This is an investment, and if you can't see that..."

"Thaddeus," a dark-haired gentleman in the middle of the screen interjects, his tone conciliatory, "I misspoke. How much more time do you need?"

Thaddeus meets their gazes with a sense of quiet confidence. "I can give you the money back after the Gala."

Chapter 38

JUDGES 16:21

The black, unmarked police car arrives at the station in Gaza.

The officers take a left around the building to pull up to the east side entrance. Ally radios in. "We're here."

The men climb out of the car. The Kashton pops open the trunk as Ally, gun drawn, plants himself into a protective stance. Samson lays limp, still unconscious. They pull him out and drag him, one on each arm, into the prison. Samson's feet scrape the ground.

As they walk down the long corridor, inmates peer out of their cells to see who is coming in. "Fresh meat!" someone yells.

When the officers and Samson reach the cell, a guard approaches them and opens the door. "What happened?" Samson is now bald; his face is red and swollen from the spray.

"He got out of hand, so we had to make him," Kashton confessed.

"Everyone thinks they are above the law," the guard sighs. He walks back to the desk and then turns around. "How can I get information from him if he's passed out? Do you know his name?"

They looked at each other, puzzled.

"Uh…Yanir," Kashton says, looking over the guard's shoulder at a form. "Yanir Brutus."

The guard writes down the name. Sliding up his glasses, he asks, "Do you know his date of birth?"

A brief silence fills the air. The officers look at each other and mumble, "Nah." Neither knew much about Samson nor had they thought about providing any information.

The guard sets his clipboard down. "At least hold him up so I can go through his pockets and collect his belongings." The two of them quickly pat him down as they prop him up. They are relieved that Samson's wallet isn't in his pocket, having fallen out in the struggle.

"What did he do?" the guard questions.

"Resisting arrest, public intoxication, trying to bribe an officer...you name it," Ally says.

"Bring him over to the table so I can fingerprint him."

"Can't you wait until he's awake? He's heavy."

"We are in a bit of a hurry," Ally says.

"Fine, I'll do it when he wakes up. You can take him to his cell." The two men drag Samson's limp body to the cell, then toss him onto a thin, tattered mattress.

Chapter 39

JUDGES 16:21

D oor's slam. Voices shout in the distance. The noise becomes louder and louder.

Samson is slowly waking up, his head pounding and groggy. He blinks uncontrollably and repeatedly rubs his eyes, attempting to bring his vision into focus. He can't see anything. Lifting his hands in front of him, he sees nothing but an empty void where his hands should be. Heart racing and sweaty palms, he stands and feels around the room, trying to decipher his surroundings. *Why can't I see anything?*

"Hello!" he yells. "Hey, where am I? *Hello?*"

No one responds although he can hear voices. Someone's footsteps grow closer. "Are you awake now?"

"Where am I?" Samson blurts out.

"In jail," the guard replies.

"In jail? For *what?*"

"You don't know? Stand back so I can open the door. I need to fingerprint you."

Samson tries convincing the guard to tell him what he is in for, but the man won't answer. Samson steps away from the voice. "This is a mistake. I didn't do anything," he pleads.

"Yeah, they all say that. Now turn around." The officer grabs Samson by the arm and forces him around to put the cuffs on him, but Samson pulls away.

"You don't have to do that. I'm not resisting. I'm trying to tell you that you have the wrong man."

The guard replies, "Shut up and put your arms behind your back." He pushes Samson back, knocking him down and onto the bed.

Samson jumps up as quickly as he can. "I said I didn't do anything. Let me go!"

The two men struggle. Blind and weak, Samson fights with everything in him, which is, unfortunately, not very much. He loses his footing and falls over, clumsily knocking the guard down. With a loud wail, the guard hits the corner of the bed and the floor. More guards run into the cell to hit Samson with nightsticks, punching and kicking him. He curls into a ball on the cell floor with his arms covering his head and his knees tucked into his chest.

"Since you want to beat up on officers, you can spend time in the hole," the bruised guard says as he slams the door behind him.

They take him to solitary confinement. The room is silent—no clubs, no voices, no footsteps. With his arms stretched out, Samson feels around the room, taking small steps and searching for the bed. Once the tips of his fingers find the mattress, he thrusts himself upon it and tries to get comfortable.

Why am I here? What is my mother going to think? Samson can't even think about calling his mother—seeing him like this will break her heart. A tear rolls down his cheek. He is supposed to be destined for remarkable things. Instead, he is blind and in jail.

His mind wanders to Delilah. He had loved Delilah, and she had betrayed him. The more he thinks about it, the angrier he becomes. He hadn't trusted anyone with his heart in such a long time. The *one* woman he let his guard down for since his ex-wife deceived him against his better judgment. *How could I have been so stupid?* He asks himself for the millionth time.

Samson lies there, mulling over his situation for what seems like hours. The sound of the slot suddenly opening on the cell door interrupts his thoughts.

"Food," someone announces.

"Wait. I need a doctor. I can't see. I think I'm blind," Samson calls out. "Can you let me see a doctor?" He hears footsteps walking away. Samson sighs and plops back down on the cot.

The abrupt pounding on his door sends shockwaves through Samson, causing him to jolt in surprise when the guards return. "Back away from the door, turn around, and put your hands on your head," commands a deep voice. Samson obeys, his heart pounding in his chest, and they enter, placing heavy shackles on his hands and feet. In silence, they lead him down the cold, dimly lit hallway toward the prison's medical center. His stomach twists with anxiety. He hopes that his sudden blindness is a temporary affliction, but the gnawing fear persists – what if it isn't?

"Wait here. The doctor will see you shortly," the voice echoes as the heavy door swings shut, leaving Samson to tap his foot nervously in the oppressive stillness.

The sound of his breath is interrupted by the door's return. "Good morning... I'm Doctor..." the doctor begins, his voice a mumble that barely reaches Samson's ears. He fumbles through the chart, flipping pages and searching for Samson's name or prison ID number.

"I can't see," Samson interjects, his voice carrying the weight of his dread. "The officers who brought me in sprayed me with something."

As he sets the chart aside, a muted sigh escapes the doctor's lips. "Let me take a look." Retrieving a small light from his pocket, he directs its beam into Samson's unseeing eyes. "Hmmm... well." Stepping back, he returns the light to its place. "I have bad news and more bad news. The bad news is that whatever was put in your eyes damaged your pupils. Even worse, it looks permanent.

"Sorry, there isn't much we can do here but monitor your progress periodically. Your eyesight will come back? You never know. Let me know if you need anything else."

Samson begins to voice a question, but before he can complete it, the office door slams shut, jolting him with surprise. "Hello? Doc?" He calls out in confusion, sitting in disbelief. The doctor concluded his examination, leaving Samson with a multitude of questions.

The door opens once more, and a stern voice breaks the silence. "Let's go, prisoner. Back to your cell."

Chapter 40

JUDGES 16:21

Samson needs to be made aware of the day, time, or duration of his solitary confinement. Every day passes in complete darkness, leaving him to pass the time by reminiscing about his parents, racing days, cherished memories, and reflecting on God's plan for his life... Abruptly, the sound of his cell door opening interrupts his thoughts.

"Let's go," a now familiar voice says.

"Where am I going? Am I getting out? Did someone post my bail?"

"You wish," the guard mumbles under his breath. "You're going on the cleanup crew."

Once Samson's arms and legs are shackled, he complies with the guards as they guide him out of the dimly lit cell, stepping into the stark contrast of the outside world. As he emerged into the open air, he squinted against the sudden assault of light, and the backs of his eyelids flooded with an intense, unfamiliar glow.

A gentle hint of foliage and the scent of nature lightly caressed his senses, carried by a warm breeze brushing against his face. At that moment, as he inhaled deeply, Samson came to a profound realization. He missed life's simplest pleasures, like the feeling of being outdoors, the soft rustle of leaves, and the caress of the warm breeze on his skin. A reminder of the world he had been separated from for far too long.

The guards lead the prisoners to a bus. After a twenty-minute ride, they stop. Samson can hear the brakes and screeching of the tires on the asphalt. The bus shifts its weight under him as an extra passenger climbs aboard. He can hear the voices but can't quite make out the words. Someone yells for all the prisoners to stand and exit the bus. Samson does as he is told.

"Hey, son, you're assigned to the blind prisoner," yells one of the guards to another one. "Help him get around."

"Yanir… Yanir Brutus, I will help you as you work. Do you have any questions?" Samson doesn't say a word, unsure if the new voice is speaking to him. "He *can* hear me, right?"

"He can hear fine. Good luck," the guard laughs. Samson realizes they *are* talking about him.

"So, what are you in for?"

"I don't know," Samson says, shrugging his shoulders. "Why do they call you *Son?*"

"Because I'm the Police Chief's son."

"But what is your name?" Samson pressures.

"Rendor," the boy replies, looking embarrassed as if Samson can see him.

"Why are you working with a blind man all day? You sound young."

"My dad and I are butting heads. This is his way of teaching me a lesson. I told him I wanted to do more than be in law, like him, and this is what he came up with. He doesn't get it, but I want to keep people out of prison, not help the business of prison. My dad believes in locking people up to reform them, but prison makes good people bad and bad people worse. I want to prove we can ensure innocent people aren't imprisoned and give the guilty a fair trial with an opportunity for reformation, not throw them into prison."

Sounds like something Asher would say. "That sounds good to me."

"Yeah, too bad my dad doesn't see it like that."

"What did you do for him to teach you a lesson?"

"Normal kid stuff. I snuck out, went to a party, and missed my curfew. Nothing major."

"Nothing major, huh?"

"I tried to talk to him about it, but he doesn't care what I have to say."

"He's hard on you because he cares," Samson replies, thinking of his father. "I know it's difficult to see when you're young, but it's true. I found that out the hard way. I did things my way and didn't listen to my parents. But I learned in the end that they were always right. They were looking out for me. I was too hardheaded to see that. He has your best interest at heart. Learn from my mistakes before you make a bunch of your own."

Hazel's concern for her son had been steadily growing. While it wasn't unusual for them to go a week without speaking, this prolonged silence was unprecedented. Doubts gnawed at her, and a sense of unease had settled deep within her heart.

She grappled with the decision each day, weighing the need for patience against her maternal instincts. She resolved to grant it a few more days, a fragile hope that there was a reasonable explanation for Samson's silence. But lurking beneath her patience was a growing resolve - if those days came and went without a word from him, she would enlist someone to perform a drive-by, determined to unravel the mystery that shrouded her son's absence.

Chapter 41

JUDGES 16:18, 16:23

Delilah is anxious about this weekend's awards ceremony. The last few months have proven to be challenging, to say the least. She thought her life would be different once she had the money from Thaddeus. But everything around her crumbles before she can pay off all her debt.

First, it's her car. She is proud of her late-model Bentley, which has the same body as the new models but at a third of the price. She hadn't considered that the warranty had expired, which now costs as much as a new one to repair. Although it is her dream car, she is considering selling it. But the Bentley is part of her image, so she can't bring herself to part with it.

Then, it's her house. The air conditioner quit, and the warranty expired. To make matters worse, the painting she'd eyed for years and finally purchased turns out to be fake when the appraiser estimates it for insurance. In her eyes, if something could go wrong, it had.

Business is also slow, which isn't helping. The one positive thing for her is that people rent her buildings for events. The government contract being awarded at the Dagon Awards Gala this weekend is what she needs to get out of this situation. Delilah feels she deserves that contract for all the hard work she has put into that hotel and all other projects she has completed. No one even comes *close* to putting in the same amount of work, time, or attention to detail as she does in her projects. *I am going to win that contract*, she tells herself. Winning will be the catalyst she needs to get back on track.

"All right, good," Thaddeus says into the phone.

"Just making sure everyone is on the same page," he continues, "Listen, I'll talk to you later. I have another call coming in… Hello?" he answers, switching lines.

"Thaddeus, are you ready for this weekend?"

"That depends on you. We still got a deal?"

"Yes, I can give you the details at the Gala."

"I'll drop the gift at the Gala," he says, holding the phone to his ear while pacing his office floor.

"Sounds like we have a deal."

The Dagon Awards Gala is a star-studded event held at the governor's mansion every four years. During the celebration, the governor presents awards to local businesses and awards all the new government contracts for the next four years. Everything from construction to food service to cleaning is an evening that shuts down the city. Everybody who is anybody is there or wants to be there.

Plush red-carpet lines the front steps of the governor's mansion, leading to sizeable wrought iron, glass double doors. The foyer is centered between two grand wood-iron staircases lining each wall. The Carrara marble floors sparkle with swirls of gray and white with hints of blue. On the oak table in the center of the foyer sits a tall, pewter vase full of white and blue hydrangeas, white roses, and yellow forsythia. Above the table hangs a massive crystal chandelier with hundreds of candle-shaped lights.

The foyer leads into a grand room where people mingle in their finest attire. The floor-to-ceiling windows in the room are draped in cream-colored silk drapes that pool slightly on the floor. A soft, amber glow comes from the antique gold sconces around the great room. In the corner, someone plays soft music on an all-white Baby Grand piano.

Chapter 42

JUDGES 16:22-23

Kneeling on the unforgiving cell floor, Samson's demeanor exudes a profound sense of repentance. His brow furrows with remorse, and he runs his fingers through the lengthening strands of his hair, a tangible symbol of his time spent in isolation. Now fuller beneath his touch, his beard reminds him of the passage of days uncounted in this dim, colorless existence.

As uncertainty shrouds him like a suffocating cloak, Samson's gaze remains fixed on an inner reflection. He ponders that his once-dark hair may have surrendered to gray during his absence, and his last encounter with a mirror is a distant memory. In an almost ritualistic gesture, he wipes his hands on the drab fabric of his jumpsuit, each movement an act of penance and a plea for redemption, his arms folded across his chest in silent contemplation.

"I don't know how long I'll be in here or if this cell will be my lifelong abode," Samson murmurs, his voice tinged with remorse, the shadows of doubt dancing in his words. Kneeling on the cold, unforgiving floor, he addresses the invisible presence of his Creator, "But, God, I'm burdened with remorse for squandering the precious gift You bestowed upon me. I've betrayed You, my parents, and my people. This blindness is divine mercy. My sight led me astray, my desires eclipsing Your divine purpose. I've fallen woefully short of the destiny You intended for me. I implore You, O God, grant me another chance!"

With a heavy heart, Samson reclines onto the harsh cell floor, his mind turning to thoughts of his parents. He longs for the soothing embrace of conversation with them, knowing that his mother must be suffering in agonized uncertainty. In the depths of his reminiscence, he conjures the image of his mother, her radiant smile framed by the kitchen window, gazing lovingly at his father as he tends to his beloved Mustang in the driveway. The yearning for his father's sagacious counsel becomes an ache in his heart, for Manoah had always held the key to life's complexities. Samson's trembling hand sweeps away a tear with the back of his hand, the cold, desolate floor bearing witness to his penitent solitude.

"Yanir."

Samson snaps to attention at the sound of his name. "What?"

"You're getting out."

Joy and apprehension intertwine within Samson, emotions tugging in opposite directions. The cell door swings open, and a guard emerges, signaling him to move toward the prison's front, where he'll be reunited with his belongings. As he traverses the prison corridor for the last time, a simultaneous wave of relief and anxiety washed over him. His mind races with vivid flashes – the uncertainty of life outside, the loss of his sight, the tasks he can no longer manage. Samson grapples with the impending reality that he'll never see again.

A voice disrupts his thoughts, and a guard beside him hands over his clothes. Samson takes them hesitantly, admitting that he can't even recall what they look like; it's been so long. Another guard steps in, ready to assist him in changing.

Once dressed, a different man replaces the guard.

"He's ready to go, Mr. Phillips," the guard reports before departing.

"Yanir, are you ready?" the man asks.

"Yes, but do you know me? Why are you bailing me out?" Samson inquires, suspicious.

"I know who you are, Samson. Come with me, and I'll ensure your safe exit," Thaddeus leans in, his voice a hushed, mysterious whisper, leaving Samson with more questions than answers.

Samson and Thaddeus arrive at the governor's mansion within twenty minutes.

The car navigated its way around to the rear of the grand mansion, coming to a halt beside a row of garages. Thaddeus took charge, guiding Samson through a discreet back entrance that led them down a dimly lit staircase, descending into the depths of the mansion's interior. As they reached the bottom, Samson found himself in an orchestra pit.

Awaiting him were two formidable figures, their faces masked by shadows, their intentions clear. They shackled Samson's hands and feet together, binding him in chains. Their stern instructions compel him to take a seat, and an undeniable resistance stirs within him as he settles, resolved to resist and await whatever fate lay ahead.

Delilah slowly makes her way up the carpeted front steps of the mansion. As she enters the iron doors, she is greeted by two attendants standing next to the table in the center of the foyer.

"Welcome. Your name, please?" one of the attendants asked.

"Delilah."

"Welcome, Delilah. This way, please. I will escort you to your table."

Delilah walks carefully across the marble floors, her stilettos clicking along the way. "Good evening. Hello, how are you?" She greets guests as she struts through the room with floor-to-ceiling windows, the moon beaming through the glass roof. She follows the attendant as they walk through a dining area filled with large, white, linen-covered tables. There are two marble pillars in the center of the room and a stage at the front with a band playing soft music. Couples dance slowly to the music as multi-colored lights flash across the dance floor. On the screen behind the band, a projector scrolls through images of completed development projects in the city.

Delilah recognizes many faces in the crowd. She smiles and nods as she catches each person's attention. Delilah arrives at her table just as the governor's red-haired assistant approaches the podium. The assistant smooths the front of her knee-length black and white gown, clears her throat, and pushes her red-framed glasses up the bridge of her nose.

"Welcome, ladies and gentlemen. Tonight, we have a wonderful evening planned for you filled with delicious food, beautiful music, and many well-deserved awards. After the ceremony, don't go anywhere; three parties will occur here at the mansion. On this level, the house band will continue to rock the house with smooth R&B.

On the second floor, a DJ plays old-school grooves in the lounge. And for those in the mood to dance, another DJ will start the party on the rooftop terrace's glass dance floor. We are expecting ten thousand people tonight. No matter which floor you decide to party on, this will be a night you never forget. So please, sit back, relax, and enjoy yourselves. Maestro, take it away."

"Sir?"

"No, thank you," Thaddeus says, waving away a server who offers to refill his glass. He continues talking with the mayor and his wife, scanning the crowd as he pretends to listen. Thaddeus can no longer hide his thoughts about not being seated with the governor. His random side-eyed glances are hard to miss. He needs to speak with the governor, but there is a waiting list to get his attention. With a smile and a nod, the governor gets up from the table and exits through a side door. Thaddeus excuses himself from his table and steps into the hall just as the governor enters the restroom.

Thaddeus hangs back a moment, giving the Governor time to finish and wash his hands. "Governor, do you have a minute?" he asks, stepping inside the restroom.

"Sure, Thaddeus." He finishes drying his hands and tosses the paper towel into the wastebasket behind him. "Enjoying yourself?"

"I am. You sure know how to throw a party."

"I mean, I try." The governor eyes Thaddeus. He pulls an envelope out of his pocket, breaks the seal, and shows the contents to Thaddeus. "I assume you didn't come here to discuss the Gala."

Thaddeus nods his head in approval. "Your present is gift-wrapped in the orchestra pit."

"Nice doing business with you, Mr. Phillips."

"Always a pleasure," Thaddeus responds.

Chapter 43
JUDGES 16:23-30

"Without further ado, your host for the evening, the governor of our great state." The room fills with claps and cheers as the overweight governor arrives at the podium.

"I would like to first thank you all for coming tonight," he begins through an overgrown mustache. "I know you are as eager as I am to commence with the awards portion of the ceremony. Let's start with our service awards for those of you who have served alongside me all these years. The following people have been on my team for five years: Sally Swift, Alvin Thompson, and Simone Rogers. Please give them a hand, everyone," he says as the three come up and stand to his right. "Now, for ten years of service…."

The Governor rambles through six more names who joined him on stage to accept their gold pins, shake his hand, and return to their seats. Delilah bounces her leg anxiously as she picks at her stuffed salmon. No one deserves this more than she does. The other people at her table are fully engulfed in the tenure awards being handed out, but she is waiting for the contract awards.

"Next, I will present the awards for all government projects up for bid this year. The first award goes to Angie's Catering; they will be the exclusive caterer for all our events. They catered to this delicious food you are eating now. Please give them a hand, everyone. Angie's Catering."

The owner of the catering company, who sits at the table next to Delilah, stands and takes her place on the stage. Delilah cringes at the caterer's frumpy appearance.

As the governor continues, she scans the room and sees contractors sitting with their significant others. It makes her heart sing. Then she spots Thaddeus sitting all smiles with the mayor.

The governor announces more awards, including an event planning business and a car service, which wins the bid for new fleet vehicles needed by the governor and his office. Delilah reapplies her lipstick, knowing her time is coming.

"Chocolate mousse cake, ma'am?" a server asks, holding three dessert plates.

"No, I'm fine," Delilah snaps, shooing the server away. She glances at the program for the hundredth time and then sips her drink.

"And now, the final award of the evening, general contractor for the next four years, goes to…drum roll, please," the governor says with a smile.

The drummer obliges. Delilah scoots her chair back.

"Thaddeus Phillips."

Delilah's astonishment was palpable as the crowd erupted in cheers and applause. She had been aware of Thaddeus's involvement in the construction business, but the victory he claimed seemed implausible. A blaze of anger kindled within her, simmering like an unquenchable fire in her chest. Rising from her seat, she began to stride purposefully toward Thaddeus, who was making his way to the stage amidst the jubilation.

However, as her path converged with him, Delilah hesitated. Her steps slowed as their gazes connected. In that instant, she realized that confronting him now would undoubtedly ignite a public spectacle. Reluctantly, she admitted to herself, "I can't approach him at this moment."

She decides to wait for Thaddeus to conclude his stage appearance. As he ascended the podium, their eyes met once more – he punctuated the moment by offering Delilah a smile and a wink, unraveling her composure.

Retracing her steps, Delilah returned to her table, snatching her purse from its resting place. Without a word, she departed the room, bound for the sanctuary of her waiting limousine.

"Thank you, Mr. Governor," Thaddeus says, shaking the official's hand.

"Thank you, Thaddeus. I look forward to working with you over the next year." He turns to face the crowd. "I want to thank all of you for allowing me to be your governor, and hopefully, after this year, you'll allow me to serve you for another four years. That said, don't feel like you are leaving here empty-handed tonight. I have an award for each one of you. Over the years, there has been one man who has continued to terrorize our people and has never been brought to justice." Silence fills the room as the party guests wait for the surprise. "Philistines, I give you…Samson!"

The grand curtain behind the imposing podium parted, unveiling a sight that left the audience in awe. Samson emerged, his figure rising gracefully from the depths of the orchestra pit. There he stood, a formidable presence, his legs bound by shackles. Despite streaks of gray infiltrating his once-youthful mane, the older Philistines in the assembly immediately recognized the legendary figure. A thunderous eruption of applause cascades through the crowd.

"I have relentlessly pursued him and delivered him to you as a symbol of my unwavering commitment to the people of this state," declared the governor. The room explodes with enthusiasm, guests leaping from their seats in a frenzy of excitement. The entire assembly, moved by the governor's announcement, rose in a resounding standing ovation.

"Now, he will face the trial that has been delayed for years. I assure you, he will spend the remainder of his days behind prison bars." The governor's pronouncement of a promise of justice was finally fulfilled. With those words, he concluded, "And with that, let the festivities commence! Eat, drink, and revel in merriment!" The crowd embraced the governor's call.

Some people whistle, others shout. The room is delighted to see Samson captured. The curtain closes on Samson as the governor exits the stage and heads toward his table. The band starts playing a hit song, immediately filling the dance floor. The party is now in full swing on all levels.

"You're *Samson*?"

"Rendor?" Samson asks the young voice as they stand behind the curtain.

"You told me your name was Yanir."

"Sorry, kid. I didn't want anyone to know who I was."

"How did you get out?"

"Honestly, I don't know. Someone bailed me out today and brought me here."

"You know they're out for revenge?"

"I heard. What are you doing here, kid?"

"My father was sick, so he gave me his ticket. I was upstairs, making my way around the party. There were so many pretty ladies. Then I saw you on the TV monitor up there."

"Where are we?"

"The governor's mansion."

Samson recalls that it replicated his building from when he was mayor. "Is there anyone else around right now?"

"No, just you and me. Why?"

"Take me to the basement."

The boy hesitates for a minute; he has heard the stories about Samson. Somehow, he doesn't think the man he has spent so much time talking to could be as dangerous as his people have made him out to be. He reaches for Samson's arm and leads him down the two flights of stairs behind the stage, his chain clanking with each step.

"This is going to sound strange, but I need you to leave," Samson instructs him.

"What?"

"You heard me. Go home."

Rendor registers the seriousness in Samson's tone. He heads toward the stairs, glancing back for a moment. Samson stands in the basement, unbeknownst to the party guests, drinking, dancing, and mingling above him.

"What are you going to do?" Samson doesn't respond. Rendor hesitates for a moment, then turns and walks up the stairs and out of the room. *What's the worst that could happen? He's a blind man shackled in a basement*, Rendor reassures himself.

Chapter 44

JUDGES 16:23-30

O utside the opulent venue, Rendor faces the valet, who extends a hand expectantly for his ticket.

"I didn't valet," Rendor replies with a shake of his head. His aging car, a blue Oldsmobile, wasn't worth the splurge on valet service. He quickens his pace, darting across the street to reach his vehicle. The car door creaks open, and he settles into the well-worn front seat, pausing for a moment to collect his thoughts. Something gnaws at him, an unsettling feeling he can't quite pinpoint. His curiosity about Samson's intentions gnaws at him, too.

Rendor couldn't resist looking back at the grand building as he pulled away from the venue. He wonders why Samson had been so insistent that he leave. After all, nobody should have known that he had escorted Samson downstairs.

Turning onto the street, he periodically casts longing looks over his shoulder until the mansion disappears from view. A flutter of unease dances in his stomach. Gazing into his rear-view mirror, his heart sinks as he sees a plume of smoke rising from the direction he had just departed. He slams the brakes, bringing his car to a crawl. The air fills with cacophonous cracks and shattering noises.

Without a second thought, he executes a U-turn in the street, forcing another vehicle to swerve to avoid a collision. Jamming his transmission into the park, he leaps from his car, leaving the door ajar. His eyes remain locked on the horrifying spectacle: the very building where he had stood just moments earlier crumbles before him. His throat constricted; he couldn't even be sure if he was still breathing. For a moment, the world seems to fall into a silent abyss.

Thoughts of the countless individuals inside the building race through his mind. Thousands, perhaps. The lump in his throat grows unbearable. He yearns to draw nearer to the wreckage, but debris swirls through the air, a tempest of danger. People from across the street start fleeing, their panicked cries and shouts breaking the eerie silence.

Samson bumps into a wall as he fumbles toward the churning sound.

In a moment of profound introspection, Samson's prayer resonated with a profound sense of regret. His voice, filled with contrition and resolve, carried his plea to the heavens.

"Lord, I humbly admit my shortcomings," he confessed. "Grant me the strength and wisdom that only You possess, just one more time. I yearn to become Your instrument of justice, to repay those who hold disdain for You and Your righteous ways. They have pillaged and taken innocent lives, casting shadows over the land," he continued, his voice quivering.

"For the wrongs they have committed against Your people, for the suffering they've inflicted upon me, for the loss of my sight." Samson's plea is a desire to serve as an avenger.

Samson feels his way down the hall and then stops. He does a 90-degree turn and reaches for the door; it is warm. He jiggles the handle. It is locked, but Samson tears it open with one tug and frames it all. Samson is hit with a wave of heat. God guides his steps to the left. Samson reaches forward and places his hands on a pipe; it is too large to get his hands around. He moves closer to the enormous pipe, places both arms around it, and yanks. The boiler shakes with its damaged pipe, the smell of gas saturating the air.

Samson carries what is left of the gas pipe into the hallway. The thumping of the music is now drowning out the hissing of the gas. He retraces his steps until he grips the metal railing along the stairs.

"Please remember me, Lord. Today, I die with the enemies!"

Samson hoisted the massive pipe above his head and, with a resolute swing, brought it crashing down on the unforgiving metal railing, generating the crucial spark he sought. In an instant, the basement transformed into an inferno.

The searing blaze roars to life, a fiery dance of orange and red. The air is thick with the acrid scent of burning wood and metal, and the basement becomes a cauldron of chaos.

Then, with a deafening eruption, the boiler succumbs to the heat, unleashing a cataclysmic explosion that sends shockwaves through the inferno. The world seems to shudder as fire and smoke intertwine.

A sudden, deafening bang shatters the rhythm of the dance floor, and every reveler freezes in their tracks. Eyes turn upward as a cascade of dust descends from the once-clear ceiling. Hairline fractures race across the glass roof above, and a palpable unease grips the crowd.

Panic spreads like wildfire, and people surge toward the nearest exit, desperate to escape the ominous rumblings within the walls. Bodies jostle, and limbs tangle as fear propels them toward salvation. Yet, fate proves merciless as the building's structure begins to splinter and crack.

Exit doors become bottlenecks, trapping those desperate to flee. Above, the glass dance floor surrenders to the pressure, it's surface bending, and buckling before shattering into a tempest of shards – a nightmare where a deluge of glass rains upon hundreds of shrieking bodies.

Below, the building's foundation, weakened by the initial blast, can no longer bear the burden. Support beams surrender, causing the structure to lean precariously to one side. Amidst the chaos, a pall of smoke, choking dust, and anguished screams filled the air.

Then, in a heart-wrenching crescendo, the building succumbs to its fate, folding onto itself in a cataclysmic collapse. The dust settles as the final tremors subside, and the once-thriving venue reduces to a haunting pile of debris. The echoes of screams fade into an eerie silence, marking the tragic end to a night of celebration.

PART IV: HAZEL

Present Day

EPILOGUE: JUDGES 16:31

Hazel reaches for the remote, then slowly falls back onto the soft cushions, which hug her as if to welcome her with open arms. Her 55" television quakes as the anchor's burly voice spills from its speakers. Startled, Hazel fumbles the remote, trying to lower the volume.

> *Good evening. We are interrupting our regularly scheduled programming for this late-breaking news. We have that thousands of people were killed tonight while attending a party at the governor's mansion.*
> *According to sources at the capital, an explosion at approximately 9:52 p.m. could be felt for miles. The explosion…wait, folks…I'm receiving updated information…"*

The reporter presses his finger against the earpiece while he receives a transmission.

Squinting his eyes, the seasoned reporter gazes vacantly at the ground, the weariness on his face belying the weight of the grim details he is about to convey. He struggles to block out the cacophony of environmental sounds drowning his thoughts, the hustle and bustle around him fading into insignificance.

In seconds, it becomes evident that the gruesome narrative he is now tasked with sharing is far heavier than he anticipated. His once-square shoulders slump and fold like a flimsy tent. With a deliberate inhale, he draws a deep, steadying breath, preparing himself to deliver the solemn news.

> *"It appears the 75,000 square-foot building, a longstanding part of Philistine history, is being reduced to rubble. According to our sources on the ground, there are no known survivors, and eyewitnesses are scarce.*

"Nothing is clear at this point. Police are scrambling for answers. What we do know is that this event boasts an extensive guest list, including prominent Philistines such as the mayor and governor. A tragedy of this magnitude is expected to have profound repercussions on the Philistine government.

"We do not yet have an exact death toll, but rest assured, we will keep you updated with breaking news as this heart-wrenching tragedy continues to unfold.

"An eyewitness account from Rendor, son of the police chief, points to a possible suspect. Rendor states that Samson, an Israelite, urged him to leave the building mere minutes before it crumbled. As of now, countless mysteries linger, leaving us with more questions than answers.

"Stay tuned, ladies and gentlemen, for more details as we navigate the unfolding chapters of this harrowing event."

"No! No, no, no..." Hazel's anguished cry reverberates through the room, her frantic movements causing objects to scatter as she desperately searches for her phone. "There must be a mistake! There is no way Samson has anything to do with this!" Her voice trembles with denial, tears well up in her eyes.

As she dials Samson's number repeatedly, each unanswered call sends a shock of fear within her. With each passing second, her breath becomes more labored, and her thoughts race. The room seems to close in around her, the walls bearing witness to her growing dread.

"My miracle child," Hazel says, looking up at the clear blue sky. The day is too lovely to be grieving over the loss of her child, yet here she is, stumbling to his gravesite. She slowly kneels in front of where Samson has been laid to rest next to his father. Behind Hazel, a silent presence lingered - the sons of Manoah, Samson's half-brothers. They had come to bear witness, to confront the undeniable reality that Samson had truly departed this world.

"Why was he even in the governor's mansion?" she complained, trembling like a fragile leaf in the wind. Her eyes glistened with unshed tears, her gaze fixed on a distant, unknowable horizon. "I just can't comprehend it." Her words hung in the air, a fragile plea to the heavens.

Her slender form knelt before the heavens, her anguish palpable in the way her fingers clenched the earth beneath her. Her voice quivered as she implored the Divine, the weight of the world pressing upon her shoulders. "God, You didn't bless me with Samson only for him to die like this. What was the purpose?" The question was a lament, an echo of her heart's torment.

Tears flowed freely down her cheeks as she cried out to the heavens, her voice strained with raw emotion. "Oh God, I pray that his death will not be in vain." Her words were a fervent plea, a desperate hope that Samson's sacrifice would not be forgotten. "Samson's reputation for standing up to the Philistines has not gone unnoticed, and I beseech our Almighty God that our people will do better now that we have been delivered from the hands of the Philistines."

She wiped away a tear with trembling hands, her fingers leaving moisture streaks on her cheeks. She took a deep breath, the air filling her lungs like a balm for her wounded soul. Slowly, she rose from the ground where she had fallen, her silhouette marked by the fading light of day, a testament to the resilience of the human spirit in the face of unfathomable loss.